A HANDKERCHIEF FOR MARIA

Charlie Garratt

Copyright © 2020 Charlie Garratt All rights reserved

The characters and events portrayed in this book are fictitious. Any similarity to real persons, living or dead, is coincidental and not intended by the author.

No part of this book may be reproduced, or stored in a retrieval system, or transmitted in any form or by any means, electronic, mechanical, photocopying, recording, or otherwise, without express written permission of the publisher.

ISBN: 9780993178443

Bunlacky
Press

For my grandmother, Kathleen Garratt, and her father, John Costello, without whom I'd never have begun this journey.

Acknowledgements

It all started with a photograph which led to a search revealing a life beyond my comprehension. Over a number of years this novel emerged and so there are many people to thank. Here are a few.

My wife, Ann, for everything. All the readers of early drafts and Susan Davis (aka Sarah Vincent) who helped with editing. Tir Conaill Writers Group for unflinching support. Nuneaton Library for the research facilities in the early days, and everyone else who helped me along the journey.

Cover photograph by Yaoqi Lai from unsplash.com

PART ONE

Day 1

Maria is late, the bus is full, and she stands all the way from the city centre, feeling faint on this muggy evening. Faint from the heat, and faint from not knowing if tonight will be her daughter's last. There are two buses each night to make visiting time at the hospital, and the first is emptier. Mothers, fathers, sisters, brothers and friends pile off and clog the pavement, crossing the road in twos and threes to dodge the traffic trailing behind when their transport rolls away. She spends another wasted moment to take in the vast, blackened exterior of the hospital, with window after grimy window reflecting the grey Manchester sky. Alice's ward is on the other side, where wide, glass, veranda doors allow sunlight to pour in on summer mornings.

She feels a tug at her elbow and turns to see a smiling younger woman.

'Come on, love, we can cross now.'

Maria breaks from her daydream and steps into the road, hardly noticing her new companion's chatter. On the other side, a question is being repeated

'Who are you here to see?'

'My .. my daughter. Alice. You?'

'My Eric. Silly sod bashed his head at work yesterday. Knocked him right out. Said they'd keep him in for a night or two just to make sure. Should be home tomorrow though. What's wrong with your girl?'

'Some kind of cancer in her brain. She's in a coma now, so no pain. Thank God.'
The woman looks away. 'I'm sorry.'
'Ah well, she's been here a few weeks so we've known this was coming. I spend my time talking to her, giving her the news. Run out of things to say some nights though.'

They walk in silence up two flights to the first floor, where Maria points down a corridor on the right. 'This is me,' she smiles and turns,' I hope your husband is feeling better, and out of this place soon.'

Maria sees the visitor's mouth start to wish her the same for Alice, then close, trapping in the false comfort.

*

Alice looks peaceful, her nut-brown hair spread across the pillow, and her white sheets tucked tight. The only sign of her serious condition is the feeding tube and funnel on her bedside cabinet. Maria bends and kisses her daughter's forehead before sitting and clasping her cool hand. She speaks to the girl, as she does on every visit, as if she is conscious.

'How are you tonight, Alice? I brought a letter from your brother. It came this morning and I've not opened it, thought I'd read it to you but now I'll leave it for a while. Which brother? Well Josie, of course, all the way from India. Who out of them would bother to write to their mam even to tell her they were still breathing? I know, I know, they're good boys. Though none as considerate as Josie. You remember I named him after my grandfather, John Joseph Byrne? I'll tell you why ... sometime.'

'Your dad, my father, my grandfather and even his father, all soldiers. Soldiers travelling to places I've never seen, nor want to see. Places you might never have the chance to see. Just eighteen and no life before you.

'At least Josie and your dad fought for their own country not some foreign power. Through all those years, hardships, Alice, always hardships. Daddy used to tell me we came from nobility. Lords and ladies all, he'd say, then slap his knee and laugh. The best laugh you'd ever hear. That's how I remember him most. That, and the cough.'

Leaden clouds have turned the sky dark and Maria sees herself in the window's reflection. Still-black hair, glasses, a solid, forty-six year old, without the curves Billy ogles in the News of the World. She looks away and strokes the creases from her best weekday skirt down towards her knees.

'Jesus, Mary and Joseph, look at the state of me. Little Tommy ran in crying when I was getting ready. The poor mite fell and scraped his knee. It wasn't much more than a wee scratch but the leg was covered with blood and he'd got dirt in it. By the time I'd cleaned him up I'd not time to run an iron over my clothes, else I'd have missed my bus.'

She reflects on the hour here and hour back, twice a week, and how she struggles to afford it on Billy's postman's wages. The bit sent from Josie' and Alan's army pay helps but the others don't bring in much. Billy nags her all the time for spending money on bus fares.

'You know, I'd been married nearly five years when you came along. Overjoyed I was, and you such an easy birth. Never gave me any trouble, only smiles. Three boys by then and me thinking I'd never have a girl. How was I to know there'd be another four girls and two boys come after you? All wonderful in their own way though. Twenty years between first and last, and Rose coming as a little present when they de-mobbed Billy after the heart attack two years ago.'

Two visitors appear at the next bed, where a pale woman, Mandy, lies barely breathing. Their faces are as careworn as Maria knows her own to be. Over the past six months she's come to know a few of the patients and their families, exchanging words of encouragement or condolence but this pair is new. Mandy would be around twenty, two years older than Alice. She'd arrived in the ward two weeks earlier, though this is the first time

Maria has seen anyone come to see her. A nod in their direction but she'll not speak, not tonight. Maybe next time. If there is a next time.

Maria sniffs back a tear as the thought escapes its cage. Her daughter's death is near and she knows she has to be strong. She sits quietly for what seems a lifetime, struggling to dredge words to get her through the visit, then heavy raindrops spatter against the glass and Maria finds inspiration to continue.

'Wasn't it warm today, Alice? Baking. Got the clothes dry with no trouble. Could be a thunderstorm tonight, I expect, sticky enough for it anyway. My dad used to say it was boiling almost every day when he was in Malta, I wonder how we'd put up with that? I don't think I'd enjoy it, everything dried up and brown. Not like home. Manchester? No, my baby, my original home. Wicklow, in Ireland. Damp, surely, but green. Ever so green. Don't you remember the stories about it? I'll tell you again soon, maybe when I come next time, would you like that?'

The girl won't answer but Maria needs to talk about something when she's there, so why not about her life? Tell a story to pass the time. Where's the harm in that?

A starched-white sister marches over to Alice's bed. She straightens the sheets, takes the girl's pulse, notes the result then turns to the mother.

'Just five more minutes, Mrs Byrne.'

Maria hates her for these words.

She takes in the ward, scanning for beds which were occupied on her last visit. Of the twenty lining the walls, two have changed. A young man had coughed and wheezed in one of them, but seemed cheery enough, so must have gone home or moved. In the other, a woman in her mid-forties like Maria, had been unconscious all the time Alice had been in this ward. She must have slipped away in the night and they've now stripped her bed, ready to prepare it for its next patient. Maria can't handle this. Every time she sees it she doesn't sleep. For weeks a picture in her head of Alice's bed the same. Empty, scrubbed.

She stands and leans over Alice, brushes her hair and strokes the girl's cheek with the backs of her fingers. A bell sounds to signal the end of visiting time. Maria struggles for something to say in the final moments.

'Oh, heavens, I didn't read you Josie's letter. Never mind. I'll look at it on the bus on the way home and tell you his news on Saturday. I have to go now, my darling. Sleep tight and you'll be a bit better by then.'

Maria stands, puts on her jacket and turns towards the doors. When they swing shut the tears flood, as they always do.

*

Maria feels like a smoke but she's no cigarettes left and no chance of affording any the day before payday. She takes a seat near the back of the bus, where she can take some relief from the humid night, pleased, at least, she doesn't need to drag herself to the top deck. The ward sister had asked her for a word as she'd finished her visit.

'The news isn't good I'm afraid, Mrs Byrne. Doctor thinks it won't be long. It could be days but he thinks three weeks at most.'

Maria bit her lip so hard the blood had run warm and sweet on her tongue.

Only weeks? How can she tell Billy she must be out every night from now on? She'd not raised it when she got home, deciding to wait until the moment was right. Surely he'll understand? She's never sure how he'll react. He's the kindest, most generous man she ever met but can be stubborn, and he thinks his word is law. She knows he'll feel Alice's loss as much as she will, and his objections are just his way of trying to protect her from the pain that's to come. Still, she wishes he'd see it from her point of view and accept she can't be away from her daughter. Not now.

She thinks of the cheaply-framed photograph on the cream-painted wall by the stove in her kitchen. Nine of her children, in three lines, the eldest boys at the back, Josie and Alan in uniform, Bobby in a suit. Alice, looking like she'd still her entire life before her, alongside the other middle ones, Ruth and Brian, then the smallest at the front, Annie, Lizzie and Tommy. No Rose, she'd be there a year after we took this picture. They'd just heard Billy was coming home. In hospital after a heart attack, but safe. Maria dragged them all to Sunday Mass to give thanks, and Mrs Parker's son, Eric, came round with his camera.

Lizzie is a trouble. She's only nine but her mother can tell there's something different. The others are bright as buttons, despite a few not liking school. The girl seems in a world of her own. Thoughtful, not practical, and not a reader like Ann either. Maria can't see how she will ever hold down a job or find a husband.

She's all ten children to worry about, half still at school or tugging at her skirt hem. Three others are fighting in the war and Alice is dying in hospital. And Billy not even able to boil a potato. Maria can't bear to think how they'll manage if she falls apart. She closes her eyes and bows her head, ignoring what other passengers might think. She needs an extra hard prayer for Him to give her strength.

Day 2

Maria wipes her daughter's mouth then strokes back the girl's hair. She wonders why she's bothering to chat away when her daughter can't hear a word nor make a reply.

'Perhaps it's me I'm helping. What else would I do but just sit here and watch you breathe? Remember I said I'd tell you about my daddy and his adventures, and about his father, who was in the army a really long time? I've been thinking about it ever since I was here, hardly slept a wink last night with it spinning round in my head. I've decided I'll put it all together for you, remind you of the stories I told you when you were small, about my life in the school, how I met your dad. Everything.'

'There's so much to tell I don't know how I'll do it. You'll have to forgive me if I miss things out, or repeat myself. There's three … or maybe four … important men I need to tell you about, and half a dozen countries, explosions, armies and wars, and hard times. And beatings. And the love of my life. Will I tell you these? What if you can hear?'

'What countries? Well England, obviously, and Ireland, where it all began, where your mammy came from. Then there was Malta, where my daddy was, like I said before, and Greece, where my grand-dad was, and he was in Egypt, and India, and Africa as well, all exciting places. You just lie back and listen, and if that nurse comes and chases me again before I'm finished I'll pick up the thread next time I'm here. Are you ready? Sure, I won't expect a reply, best just get on with it.'

She shifts her chair closer to the bed, takes her daughter's clammy hand and allows her words to begin to flow, as free as the river running down the valley her people left.

*

I've lots to tell and no clue where to begin. Gone over and over it in my head trying to make sense and there's not much of that in it all, so it's probably best to tell you where it all started. You'll know then where I came from. Where you and all your brothers and sisters came from.

The Avonmore, that's a river, bubbles out of an old, old lake, Loch Nahanagan, high up in the Wicklow hills, then twists and turns its way down to the sea at Arklow. A town where I had some real hard times. We'll get to that one day, God willing.

Ireland is a land of fairy stories and this lake is no different. Daddy told me its Irish name tells us it was the home of a water monster, which lay coiled and sleeping at the bottom, waking every few years to take its fill of cattle and anyone it might catch unawares. They say it was only banished when Saint Kevin walked barefoot along the river from Glendalough and prayed for an end to the creature's shenanigans. It rose fifty feet out of the water and opened its mouth to swallow him but sensed his holy strength so slithered off to some other dark place.

Imagine that, something so big and fierce being driven away by a priest. I'd be scared enough of Father McSorley but surely even he'd have no effect on a water monster.

The other story is of a strange boulder in the lake which only appeared from time to time and it was said to be full of anger and bad luck. The rock was close in by the shore and if any man hit it with a stick, cursed it or even looked at it in the wrong way, rain would pour down, only stopping when an apology was made. For years the locals left offerings at the lakeside, unable to tell the difference between the bog's natural showers and those coming from that old bad-tempered rock. From what I hear, despite all their prayers, the rain still falls almost every day on the Wicklow hills.

As the river makes its way down it sparkles as it trickles over gravel, or takes a turn when its path is blocked by harder ground. Up near the source it cuts through the bog over stones but, lower down, it's overhung by green branches where there are calm pools, and tiny trout hover just below the surface.

Past Glendalough, the Avonmore, still only twenty feet wide, wanders down the valley to Rathdrum. That's where I was born in a tiny railwayman's cottage, hard by the station. Daddy was so happy then.

Four miles below the town it joins another river, the Avonbeg and becomes the Avoca, at a spot called the Meeting of the Waters. What a lovely name for a place to live, not harsh like Clayton where we live, is it? I went there once. The sun sparkled on the water and my daddy sat on the grass with a bottle of beer. It was when he was ill and we'd been to see Auntie Bridget. I remember they argued and Daddy said he needed a drink after all that, so he borrowed a cart and off we went. He wouldn't say why they'd crossed words but maybe it was because he wanted her to look after me and little Jimmy, and she wouldn't. I've thought about that a lot over the years.

It's a beautiful spot but men used to mine for copper, lead and sulphur only a mile from there. Not far away, near Ballinagore, gold the weight of three full grown men was panned from the waters one time. It's said there were nearly a thousand carts a day hauling minerals from the Avoca mines to boats in Arklow port. When the river reaches Arklow it's a hundred and fifty yards wide and passes under a bridge with nineteen arches before it glides past the quays and the harbour out into the Irish Sea.

What a sight that would be to see, eh? Gold, and copper, and so many carts, and so many ships.

My grandfather, John, worked in the mines. Hard, hard, work. But a living. Shame he gave it all up and joined the army, coming back poor and injured.

*

'Name and age, lad?'

'John Byrne, sir. Nineteen years, sir.'

'It's not "sir", it's Sergeant. "Sir" is for them that buys themselves in. Or out. The ones in the posh uniforms. The likes of me and you, we take the Queen's shilling, do as we're told and collect our pay every week. So what have you been doing these nineteen years, Byrne?'

'I was in the mines since I was fourteen, sir … Sergeant. Up the Avoca valley."

Sergeant Collins eyed all five foot nine inches of John up and down.

'So why are you leaving that good honest trade and coming to join us?'

'Do I have to say?'

The recruiting sergeant raised an eyebrow. John squirmed.

'Something happened and they let me go. Thought I might try soldiering like my Da did. At least I'll get fed.'

What my grandfather didn't tell the sergeant, though I suppose he guessed, was he'd got caught up in some trouble. He'd had an argument with another man and the following week some tools were stolen from the mine stores. The next day this man lied to the boss he'd found the tools in among granddad's things. He was hauled into the office but thumped the boss then ran away and hid for a few days before he went down to Arklow to the recruiting station. My dad always said it was a good thing granddad did because without a job he'd have starved at that time, then we wouldn't have been here, would we?

Collins never faltered for a moment.

'You'd not be the first, and doubtless won't be the last young feller who joined up to keep his belly full. So let's get you measured up then you can sign the papers to give yourself over to her Majesty.'

Later in 1847, the same year John joined the 91st Regiment of Foot, a local newspaper carried the story of the biggest sawmill in the land having been working flat out for eight months, using sixteen to twenty saws at a time, to keep up with the demand for planks for coffins.

John didn't see that newspaper, nor could he have read it if he had. At the time he was hanging on for dear life to other planks, those making up the deck of the SS Royal William which was battling the waves between Dublin and Liverpool. He'd never been on a boat before, like most of the new recruits sharing his misery for the last ten hours. He was sure it would have been better in the cabins below, where the paying customers had the luxury of a bunk and a toilet, but the thirty soldiers groaning beside him were not seen worthy of such expense. He'd been told there were another four or five hours to go and he felt like he'd never make it, with his stomach churning like the vast paddles on either side of the packet ship.

Only a small number of his fellow travellers seemed to be coping with the conditions. These took the opportunity to lord it over the rest, swaggering along the deck and stopping by the most bilious-looking. They'd then adopt an exaggerated swaying motion to make the poor souls feel even worse. One man stayed apart, leaning confidently with his face set into the storm. After a while, he squatted on to the boards beside John, and pointed at the play-actors.

'Fools, aren't they? Should remember first time they was out on the sea. Bet they puked as much as this lot.'

John nodded, too grim to speak. The soldier stuck out his hand.

'Patsy Finn. What's yours?'

He was a big feller, half a foot taller than John, and with well-muscled shoulders and thighs. His cornflower blue eyes sparkled through a fringe of blond hair and a first glance told you he'd never want for female company. In fact, he never had, and this was the reason he was sitting alongside John on the boat. He'd married a golden-haired seventeen year old, Jenny, after her father discovered them in the cornfield after mass one Sunday. The man then threatened, for the second time, to take the shotgun to Patsy when word of his son-in-law's affairs reached his ears. Although this in itself was frightening enough, it paled into insignificance when Jenny and her best friend, one of his little indiscretions, confronted him and insisted he make a choice. The decision was easy, especially when the recruiting sergeant was in town and the Queen was offering food and lodgings in places where neither the ladies nor their fathers could get to him. He'd packed his bags, signed up, donned the uniform and was soon introducing himself to another soldier on the deck of a boat tossing the waves between Ireland and England.

Patsy's new companion looked green and shook his hand limply. 'Byrne. John. 'Scuse me.'

John stood and heaved in vain over the side, his guts aching with the endless retching. He held the rail for a moment facing into the wind, taking great gulps of air before slumping back down by the soldier called Finn.

'Pleased to meet you, Patsy. How do you manage it? Stay from being sick I mean?'

Finn cracked a generous smile.

'I was on the sea for years so it's no great hardship now, though this is a rough one and that's no lie. My dad was a fisherman out of Arklow so I've been knocking about boats half my life.'

'Was a fisherman? You said "was".'

'Had an accident last year and hurt his shoulder. Not fit to haul nets any more. He and the mammy sailed off to Canada a few months back but couldn't afford the fare for me and my brother so just took the little ones. Said we'd be better off making our own way in the world. Things were going fine until I got a little too friendly with a pretty girl' Patsy smirked 'or two.'

John groaned again though this time managed to avoid the embarrassment of leaping up to lean over the ship's side for what seemed like the hundredth time. Patsy clapped him on the shoulder.

'I'll keep my mouth shut for a while now, John Byrne, and get my head down for a nap. We should be hitting sheltered water before too long and perhaps you'll feel more like chatting when I wake up.'

John was sure he'd never feel well again.

*

Maria feels the need for a cigarette tonight after her visit, so lights one in the company of other smokers on the top deck of the bus. She's not a regular smoker, Billy doesn't approve, even though he goes through forty a day himself. His family never had two pennies to rub together, much the same as her own, but still he clings to his odd ideas about manners and decency. Always going on that a woman shouldn't smoke, "not ladylike" he'd say. Not that "ladylike" was much used to describe Maria Ann Byrne but she's happy if she's a lady in his eyes. Maria knows he's always done the right thing by her.

She overhears an elderly woman complaining to her neighbour.

'Wish they'd let us smoke downstairs, this rocking is making me ill. So many things not allowed. How did they come up with this one; do they imagine the bus might catch fire? I feel sick enough already without the bus's swaying from side to side.'

As they pull away from a stop, thick droplets of rain fall on the window then stretch horizontally, the lines becoming longer and longer with the gathering speed. A double flash of lightning is followed by a massive crack of thunder and several of her fellow travellers draw breath, then laugh nervously. Others strain to see which building bought it. This was what the war had done to them. Always scared, always relieved when they open their eyes to find someone else has been hit.

A couple sit across the aisle from Maria, totally absorbed in each other's company. The woman, in her early twenties, is in the navy uniform and white cap of the Wrens, the man in civvies. The empty sleeve of his suit jacket explains why. Maria looks away. She prays her sons come home in one piece. Maria's heard they're all safe but anything could happen while they're still in the forces.

The bus jerks to a stop outside St Clements. Maria almost misses it and only makes it down the stairs at the last minute when she shakes the image of Bradley's funeral home on Clayton Lane from her mind. It's nearly ten o'clock but the church door is open as always. There'd be no Father McSorley on duty at this time of the night but Maria is sure another prayer could do no harm. She searches her near-empty purse, drops a few pennies in the box, and lights a candle from another on the tray. A quick bow of the head before taking a seat below the statue of the Virgin and Christ-child. Two decades of the rosary pass through Maria's lips, then she looks up into the eyes of her name-saint.

'You know what it's like to lose someone you love above everything, don't you. So if you have any influence, any at all, with the good Lord, please, please, please, ask him to spare my lovely Alice. I know if he takes her it will be because he wants her at his side but I don't want her to go. Not yet. Not before me.'

She holds the marble's lifeless gaze for a full minute then drops her chin to her chest in submission.

A creak from the porch door startles Maria in the darkness.

'Who's there?' A male voice. Irish with a slight

tremor.

'Father - is that you?'

An elderly priest, in dressing gown and slippers, points a torch from the doorway.

'Maria? What on earth are you doing here at this time of night? I thought we had a burglar.'

'I'm sorry, Father. I've been to the hospital and hoped I'd get a little extra help for Alice.'

'Well I'm sure another prayer never goes amiss, Maria. Was it bad news tonight?'

The two sit on the back row and Maria pours out her heart to the cleric, fears she'd not been able to share with anyone, not even her Billy, since Alice had been diagnosed with the growth. She tells again how the girl's headaches had started eighteen months earlier, how the doctor had charged her a shilling just to tell her it was a cold, how it didn't get better. Then the fits began and he gave her medicine which made her sick all the time. Maria knew it was serious when her quiet daughter became bad-tempered and couldn't remember what day it was. Finally, the hospital had taken her in and cut open her head, then stitched it up again. Now they are telling Maria that it is too late, there's nothing more to be done.

Father McSorley says what he always says in these circumstances, that the Lord's will is not for us to question. After ministering to his flock for nigh on fifty years he is no longer sure he believes this himself. Every day he read his Gospels and every day he tries to make sense of them in the real world he inhabits, surrounded by the poverty of the many and the greed of the few, where those who are sick can't afford the treatments, and where the ungodly live just as long, or just as short, a life as the devout.

Maria shakes her head. 'I understand that, Father, but why us? Why always us?'

She runs dry of emotion, thanks her confessor for listening and stands to leave. The priest asks her to kneel a little longer and share one more decade, Perhaps he's fearful he'll lose this soul from his flock if he doesn't do something to hold on to her. She complies and takes strength from their prayers, as she always has in the past. When she stands again the steel has returned to her spine, so she has no need of his hand on her elbow as he lead her outside, but she accepts his support in the spirit it is given.

From the step she can see a light escaping from her kitchen curtains across the gardens between the church and the back of her home.

'So, Billy's still up, Father. Best get round there and share our bad news. I expect there'll not be much sleep between us tonight.'

The old priest pulls his dressing gown tighter round his substantial waist and ambles towards his front door.

'Goodnight, Maria.'
'Goodnight Father. Thank you and God bless.'

Day 3

I called in to church last night, Alice, said a prayer with Father McSorley. You know, that man can preach all kinds of fire and brimstone from the pulpit but he can be a very decent feller when you have him on his own. Still, like all of them, I don't think he really understands the likes of us.

So, when I left last night we'd left my granddad clinging to the ship's rail and dying from seasickness, with his new-found friend. Needless to say, he survived and they landed in England safely enough a few hours later.

*

By the time John had disembarked and stood in line with the rest on Liverpool docks for half an hour he'd regained his legs and some of his confidence. They'd an hour's march to the barracks at Walton on the Hill and they were kept in strict formation, fifteen rows, two deep. Often the column would be four men wide but the streets here were so busy with every form of waggon and carriage it had to stay narrow. When they'd cleared the yards the word came down the line that they could drop to walking pace until they were in sight of the barracks. Patsy Finn had taken his place alongside John in the ranks when they'd formed up on the docks and until this order came they'd marched in silence.

John offered his new-found friend a cigarette,

which he refused.

'Never bothered to start with 'em, you know. Tried it once when I was a lad but did nothing for me so couldn't see the point.'

'Christ, I couldn't get out of bed in the morning without a quick drag. I'd be sour all day '

Patsy laughed. 'Each to his own I suppose'

Even though they now had the sergeant's permission to talk neither seemed able or willing to begin a real conversation. Instead, they passed the occasional comment on the sights and sounds of the city. John, in particular, had only known the Wicklow countryside and army camps before. True he'd been to Arklow and Wicklow Town on the odd time but they didn't prepare him for Dublin or Liverpool. The sheer numbers of people, horses and waggons took his breath away and the variety of shops, factories and houses drew a "look at that one" on every corner. Finn tried to play the unruffled town boy but John could tell he was just as overwhelmed. After a while when they'd settled into this pattern and the words came easier John ventured further.

'What about this fishing life then, didn't you fancy taking it up yourself?'

'Seamie, my brother, decided he'd have a go and asked me to join him but I'd had enough of that old place and wanted to see the world. So far I've seen the parade ground, Enniskillen and Dublin.

Now this. Not very exotic is it?'

'Well if it stays this quiet it will be fine with me, I've no desire to be shooting or being shot at. Three square meals a day and tramping the green lanes of England or home will be good enough.'

Patsy grinned. 'I'm pretty sure her Majesty won't be too keen on that arrangement. She's an empire to run and we're the boys to help her to do it. It won't be too long before we're sent off to far flung places I'll bet you'

'Aye, I know. My own father was in Bermuda and Canada keeping King George's peace, but he told me he'd been glad to be there and not taking on the rebels at home. Dad grew up with lads of that persuasion and never knew how he'd have gone on if he'd been ordered to point a gun at them.'

Both men now walked in silence again, sobered by the talk of fighting, whether at home or overseas. They knew enough of the starvation and mass evictions in Ireland to worry about another uprising. One they'd be expected to put down.

Rain began to fall, large drops splattering the leaves of overhanging trees before dropping onto the soldiers' caps. Behind them the clouds scudding in from the sea grew darker and darker with their every passing step and the men cheered when they heard that the barracks were in sight and that they must fall in to strict formation. Thunder exploded just as they reach the gates and the column was drenched to the skin by the time they'd formed ranks on the parade ground before being directed to their quarters.

John took a bunk in the long narrow room as close to the stove as he could, ripping off his soaking jacket and hanging it to dry near the flames with the other uniform parts already discarded. There were twenty beds on each side, with several still empty at the far end but Patsy was towering over John's neighbour in earnest conversation. After a minute or two the smaller man gathered his things and moved to an empty bunk at the other end. Patsy dropped his pack by the now vacant one next to John's. John raised an eyebrow.

'What was that all about?'

The big man grinned. 'We had a quiet word and he thought it would be much handier if I slept here.'

*

John soon began to believe that the dreariness of army life was intended to give the soldiers a willingness, even a desire, to go into battle. It seemed he wasn't the only one to feel bored and the grumblings from the recruits who'd travelled with him from Ireland grew stronger every day. Up at first light, inspection by the sergeant and one officer or another, then some mind-numbing work in the camp or around the town if he was lucky.

Those who could read or write well were given clerking jobs, recording every detail of the life of the battalion. Denny McGann, the man faced down by Patsy when he'd claimed the bunk, was one of these clerks and showed John one of the ledgers he was required to keep. Column after column of words and figures, most of which John couldn't make head nor tail of until Denny explained.

'This one's who's been paid, and, here, how much. This is who was sick, how long and why. This here's a good laugh, it's who's been in jail. See, Eric Potts, he's in the next hut to us, got forty eight hours for falling asleep on guard. Silly sod. It was during the day as well.'

One of the books listed all of the transfers in and out of the barracks and John was able to find his own name in there. He couldn't wait for the entry to be made when he'd been moved on. He also thought it staggering that week after week different soldiers were writing down everything anyone would ever want to know about every officer' and man's life in the army. The clerk clearly shared his view.

'Shame there's nothing very juicy in this lot,' McGann waved at the shelves of ledgers 'a man could have his fortune made with a word or two in a guilty ear.'

John decided Denny McGann was a weasel and was glad Patsy had replaced him in the next bed.

For two years, those soldiers, like John, without sufficient book learning, cleaned kit and weapons, laboured wherever they were needed or, most boring of all, carried out guard duty. It was no surprise that Potts had nodded off when he was doing it. Almost everyone in the barracks looked forward to getting away from this monotony and into battle. The ones who didn't were either in cushy office jobs or had fought before. Corporal O'Grady, a fellow Irishman from Queen's County, was one of this second group. He'd seen action in China and Afghanistan, and was always ready to point out the perils of facing the enemy in hostile conditions and a hostile landscape.

'You think about the way we practice here, my boys, ranks neatly lined up across green fields, all easily in view. Then think about a different picture. Heat to melt you, dust in your face, and you half dead from dysentery. Shots or spears coming from every bush and rock, and no place to hide except behind the dead bodies of your mates. Pray to God to stay home in this place, boys, and no doubt about it.'

Several of the men jeered every time O'Grady came up with this speech, bravado being in greater supply and brains than on their part, but most stayed quiet, knowing his words had the ring of truth.

One of the brave lads, Fitzpatrick from County

Cavan, was always boasting of what he'd do when he had the enemy in his sights or, better still, within reach of his knife. Everyone was convinced it was all blather and wasted no time in telling him so.

What did they know eh? Appearances are just that. Men deal with their feelings in different ways and Fitzpatrick would prove a better one than most in the end.

One day the shout went up for them to pack and make ready to move on. Speculation spread wildly.

'Sure boys this is it, we're off to do what we're paid to do. Bombay is where we're going or I'm a Dutchman.'

But it wasn't Bombay, it was to Dover they went, and no further. Eighteen months on the Heights doing what they'd been doing in Liverpool, only now, every day, they could see all the way across the Channel to where, only ten years before John was born, Napoleon's empire had come tumbling down in bloody battle. A war in which men of their own regiment had fought and died.

It was on a thundery Tuesday, with the French Emperor long dead, when another move was announced, with another wave of excitement breaking through every block. Another false alarm. This time the move was to Portsmouth. An outbreak of cholera had weakened the garrison there so the 91st had been requisitioned to fill the gap. Rumours were rife that they'd all be on troopships when the stint was finished, though John had to wait yet another year and a return to Liverpool before that particular wish was fulfilled. It was finally in October 1851 that the SS Phoebe sailed out on the Mersey, leaving the strains of the military band on the quayside. John and several hundred companions, every one of them bored with life in an English barracks, were on their way to the Cape of Good Hope.

*

Maria stands, then slips on her coat and hat. She turns to leave but instead walks to Mandy's bedside. The girl's had no visitors this evening and is sleeping, rosy-cheeked. She's due to go home in a couple of days. Home to a family who seem to love her but who live too far away to visit often. Maria returns to her daughter's bed holding back the tears. She sits again and then lifts Alice's hand to her cheek.

'We're getting through the story, Alice, slowly but surely. My granddad had an interesting life, don't you think? And a dangerous one. I'll tell you more of his adventures next time but I've got to go now, else I'll miss my bus.'

Maria lays her daughter's limp hand back by her side, kisses her forehead and walks away, shaking so much inside she wonders how she'll make it out of the ward.

Day 4

It is silly telling her all of this. Most of it isn't even true, but what else do I do? Stories, nothing but stories. Snatches of tall tales told by my daddy to keep me quiet when I was missing Mammy. Stuff told to him when he was small, half-remembered and passed down to me. Now I am doing the same for her. Give my darling adventures she'll never know for herself. And some things I need her to know. I can't jump right in and tell them. She needs to understand how they happened. Why they happened. Perhaps she can't even hear me and it's all a waste of breath but it does no harm for me to talk about it, even for my own benefit. Get it straight in my own mind.

What if Alice can hear, then wakes up and remembers? What if she's shocked and hates me for it? It wouldn't matter, not one bit, not if I could have her back. I probably would have told her one day anyway.

Would I though? I haven't told Josie and he's the one affected most. I haven't even told the whole truth to Billy and he deserves to know.

What is it with me and the romancing? I tell myself they're not real lies, just fibs to avoid hurting people's feelings and to cover up the fact that I don't know half the time. The other half I do know but still don't tell the truth. I think it might be because I enjoy making things up. I always have.

At least since I went into that place.

I even told one of the boys that my mammy died when I was born. How can that be? I remember her clear as day so why make such a thing up? I told two of the littler ones that both my parents were killed in a car crash. Car crash? They could barely afford a bus fare most of their lives.

*

John tossed a cigarette to the poor lad on duty at the gate of Brown's Farm fort. The finger across John's lips told the guard to keep his mouth shut about the evening walk down the hill.

The track was dusty and well worn, caked hard by the hundreds of boots, waggons and horses that had passed over it since the winter rains. At that time of year it was a mud bath, a danger to man and beast trying to get into the fort but the last five month's scorching sun had remedied that. Where the ground levelled out, a hundred yards from the gate, the track turned sharply right in the direction of Fort Beaufort, a day and a half's march to the west. John continued straight on, taking the narrow path towards the firelight of the village. The sixty mud huts, each with a straw roof, reminded him of the thatched cabins of home. The parched earth and the colour of the skin of the babies crying outside may have been different but John still recognised the same squalor and poverty. He wondered if this what the English brought with them everywhere, or just what they found when they arrived.

He shook his head and ambled to the last hut in the village, where a young woman smiled as he approached. She was pretty, short black curls, high forehead, high cheekbones and her dark skin shone like a rabbit fur. She was naked from the waist up and her belly was swollen with John's child. He had no way of being certain but Esihle had told him her grandmother said it was a boy. He had no reason to disbelieve this. Weren't the old women at home able to divine the same kind of thing, a mystery to men the world over.

Esihle raised herself from her knees with care, because she was close to her time, and wrapped her arms around the soldier's neck. 'John, you come to see me after all.'

'I didn't think I'd be able to get away. We've been told to be ready to move out at any time.'

'You are here now, and that is all I ask. It is good for you to come.'

She spoke a broken English, like everyone else in the village. Her people, the Fengu, were allies of the British and the settlement had grown up to serve the fort, the men to labour, fight alongside the soldiers when necessary, look after the horses and provide fresh meat. The women washed, cleaned, grew vegetables, and carried out other services such as are needed by young men all over the Empire. This was how John and Esihle had met but soon it grew into something. He'd liked her and wanted it to be more than a financial arrangement. She was gentle and kind, and had been happy to stay with him when other girls had left as soon as the business was done. When he'd been with her a few times she refused his money but John always insisted that she take it. The sum was nothing to him though he knew she needed it to support her parents and younger brothers and sisters.

Whenever he was able, John would escape the card games and drinking in the fort to wander down to see her. Sometimes they'd just walk the paths through the scrub down to the river and John would tell her of the river near his home. How lush the growth was beside it, how the rain fell every few days and kept the land green. Esihle couldn't believe in such a place, where it wasn't bone dry for months on end. At other times, they'd lie in the dark hut talking about their future together. John knew it was just talk, and hoped with all his heart Esihle knew this as well. She had been with soldiers before, probably lots of them, and she must know they move on when ordered to. He would've been happy to marry her, to take her for wife, especially with the baby, his son, on the way, but it was impossible. There wasn't any way she'd be allowed to accompany the regiments, only the senior officers' wives could do that, and even they were discouraged. He could hardly arrange to have her sent back to Ireland to live with his parents. A beautiful, young, native girl with a small child. He smiled to think what his mother and the neighbours would make of such a thing.

John had considered desertion, more than once, but what would be the use? He'd be caught anyway. God knows how many thousands of miles from home, with only a small amount of savings, so how would he make his way back with a pregnant wife? Not to mention the Xhosa who'd be on the lookout for any white man, in uniform or not. Esihle would be no protection. The Xhosa despised her people's complicity with the British as much as they hated the British themselves.

All he could hope was that when the time came to leave he could provide Esihle with enough money to keep her from starving until the child was grown enough for her to work again. John shuddered when he thought about that work but he couldn't see any other way forward.

Then the day came soon enough. The battalion was moving to Fort Peddie, over forty miles to the south, with no way for John to get back to see Esihle and no way for her to follow him.

Whilst she lay in his arms, John could hear the grunts and moans of his fellows in the back of the hut, taking a last night of pleasure from the women who plied their trade in there. None of the men knew what the next few days might hold until they reached the relative safety of Fort Peddie. The terrain was difficult between the two forts and everyone was aware they'd be ripe for ambush on their march.

'Tomorrow?' Esihle whispered.

'First light'

She'd already have heard, there were few secrets in the camp, but perhaps didn't want to believe it until hearing it from his lips.

'Will you go?'

Another question to which she already knew the answer.

'I have no choice Esihle. I'll be found, arrested and locked up if I don't'

'But what will become of me?'

He pulled her closer and wiped a tear from her cheek.

'I will leave you money, plenty of money.'

She sat up, breaking his embrace.

'I don't want your money, I want you. You said you love me.'

'And I want you.'

John reached up and stroked her shoulder. 'Please don't be angry, not on our last night.'

He heard her sob in the darkness.

'I will come back for you. Somehow. I promise.'

His lie was as quiet as her whisper.

Day 5

Maria pulls a pencil and a folded envelope from her handbag and reads the words she's scribbled on the back. She ticks off two lines and, satisfied, returns the notes to where they came from. She pulls her chair closer to her daughter's bed.

'Fancy that eh? Granddad having a black baby. Whatever would've happened if he'd stayed there? Stayed with that African girl. There'd be no me and no you, I suppose. Or we'd be darkies. Still, the sunshine would be nice, wouldn't it?'

As if in answer, the sun comes from behind a cloud and beams through a window on to Alice's quiet face.

'What do you think might have happened to her? I like to think she became a princess and lived in the biggest hut in the village, but that might just be another of my whimsies. I get my making up stories from Daddy I expect, he was full of them you know, especially after Mammy was taken from us. When he was well he'd sit little Jimmy on one knee and me on the other and tell us of his time in the army, and on the railway. Sometimes he'd talk about how he met Mammy at the crossroads dance, how she had been the only girl not to ignore him when she heard about his consumption. I expect she loved him a lot. After all, Mammy died from it years before he did. I hardly remember her, you know, I was only five when she went. Sometimes if

I close my eyes really tight I think I can see her face but I don't know if she's real or just someone I've made up. The woman I see is young and beautiful and now I think of it, she looks a lot like you.'

Maria leans back and closes her eyes. She rubs the muscles of her back, weak and aching from years of childbearing and her face is as sad as ever it has been. A trolley stops by the bed and a woman's words seep into Maria's consciousness. A soft, supportive voice.

'Penny for them'

'What? Oh.' Maria chuckles. 'Sorry, I was just lost there for a minute.' She scrabbles in her purse for a few coppers and holds them out in her palm. 'Let me have a cup of tea will you love. Is this enough?'

'It will be surely.' She throws the money into her tin without counting it, then pours tea from a large metal pot, adds sugar and places two Digestives on the saucer. 'Have the biscuits on me, dear, you look like you could use them. I'll bet you've not eaten for hours.'

That is true enough. By the time she'd prepared meals for Billy and the little ones she'd no time to eat before running for the bus to make evening visiting. There's no spare money for Maria to buy anything in the canteen, nor does she want to spend precious time away from her daughter.

'You're very kind.'

'Not really. I've been here myself. Twice. First with my husband then, just three months later, with my son. More weeks sitting hopelessly by these beds than I'd want to count. When Ken went I'd time on my hands so offered to help out in the hospital, they'd been so good to me. With so many nurses away in the War they were glad of the offer. Just doing my bit, you know.'

The trolley rattles away down the ward to the next visitors and Alice coughs. Her mother leans forward to wipe her girl's lips. She consults scribbled notes on an envelope, dunks a biscuit in her tea and, when she's dabbed the crumbs from the edge of her mouth, continues her story.

*

John mopped sweat from his forehead then scooped up the pennies from the centre of the table and added them to the neat piles arranged in front of him. He shuffled the deck, began to deal, then paused on the second circuit, turning to the man on his left.

'Lucky you say?'

Wilson, the soldier he addressed, wanted to say 'bloody lucky' but they'd been drinking and he wasn't sure how short the corporal's fuse might be in the sweltering Indian night. He settled for a disgruntled 'Aye'.

'I'll tell you about lucky, Wilson. Did you ever hear tell of *The Birkenhead*?'

'It's near Liverpool ain't it?'

'Not Birkenhead you idiot. *The Birkenhead*. It's a ship. Well, was a ship.' John nodded to his playing partner. 'Patsy here and I know all about that, don't we, Patsy? Eight years ago we were told we'd be going off on her to the Cape, then the plans changed. There were suddenly twenty spare places on a boat called *The Castor* and some of us were sent out from Chatham two months early. Now that's what I call luck, not winning some poxy card game. *The Birkenhead* was the next boat out and it sank with over four hundred men drowned or killed by sharks, only half a day's sail from Cape Town and within a mile of the shore. If Patsy and I hadn't been picked to leave early we'd not be here in Kamptee robbing you of your hard-earned cash.'

John started to deal again. 'Anyway, I've had enough of this game. Let's say we pack it in after the next round.'

The man who'd been losing heavily started to object but John cut him off.

'Now don't you be worrying where your next packet of fags is coming from, Wilson, I'll give you your money back when we're finished.'

Patsy Flynn laughed.

'You are crackers, Byrne. You do it every time. Do your damnedest to take every penny off whoever you're playing then dole out your winnings as if it doesn't matter.'

'Oh, it matters, Patsy. Always. I don't really care if I win or lose but as long as I am playing I'll do whatever it takes to make sure the other feller doesn't get the better of me.'

John's friend shook his head. 'And it's not just about cards is it, you're like that with everything.' He turned to Wilson and the other soldier, Carrick. 'When we were coming over here, we'd been in Kefalonia and landed at Alexandria. Eighty degrees and they fed us Irish stew. I ask you. Then nine hundred bloody donkeys they had waiting for us, lined 'em up thirty wide and ordered us to climb on from the back. After we'd watched the fiasco with the first couple of rows the blokes decided to have a bet on who would get on first when we went forward. John here was off the blocks quicker than you could say Jack Robinson. On his donkey before any of the other fellows got close. Mind, loads of them couldn't climb on for laughing after that. He won the bet but bought everyone a drink with his winnings when we arrived at the other end.'

John smiled and thought about that trip across the desert from Alexandria to Suez. Almost a thousand soldiers riding donkeys in formation, a column half a mile long with hundreds of camels carrying packs alongside. Sure, John had seen enough donkeys in his time but never the other creature. Strange, ungainly beasts, bad tempered, always roaring and snapping at their companions.

Nearly five days they'd ridden like this before arriving at the port at the head of the Red Sea to wait for their transport to Bombay, another five weeks away.

*

Ten miles they'd marched that day through heat and dust with full kit in a land as different from John's own as he could imagine. The ground was dry and hard; the grass so brown and brittle to the touch he wondered how any beast could find sustenance there. So unlike the lush hills of his home that John almost wept for his missing of it. Even the boglands high in Wicklow's mountains offered more eating for sheep than this place.

The order came down to make camp and all of the men fell to the ground exhausted, preferring to remove their packs and take their breath for a while than to prepare the overnight shelter or begin work on the evening meal. Even Sergeant-Major Brennan sat down on a rock, threw off his hat and mopped his face with his handkerchief. He knew that ten miles march would go into the record but, truth to tell, the last three had been a stagger, man supporting man, wheezing and coughing through the relentless sun.

Eventually John, like the rest of his group, got up and started to arrange the area into something more like a military camp than a battlefield and he set up details to gather materials for a fire, collect water, and run the night watches. At thirty he was one of the oldest and this was almost enough to give him the respect he received, though his sergeant's stripes certainly helped where his age wasn't sufficient. All the men were tough, one or two made so by the gruelling marches and fighting but most had already been fit and strong farmer's labourers when they joined up. John had once laboured in the mines rather than on the land and though not a tall man he was solid, with the inner calmness seen in men used to working with their body rather than their brain. For the last five years he'd seen action all over India, tramping northwards from Bombay, fifty miles here, fifty miles there until now he was over a month's march from the port where he'd arrived.

Within an hour, each of the units had set out its own section of the camp to suit its needs. John's infantry, the 91st Foot, in a square of tents, eight rows by eight, with three large ones at the centre, the two messes and the command tent. Cureton's Mooltanees, the native Lancers, constructed their tents alongside the animal compound, with Colonel Tombs' Horse Artillery on the other side circling the eight- and eighteen-pounders, the howitzer and mortars.

John could see all of these from their position on the hill next to a wing of the 60th Rifles. On the other side the Caribineers were cleaning and oiling their carbines ready for the action they all knew was close. Everywhere was the smell of woodsmoke and cooking.

Captain Lambert had sent instructions that all the men should get some sleep because they'd be moving out in a few hours. Even exhausted as they were from the march, it was only the lucky few who would manage any. Most of them wouldn't be able to relax enough to get more than a few minutes shuteye with what they knew they'd be expected to do next day.

John dropped off at around eleven o'clock and was woken by the bugle call two short hours later. He made sure that the rest of his troop was awake, went outside to relieve himself, and then made his way to the command tent.

Captain Bingham stood outside smoking, mopping his forehead. 'Morning, Sergeant Byrne, bloody warm don't you think?'

John shrugged. What Bingham said was right, but anyone with an ounce of sense wouldn't bother to comment. He had little time for English officers. Some of them were good men but this one was a young idiot. Public school, privileged upbringing, and sent out by his father to take in a little experience of the world. John hoped he was enjoying it.

Inside the tent, the sergeants were grouped around their individual commanding officers, each at a trestle table draped with roughly drawn maps of the action ahead. The plan was for John's infantry company, along with the Caribineers, to go into the town, only backed up by the artillery and cavalry if they faced significant resistance. The air was full of sweat and nervous chatter. The men were not frightened, they'd all been through this before, but almost every one would be anxious about the unknown. In a war the armies would line up and face each other, heavy guns firing from behind them. Both sides could see their enemy. Here it was different. Whilst the British army still fought in formation, the rebels preferred the surprise attack, the ambush and infiltration.

At two in the morning the force moved out to cover the remaining ten miles to Madapura. It was still over eighty degrees but at least they were spared the blistering sun. The march would be easier, though John couldn't help wishing he'd the luxury of the officer's horses rather than his worn leather boots and shank's pony.

Around a quarter of a mile from the town, shortly after dawn, a cavalry unit of about a hundred rebels, supported by two guns, charged from a group of buildings to the west and the Multanis, horse artillery and Caribineers had to be deployed to disperse them. There was some initial firing on both sides but only a few men took minor injuries. The superior British numbers made the enemy flee, leaving the two brass guns behind them. John's company and the native rifles were sent into the outskirts of Madapura to clean up. They found the town deserted and quiet other than for dogs darting out to bark at the strangers on their territory.

John led his squad down streets behind the market place, with Patsy Finn, now a corporal, watching the rear. Most of the men had rounded a corner when a shot rang out behind them. Patsy had taken a hole in the chest and was lying still, ten feet from the safety of the building, blood mingling with the dust on his jacket. The sniper was in the upstairs window of a two-story house fifty yards along the street, the long barrel of his musket catching the sun. John dashed to drag his friend behind the wall but was stopped in his tracks when a ball grazed his knee, ripping his trousers and bringing him to the ground. Crawling on all fours he reached Patsy, just as the final breath left him, scarlet specks splattering John's face.

John glared up at the white-turbaned Indian lifting the barrel of his weapon to take aim again. Behind the rebel something glinted for a second before he slumped forward. Two shots from John's squad smashed into the wall beside the window.

'Stop, lads! Stop firing. It's me.' Eddy Fitzpatrick waved a hand 'I got him'.

It turned out Fitzpatrick had slipped round the

back of the buildings as soon he'd spotted Patsy Finn's killer and managed to sneak up the stairs without being heard. His clean, sharp, bayonet was all it took. He was lucky it was a lone gunman, else he'd have run into trouble himself.

Back at the camp, John's wound had been cleaned and bandaged, and he'd been declared fit for duty again. Captain Bingham was addressing the company.

'The town is clear. Only one fatality on our side. Well done.' He consulted a sheet of paper. 'Orders are that we now go into the town and burn every public building we can find.' There was a murmuring from the men. Bingham raised his hand to quieten them. 'Is that clear? Every one.'

As they dispersed, John approached the Captain.

'Is this necessary, sir?'

'Of course it's necessary, Sergeant Byrne, have to teach these boys a lesson.'

'But it's not the rebels we're hurting is it? It's the poor buggers from the town who've run away and hidden while we fought it out. If we now destroy what they have they're more likely to back up the rebels next time, aren't they.'

'Listen, Sergeant, this order doesn't come from me, though I do agree with it. It come from on high and isn't for the likes of you and I to question. So take your men and get on with it or you'll be in front of a court martial. Do you understand?'

*

It was only a short time before the town was cloaked in smoke, choking the soldiers as they went about their destruction. John's unit had been sent to burn a minor set of offices which was next to a temple and it was clear to all of them it would be damaged if they set a fire in the public building.

'What do we do, Sergeant? Do we go ahead?' Corporal Des McGill was leading the men setting the fires in this section of the town.

'You know the orders, Des, though I've no stomach for such things. For sure, I'm not lighting it. You take half the men and stack up all the paper and timber you can find, anything that will give the fire a good start. Shout when you're ready. I'll send the others to do what they can to stop the bloody temple burning down.'

Fifteen minutes later, in the dark house across the street, John could hear the flames crackling and spitting above the cries of the group dousing the place of worship next door. As the flames soared from every window of the offices he lay curled like a caterpillar in the corner, mourning his friend and the loss of human decency.

*

'That was a brave thing you did earlier, Fitz.'

'Couldn't have you getting killed, could we, Sergeant? Who'd we have to tuck us up at night?'

Several of the marching men laughed at Fitzpatrick's joke, but they knew it had taken real courage to do what he'd done. There'd be no medal, of course, there never was for the likes of them, but he'd gained the respect of his comrades-in-arms and that would be all most of them asked.

John tugged his saviour's elbow and pulled him aside from the column.

'No, seriously, it was brave. Damned brave. And I'm grateful, I could have ended up like poor Patsy.'

The two soldiers chatted for a while, then Fitzpatrick asked John what he thought of what they'd done to the town.

'Tell you the truth, I've had enough of it all. In Africa and here, all I've been doing is killing for killing's sake. What's two true Irishman like us doing propping up the Empire so's the likes of Bingham and the rest of them can live in the lap of luxury? Tell me that if you can. In a couple more years I can get out and believe me I will. Just watch me.'

*

'Every time I come to this awful place, I could catch the disease and I'm sure that's why your dad won't come. Even Alan is the only one of the boys who's visited. Remember he came in with me the night before his leave ended and he went back to France, said if he'd not been scared of Germans he shouldn't be scared of germs either. Made me laugh. He is the one most like me. Tells lots of lies, and is as wilful as can be, always doing things he shouldn't. He is a trouble sometimes but of all the boys, Alan is the one who looks out for me. When Billy has had a pint too many and tries to pick a fight, Alan is the man to face up to him and calm him down. Mostly it's with a joke, or a silly story, but I know he'd not be scared to use his fists if it ever came to that. Not that Billy has ever hurt me but he can be so bad tempered when he's a drink taken and he scares me sometimes.'

Maria looks up as the door of the ward swings open.

'Here's that crabby sister to chase me out again, Alice. I'll have to think about what I'll tell you next time. Maybe I will carry on the story I was telling you about my grandfather, or perhaps I can talk about my father and mother, maybe even about how I met your daddy. That will be something to look forward to, won't it.

'I might tell you that I grew up in a pretty cottage with flowers all around the door, and every meal with fresh vegetables dug by Daddy from the garden, and plenty of meat from the chickens, pigs and cattle we kept. And the sun always shining. But it wasn't like that. Not a day of it.

'Anyway, it's getting dark and I'd better be off for my bus. The nights will be drawing in before long. I'll see you soon again my baby.'

*

Maria passes the steaming mug of tea to Billy and he holds on to her fingertips for a second as he takes it.

'How was she tonight?'

His wife's more tired than usual and has felt her strength ebbing, so is glad for her Billy's rare show of tenderness. Maria remembers when they met, he in uniform, she on the road. She's not sure he'd fallen in love with her then, that was later, but fell for her he did. Headlong. After the abuse she took from neighbours, the escape back to England, and nine kids later here they were, still together. Both readying in their own way to grieve their daughter.

'I thought she looked a bit better. More colour in her cheeks.' Maria sits by the wireless and her eyes focus on the Blessed Virgin above the fireplace. 'You'd know better how she was if you'd come in to see her with me. Why won't you, Billy?'

He's usually quick-tempered when she asks him this but tonight he sighs and shakes his head. 'Don't go on about it, love, we've been there a hundred times already. I can't.'

'But why? I just don't understand.'

She never will understand, not properly, she knows this. It's clear he loves Alice, their first daughter, at least as much as she does but he's seen so much death in his life, in the last war and the beginning of this one. Lost so many friends and family, lives wasted with no rhyme or reason to it. Probably he can't sit by the bedside and watch another one slipping away. Billy always tells Maria he's too tired to spend the hours on the bus to the hospital. Becomes angry when she presses him. Pretends he doesn't care.

Maria straightens her back and catches a reflection of herself in the mirror. The worry is taking its toll, the lines on her face growing deeper day by day, her skin ever more ashen, the odd grey streak appearing in her once black hair. True, looking after the children doesn't help, even with the older ones taking some of the strain, but it isn't all of it. Alice's sickness, and three lads in the forces, are almost as much as anyone could stand. Billy's voice breaks through her pain.

'I know you don't understand. That's why it's no good going on about it.' He hardens his voice. 'So leave me to get on with my paper.'

Maria goes back to the kitchen to hide her tears She's seen the photograph her husband keeps in his wallet. It shows a blond girl in a flowery dress, standing in the park beside Maria, ten years earlier. Alan, the second eldest, had taken it on a box camera he'd borrowed from a friend for the day. Maria has spied Billy study the creased picture more than once and likes to imagine he has looked at it every day since their daughter went into hospital.

Day 6

These stories just keep coming to me when I'm on the way to the hospital. There's only so many buildings can be interesting from the top of a bus and I can't count the ones I've looked at over the past few months. What else have I to do but think of ways to take us to somewhere else?

I nearly didn't come tonight. The two little ones have caught colds and your dad was out of sorts with me for leaving them. The other night when I asked him to come he refused. Said he has his reasons and that's that, then he stopped talking to me and stuck his head behind his Evening Chronicle. I left him to it and sat in the kitchen in the dark.

I don't want you getting mixed up over all these people. It's simple enough I suppose. There's my father, my mammy and my granddad, John. Later on I'll tell you about me. I'm not sure about all of the names and places so I might have made up a few of them. Still, it makes it interesting doesn't it?

*

A robin pecked away at the ridge, it's russet breast bringing a hint of autumn to the bare ground while the worm in its beak held on to the dark Wicklow earth, stretching to double in length before giving itself up to its feathered captor. The bird gulped down the morsel and hopped expectantly in the man's direction.

John lay down his mug, rubbed his throbbing knee, a legacy from his final weeks in the army, and surveyed progress. Four ridges dug today and already they were covered by brown, wind-blown leaves from the poplars shielding the cottage. He didn't mind. The surviving worms would drag them down over coming months and enrich the soil ready for planting in the spring. He took a bite of bread, rubbed his knee again, and thought of how he would like to be put to such use when he went, rotting in the ground to feed the grass and trees above him. His mother came to the half-door beside him.

'It's going well, son, you'll soon have the lot dug. I don't know what we'd have done this year if you hadn't come back, your daddy's not fit for it any longer.' The stout woman brushed the flour from her apron and shook her head. 'Not fit for anything anymore.'

She stepped outside and sat on the bench by her son, linking his arm. 'It is good to have you home, John. So many, many years away and such strange places you've been, I can't imagine.'

'Not so strange really, same as here in many ways.' He looked up at the clouds, grey behind grey. 'A bit warmer, I'll give you, but still filled with poor people scratching a living from the earth while the few live high on the pig, never doing a decent day's work in their lives.' John nodded to the line of trees across the field. 'Just like his lordship over there. It took me too long to work that out.'

John stood and helped his mother to her feet. 'Best get on. If I put my back into it I'll get another couple of rows done before the rain comes.'

He lifted his spade from against the wall and limped over to begin his labours once more.

*

Eight or nine men sat along the bar, each with a glass of stout in front of them, in varying degrees of emptiness. This is how these boys saw it, not as a drink to be enjoyed, but a pathway to blessed oblivion. John wasn't like them. All in all he felt content in his life. Good health, apart from the knee which he was well used to by now, and an army pension, not a fortune but enough for a few pints every week after he'd passed most of it over to his mother. The only worries he carried were his father, now laid up with a bad heart, and, when he remembered he was forty years of age, the lack of a wife to keep him warm at night. His father, he could do nothing about, the wife was a different matter and John was certain some nice woman would turn up before too long, looking for a man well set up and with experience of life outside Arklow.

'You playing this game or staying inside your

head?' One of John's three companions threw a two of clubs on the table to begin a new round of Slippery Ann. The other two laughed.

John pulled a watch from his waistcoat pocket and tapped the glass. 'Half past eight, lads, one more game then I'm for home. Mammy likes to have the house closed up by ten.'

This drew even more laughter from his friends, taunting him about being on 'the mammy's skirt hem' until the look on the ex-soldier's face told them they should stop. John slapped down the ace of clubs. 'Come on then. Let's get on with it.'

A blast of wind from the door riffled the two cards on the table top and the four men turned to greet Peter Keogh, John's nearest neighbour.

'John, come quick. It's your da'.

*

Most of the crowd had left the graveside, some heading home through the drizzle, some to continue their conversations and condolences over a pot of tea tended by John's mother. The only ones remaining were John, the gravediggers and a tall, slim, man in his eighties, his expensive coat, hat and brown leather shoes had set him apart from the other mourners. This was Charles Francis FitzTemple, ex-Colonel of the 98th Regiment of Foot, Earl of Rathnew and John's father's commanding officer when they served in the East India Company. His family seat, Skaleham Abbey, was less than a mile from the Byrne's cottage as the crow flew, though a thousand miles in terms of status and heritage. He lifted his hat to John.

'He was a good man, Sergeant Byrne. Safe to have at your side.'

'Aye. We all have our own memories, my lord. Thank you for coming. It's kind of you, and Mammy appreciated it.'

'It was the least I could do. He saved my life once, you know. Did he tell you that? Killed a Frenchie who was about to blow my head off in Sicily. Best damn shot I ever saw. Tobacco?'

John lifted a pinch from the proffered calf-skin pouch and filled his pipe. Both men lit up and stood in silence for a few moments as the smoke spread around them. His lordship was first to break the reverie.

'It was lucky for your mother that you came back when you did, Sergeant.' He pointed his pipe-stem at John's leg. 'Was it the knee? I heard you were shot.'

'I was, sir, more than once. Last time it went bad on me and it seemed like a good time to finish. I'd the twenty-one years served so knew I'd get the pension. I was going to come back after my second term but heard there was no work around Wicklow so I stayed on.'

'And have you work now?'

'Not yet. I've been trying to help Mammy get

the place back in order since I got back, the fields and pigs were too much for her on her own without Da to do the heavy jobs. The army pension helps but my savings won't last for ever so I'll need to be finding something soon.'

'Perhaps I can help you there. I'm in need of a new lodge-keeper. Nothing too heavy. Keeping the entrance tidy and the riff-raff out. Pointing guests up to the house, that kind of thing. Interested?'

'That's very kind of you, sir. It'd be close enough to keep an eye on Mammy and I shan't say the money won't come in handy. When would you be wanting me to start?'

'Soon as you can, Sergeant. Of course you'd need to live in the lodge and there's one other thing …' FitzTemple paused, choosing his words 'you'd need to be married - not right away, but we need a woman in there. Steadier, you know, shows we're respectable. See what you can do.'

*

The back of Skaleham Abbey was plainer by far than its massive ornate frontage, but John still marvelled at the opulence of the windows and stonework when he pushed his barrow towards the kitchen. The estate manager had told him he must always come round the right hand side of the building, staying away from the grand drive which circled round from the left. This way he'd be out of sight of the carriages either sweeping down to the lake or into the coach-house. On that side, the stables hid the working parts of the mansion so as not to offend the eyes of noble and wealthy visitors.

Martha Costello flung open the door and threw her easy smile in his direction. John had met her a month earlier, two days after he'd taken up his post in the lodge, and he'd liked her right away. Although she was plain her infectious laugh left those around her shaking their heads in amusement. He sensed she was perhaps too exuberant for a life below stairs and the cook told him the girl was on trial with her. She'd gone to the Abbey as a parlour maid, then banished to upstairs before being sent to the kitchens as her last chance. John thought poor Martha would soon be given her marching orders, despite the light she brought to the house.

'So, it's you Mr Byrne, is it? What have you for us today?' The girl collapsed in a heap of giggles for no good reason that John could see.

'Carrots and cabbages. Last of the lettuces. Shall I bring them in?'

'You will not. Not in those mucky boots. Cook would have me on the street quicker than you could wink. Give them here and I'll put them inside.'

John waited while Martha made five trips to place the vegetables in a basket by the sink, in readiness for washing before preparing them for dinner. Each time she returned he made an offer to help but she scolded him on every occasion, her broad grin showing him the chiding was just in case the cook was in earshot. When she lifted the fifth consignment, John crooked his finger to share a confidence.

'When is your day off?'

Confusion flitted across Martha's face. Then she raised an eyebrow.

'Why would you want to know, Mr Byrne?'

'I wondered …' he coughed 'I wondered if you might like to walk into Arklow to Mrs Callaghan's tearooms? We could go to the Temperance Rooms if you'd prefer.'

And that was it. My granddad and grandma getting together over a basket of vegetables, him in his forties with a gammy leg and her barely twenty. He probably only asked her because that Viscount feller told him he'd to get married, but why would she go with him? Maybe she knew she'd be out of a job before long with all her giddiness. Still, they made a go of it, with three children, including my daddy. Did granddad ever tell her about his black baby in Africa? I bet he didn't. Men always get away with that kind of thing. It's us women who get stuck. Don't I know it.

I remember him as a kind man in his way but sometimes stern and a bit quiet. Perhaps he was hurt by the things he'd had to do in all those foreign places. It would be hard for him, as well, trying to settle back in the Wicklow countryside after so many years travelling the world. I'm sure I'd never want to go back there. Maybe for other reasons, but I still wouldn't want it.

I was only young when they both died. Even though granddad was so much older, she went first and Daddy never got back for her funeral because we were living in Liverpool then. Sad that would be. Something else I know well enough.

Day 7

I want to skip forward so much, to explain all about what happened in my life, but none of it makes sense, not to me anyway, unless I go through it all. It's like a train track, or those wires the trolley buses follow in to town. They can't just jump from beginning to end. One stop leads to the next, then another, and another, so when you get to your destination you'll know how you got there. The journey might be enjoyable, or it might not, it doesn't matter.

So *our* next stop is with my father, Edmund, his name was, and granddad never wanted him to join the army.

*

'You can't go, Edmund, it will break your mother's heart.'

Even at sixty-three, John Byrne was still a man to be reckoned with. He may have left the army over twenty years earlier but he'd lost none of his tough sergeant's presence. Edmund didn't often cross him, not because he was physically frightened, he was well able to look after himself in that respect, but because his father had kept his ability to command. If he stood and looked you in the eye, you did as you were told, no argument. Edmund had seen him do it to men on the estate a number of times, men over who he had no official authority, he was just the lodge-keeper after all, but everyone knew where he'd been and what he'd had to do in the service of the Queen. If John Byrne asked you to do something, you did it.

Edmund couldn't give in this time though. At last training camp, Corporal Kearon had said he was doing well in the Militia and he should consider joining up full time when the next recruitment day came around. It was due this Saturday in the town. He'd been waiting for the right moment to tell his father, and the older man's good humour when they sat down to share soup and tea looked to offer the opportunity. Five minutes later he knew he'd been mistaken.

'And it will break my heart if I stay here. There's nothing for me.'

'Nothing for you? You've a decent job, nice and steady. You've your family, Bridget, Mick, me and your mother. Is that nothing?'

'I hate the job. Labouring all the hours God sends and for what? Barely enough to get by every week. Doing another man's bidding day after day.'

John smiled. 'And you think the army's going to be any different? I'd spent more than half my life in uniform when I left -'

'But you were giving the orders.'

He snorted. 'I was passing on orders, from the imbeciles at the top to the fools at the bottom, that was all, doing what I was told just like everyone else. The only thing kept me going sometimes was the knowledge that my few bob would be helping out at home.'

They battled on like this for another quarter of an hour, both becoming increasingly frustrated with the other, before Edmund stormed out, leaving his lunch uneaten on the table and his mother weeping in the kitchen.

*

Edmund had only been in Malta a month but he disliked Fort St Elmo almost as much as he'd hated working the fields at home. The island had been hot and sticky since he'd arrived, day and night, and the only respite had been to go down to the sea and immerse himself in the filthy water whenever he could. Tonight it looked like the weather might break. To the north, on the horizon towards Sicily, thunderheads were gathering and Edmund thought he could hear the occasional rumble above the noise of the city behind him. From his station on the battlements he had a good view in all directions, out across the sapphire Mediterranean, Marsamxett Harbour on one side and the Grand Harbour on the other, with Fort Ricasoli guarding the southern bank. Whoever had designed the place knew what they were doing, the whole set up had made Valetta almost impregnable. For the hundreds of soldiers stationed here, however, there was no invasion likely, so the guard duty they did every day was a waste of time. The only reason for the garrison to be maintained was to provide a base for actions elsewhere, a stopping off point for troops keeping order in the Queen's empire.

Edmund was not just hot, he was bored as well. But he'd rather be outside than in the stifling barracks below, where it stank of sweat and piss, where there was no privacy, and where half the men were coughing up their lungs all night. Another rumble, this time much louder, and Edmund saw lightning spark from the heavens to the sea. He didn't like thunderstorms, it seemed to him the very air lay heavy when they were around, but if it meant relief from this humidity he'd welcome one soon. Four nights earlier it had threatened the same, then simply moved off and dropped its deluge on Greece, far away out of sight, and the next morning had been as steaming as the one before.

In his pocket, Edmund kept two things at all times. One was the St Christopher medal his mother pressed into his hand the day he'd left, telling him to look after himself and to come home safe. He lifted out the second keepsake, a cardboard-framed photograph of his sister, Bridget, only a year older than him and taken as a present when she'd visited Wicklow Town the previous summer. She beamed out from the oval, her dark hair tumbling over her shoulders, reminding him of both of their parents, sharing their mother's eyes and their father's rounded face. Beside her was a friend. Bridget had told him she and Hannah Quinn only had enough money to have one photograph taken but the man had been kind enough to make them two prints. The slightly younger Hannah would surely have been the cause of the photographer's good nature, her pretty face making his sister look dowdy at her side and Edmund knew Hannah could charm the birds from the trees when she set her mind to it. He'd been victim of it more than once.

He smiled and put the photograph back in his top pocket, then shivered as the first drops spattered on the dusty ground.

*

It had rained, on and off, for three weeks but, despite the temperature dropping like a stone, Edmund was still waking with the sweats every night. The tightness in his chest was getting worse and he'd have to see the doctor before long. A fortnight earlier he'd thought it was just a summer cold and thrown down a daily dose of whisky in hot water in the hope of clearing it up. It hadn't done any good and now he felt so weak he could hardly drag himself on duty.

He collected his ration of bread and stewed tea, with little appetite, and sat amongst the other soldiers assigned to a pointless day patrolling the walls of the fort, watching for non-existent enemies of her Majesty. His neighbour on the mess bench, Nobby Jackson, glanced round.

'Jesus Christ, Edmund, you look rough.'

Instead of replying, Edmund rolled backwards from the table, only saved from smashing his skull on the stone floor by Jackson grabbing a sleeve in time.

*

Twenty beds in the ward and every one occupied, all but two by men with various degrees of fever. The others were a man called Jessop, with a broken arm, and Bragg, whose leg had just been cut off, gone bad after he'd banged it on a gun placement. The heat had returned and the coughing and foul air were even worse in here than in the barracks. Bragg began screaming as the ether's effect faded. Surgeon-Major Griffiths, white coat still flecked with blood and sinew from Bragg's amputation, stood at the head of Edmund's bed, reading the notes made by Nurse Grady overnight.

"Came in yesterday? Fainted?' Griffiths said.

'Yes, Doctor.'

'Sweating a lot I see, Nurse. Any other symptoms?'

'A lot of phlegm. No blood, though. Tells me

he's lost weight, but that's only to be expected. I've given him a linctus and cod liver oil as usual. Anything else you'd recommend?'

'You'd best give him zinc oxide for the infection and belladonna for his sweats when he needs it.'

'Not much more we can do, sir, same as the others. Keep them comfortable and hope they get better.'

*

Edmund woke up on the fourth day to see the sheet had been pulled over Bragg's head. Nurse Grady said he'd gone in the night. The poor soul had moaned and sobbed constantly since his operation, infection creeping through his veins as the blood and pus seeped from his stump. In many ways it was a blessing. He'd only a few months service and his wound would be called self-inflicted, they always were, so there'd be no chance of a pension. A crippled soldier would find no work and Bragg would just have ended up sleeping rough and dying on the streets of Newcastle or Birmingham or London, wherever he found himself.

After six days, Edmund was well enough to be wheeled outside into the fresh air, to join the other five beds on the veranda where it was cool under the shade of the stone canopy, looking out over Valletta. Some of the men were sleeping, breathing more easily than they had indoors. On one end of the row, Gunner Mark Timony looked up from his newspaper and waved before getting back to it. The orderly lined up Edmund's bed alongside Stevie Kilfoil, a range-finder from No. 2 Company and a fellow Wicklow man who'd been in Malta for three years.

'You're feeling a bit better, Edmund?'

'A bit. Awake at least. What are you in here for?'

Kilfoil snorted. 'Pox. Damned pox.'

Had he not been so weak, Edmund would have been amused.

'My own fault, I suppose, should keep it in my pants. But what's a feller to do? March here and march there all day and then settle down at night with his thoughts and a mug of tea? Anyway, I heard they're supposed to examine these girls, make sure they're clean. When I came in, that nurse told me there's half a dozen fellers a week getting treated. No wonder the women can't keep free of it.'

Edmund had hardly had time since he arrived to take the pleasures of Molly Brown's, Angioletta's or any of the dozen other houses catering for the men from the fort. He'd told himself when he set sail from Cork that he'd keep away from these ladies. He hadn't done such things at home and had no desire to end up like Kilfoil, covered in sores and his guts flushed out with calomel. He also needed to send as much money home as he could, to demonstrate to his father he'd made the right choice in joining the army.

The two men settled down to talk of families they'd known back in Ireland, and for a while they explored the connections they might have in common, but there was nothing. Kilfoil was from the north of the county closer, to Dublin than to Wicklow Town and his father had only moved down from Mayo to take over the farm when the wife's father died. There was a distant cousin walked out for a while with a friend of Edmund's sister, but that was it. Kilfoil dug and probed for a full three quarters of an hour before Edmund said he needed to rest and his erstwhile companion left him be.

The red glow through Edmund's eyelids took him back to autumns spent in his grandmother's orchard behind her cottage. Younger days when the sun struggled against the coming winter and the air smelled sweet from wasp-bitten apples. Days when his parents carried all the worries and all he had to do was eat his meals, or play amongst the grass, or stride alongside his father through the fields. Days before the cough racked his every hour.

*

Every day, as he grew stronger, Edmund would see the Surgeon-Major sit by the bed of one of the sicker men, filling out paperwork. Then the man would be gone, sent home as an invalid. In this place they might not be at war but they had a constant battle with fevers and consumption. There were a hundred and eighty soldiers in Edmund's company, and more than half of them had been in the hospital in the last year. Six had been sent back to England. Times that by the six companies on the island and it was a lot of casualties for the army to deal with. Just as well there was a good supply of hungry young blokes at home willing to join up and replace them.

After twelve days he was well enough to return to duty, with a recommendation he be billeted in the tents for a while, rather than the stinking halls below the battlements, so at least he'd be able to breathe under canvas.

Edmund was in the hospital five more times , once with broken ankle where he'd gone over on the cobbles in the town, the other four were a worsening of what had been diagnosed on his third admission as tuberculosis of the lungs. Then, one day, a Surgeon-Major was sitting by his bed with the forms in his hands.

'You'll be going home, Byrne, soon as we get these filled in. The Contentment is away in a couple of days back to Portsmouth, then they'll get you … where is it?' he rifled through Edmund's record. 'Aah, here it is. County Wicklow, Ireland. Nice there is it?' Surgeon-Major Baxter didn't wait for a response nor did he seek any agreement from Edmund on what he was writing down. He was a doctor and an officer after all so why should he discuss his opinions with the lower ranks.

'Will I get a pension, sir?'

'I shouldn't think so, Byrne, why would you think that?'

'Because I caught this thing, this consumption, in the army.'

'Nonsense man. You could have got it anywhere. What's to say you didn't have it when you joined up eh? Army can't be held responsible for every man who comes down with a fever. We'll just put down here we don't know what caused it, probably the climate not suiting you eh?'

'But loads of the fellers have it, sir, catching it from each other, must be. Nearly every soldier here has a cough. Something in the air, I was told.'

'Well you might think that, Byrne, but I'm the doctor and I don't agree so can't write it down here now can I? You just get yourself ready when I'm gone, then get back and pack up your things ready to leave on Thursday. The nurse will give you medicine, and you remember to take it.'

There was no more to be said. In two days, Edmund was on the deck of the Contentment, steaming westward across the Mediterranean on the long journey back to England, staring at the photograph of his sister, Alice, and her friend, the lovely Hannah Quinn.

*

Edmund and his father dumped the last stones from the back of the cart on to a pile by the road then the older man tied the horse to a tree. The two men stood back and admired their work. The new walls, stretching twenty yards either side of the four grand gateposts which had guarded the entrance to the estate for the last two hundred years, were straight and a fine example of the stone-builder's craft.

'Should be finished today, son, if the weather holds off. Your mammy heard from cook, who heard from that Jenny, the parlour-maid, who overheard at tea, that his lordship is pleased with what we've done so far.'

'Already said I can't see why it needed to be done, the hedges were well laid and kept the animals in. Waste of good money if you ask me.'

'Well it's not your money to worry about, is it. With his father gone he'd want to make his mark as the new Lord Rathnew wouldn't he, it's only natural. Every generation of the family has added something. I'll bet this wall is only the start. There'll be a new wing to the house or bigger stables before too long, I wouldn't be surprised.'

The two men set about their work, John piling stone upon stone to build the final column, Edmund selecting each one from the mound they'd unloaded, then hefting them to place in his father's hand. Occasionally, John would reject one, with 'a bit shorter, if there is one' or 'not quite so thick this time', knowing the son would respect his eye and judgement without taking offence. Edmund would need to rest from time to time when his lungs could no longer feed the labour his body had to do. Though he'd grown stronger in the country air, his breathing was still shallow and, on bad days, the cough left him gasping. For these breaks, John would grab a smoke and Edmund would lean against the wall, upwind from him, keeping an eye on the drive and the road in case anyone would come along and find they weren't hard at it.

When they'd finished the column, Edmund lifted a billhook from the cart and began hacking the blackthorn, laying the hedge to tie neatly against the new structure and repairing the damage they'd done during the building.

'You head on back to the house, I'll finish off here, there's no need for the two of us. I'll see you back there in a while.'

John didn't argue. Instead, he stretched his aching back, then stood in the lane, scanning the wall for faults one last time and finding none, before leading the horse up the long drive winding to the Abbey. Edmund could hear him whistling the air to *A Nation Once Again* and smiled, though hoped he'd change the tune before his father arrived in earshot of the master.

The sun was dipping behind grey clouds by the time Edmund finished his task, and the treetops were swaying in a breeze freshening with the shower which would surely come soon. He gathered up his things, turned up his coat collar and followed the path of his father. As he rounded the bend which skirted an ancient oak, a young woman stepped from behind its giant trunk.

'Oh, Edmund, it's you. I heard the steps and didn't know who could be coming up the drive at this time of day.'

Edmund laughed. 'Frightened you did I, Sally?'

Sally Dalton lived in the next townland to the Byrnes, she and her mother embroidered linen and the daughter was charged with going from door to door trying to sell their handiwork. Edmund knew they had an arrangement to supply the Abbey's needs for pillow-cases, runners and tablecloths in the minor parts of the house, where less important guests might sleep and dine. It would be a useful source of income for the Daltons, when the money earned by Sally's father digging ditches ran low in the winter months. She may have lacked wealth but made up for it in her ability to attract young men around her. It was as if she willed the blush to her dimpled cheeks when Edmund spoke to her.

'You did not, Edmund Byrne, I was just wondering, that's all.'

'Then why were you hiding behind the tree, I ask you?'

She giggled. 'Oh stop will you. Anyway, what are you doing rambling about like you've not a care in the world. Have you no work to be at?'

He told her what he'd been doing and they chatted under the branches for a few minutes with the rain beginning to spatter the leaves above them. It grew heavier and Sally said she needed to head home before it got any worse.

'Before I go, can I ask you a question?'

'Ask away. I can always say "no".' Though Edmund knew he wouldn't be able to refuse her.

'Would you come with me to the dance on Saturday? Marty Reynolds says he'll take the cart and there's a few piling in but they'll all be in couples. Say you'll come, it'll be great craic.' She tilted her head, the brown curls tipped from her shoulder, and the last nail was driven home. 'Pleeease.'

*

Whether Sally Dalton had invited Edmund simply to make another young man jealous or because she genuinely wanted him to come, he couldn't tell, but from the minute he joined them at Ballyduff bridge she was distant, talking all the while to another girl and flashing her eyes at a dark-haired stranger further down the cart.

By the time they arrived, the dance was in full

swing and Edmund's mood was darker than the shadows outside the hall, though it lightened a little when Sally took his arm to walk inside.

'Now young man, you go over and buy us a drink, and I'll try to find us a spot to sit. Or at least somewhere to stand where we can hear the music and not be trodden on by these great lumps.'

From the bar, Edmund saw her place her coat and hat to reserve two spaces on the bench along one wall, then go over the man she'd been admiring on the journey. They joked for a minute or two until Sally glanced round and looked in Edmund's direction. She waved as if she'd been waiting for him, indicating where the seats were, then turned to go back, brushing her companion's arm ever so slightly as she left him. Edmund downed his pint and ordered another.

He sat next to Sally, unspeaking, for the next fifteen minutes, feigning an interest in the musicians and dancers though, in fact, he was staring straight through them. Sally sipped her drink, breaking off to exchange greetings with friends as the passed, until his silence grew too much for her.

'Are we going to dance then?'

'Hmm.'

'What?'

'You'd best go ask yer man.' Edmund nodded in the direction of his rival. 'There'll be no dancing with me tonight.'

'Who? Malachy? He's married.'

'I can't see that stopping you, you've been all over him since Marty picked me up, even earlier for all I know.'

'How dare you say such …' Her voice rose in volume just as the music stopped and heads turned in their direction to see what was going on. Sally's face flushed and she paused, then continued through gritted teeth. Edmund thought how unattractive this made her look. '… a thing. If that's how you feel I'll just go and sit somewhere else.'

Edmund stood. 'I wouldn't want to be seen depriving a lady of her seat, you stay there. I'm sure your friend will join you shortly.'

He considered the possibilities. Head off into the night, hoping to pick up a lift part of the way, or stay at the bar until someone lifted him dead drunk on to the back of Marty's waggon at the end of the night. He decided he didn't fancy the long walk home. On the other hand he didn't fancy the head he'd have in the morning if he spent his evening pouring pints of stout down his throat. Still, the bar won, softened by the promise to himself that he'd take it easy.

An hour passed and Edmund was staring into the bottom of his fourth glass, not drunk but edging towards it. He felt a tap on his shoulder.

'Someone's not very happy tonight.'

The woman was slim, blond, nice figure, fuller than in the picture he'd kept for so long. Mid-twenties, same as himself. Beautiful smile. 'Hannah?'

'Don't tell me you've forgotten me?' her eyes twinkled 'I know you've not seen me since you got back but still ...'.

Edmund sat up and gave her his best beery smile, throwing an arm around her shoulder. 'How could I forget you?' he thought of the guilty photograph in his jacket pocket as the drink made him brave, and he strained not to slur his words 'you're ... you're always in my thoughts.'

'Edmund Byrne, you're a wicked man. What a thing to say to a girl. I'll tell your mammy.'

The two burst out laughing as the band started another reel. He grabbed her hand and tugged her away from the bar.

'C'mon, let's have a dance. That's what we're here for isn't it?'

*

So he'd met my mammy. Fine and young and fit she was then. Didn't know what was on the horizon, poor woman. Auntie Bridget told me she'd had a crush on Daddy from the minute they met, kept asking about him all the time he was in the army, and didn't know that he felt the same. I wonder what she'd have thought if she'd have known he kept her photo all that time.

They were married not long afterwards in the church in Newbridge, up by the lovely Avoca, the river I told you about, and I was born the following spring. I do wish I'd known her longer. I was just a kiddie and then one day she wasn't there anymore. On that evening at the dance, I bet she kept him on the floor and away from the bar all night. I can just see Daddy walking her home then getting back to Granny's as the sun came up. That's the picture I keep in my head anyway.

I've got to go. I don't want to, but I have to else I'll miss my bus. So many stories still to tell and I need to get them straight in my head if we're going to get through them all.

Day 8

Maria waits twenty minutes for the bus in the rain and smokes her last cigarette before it arrives. No more until she can wheedle a few bob out of Billy, but fat chance for a day or two. The reason she missed the previous bus was an argument with him about leaving everyone again. He woke up from his afternoon nap in a foul mood, picked and complained about his tea, then started moaning about money when she slipped on her coat.

'It can't go on, Maria. Spend, spend, spend, and for what?'

'I have to see my girl. *Our* girl.'

'No you don't. Neither of us do. Being there all the time isn't going to make her well. Nothing will. And we can't afford it.'

She held back the urge to strike him.

'We've .. I've found the bus fare so far, and that's all it is for God's sake.'

Billy dropped his head.

'Well you'll be hard pushed to find it in future.'

'Don't you threaten me, Billy Garner.'

'I'm not. They've cut my hours.'

Maria felt her colour trickle away. One second flushed with anger the next like a sheet. She grabbed a chair back to steady herself then slumped down.

'What? How?' Oh Billy.'

'Timmy Nichols called me in when I got back

from my round. Said I'd been taking too long and he'll have to bring me in to the sorting office. Something lighter that I can manage. Trouble is he doesn't have a full-time job for me, just four days. Even said I should be grateful for that.'

Maria had feared this day would arrive, ever since Billy came home after the heart attack. Getting his old job back with the Post Office had always been too good to be true. She'd no strength, nor will, to fight him any longer about money, so just hugged him and said they'd talk when she got back.

*

Without a cigarette there's no point in Maria climbing the stairs to the top deck but downstairs is full. The conductor waves her along the aisle and whispers to two young men, a soldier and a sailor, who stand and point to the seat.

'You sit here, love, we're off at the next stop.'

Maria thanks them and settles to watch the seats flit by.

At the terminus, the memory drags a smile from her as the bus shudders to a halt, like some giant beast in its last throes. She joins the queue shuffling off into the muggy evening, making her way across the square to catch the bus for her next leg. The rain has moved on and Piccadilly Gardens is crowded with couples, some chatting on benches, holding hands, others pushing prams along the regimented paths between ornamental beds full of colour.

The walk takes a little over five minutes from bus-stop to bus-stop, leaving Maria a few minutes more to look around the square. When she started these visits there were no lights in shop and office windows, nor in the Portland Hotel on the corner, but now, with the blackout ended, they'll be shining after dark. Piccadilly, the heart of the city, still bears other scars of the war, bombed out buildings and pavements lined with shelters, but it is coming back to life.

Right on time the bus draws up and Maria finds a seat by a window.

*

Wish I'd time to stay and take in the flowers. Just for a while. Maybe Billy will bring me soon. Leave early, bring the wee ones to wander round town for a bit. If I suggest he has his pint down here rather than the Labour Club he might go for it. Then we can walk through the gardens before heading to see Alice.

Isn't it funny. Small acts of kindness. Seem like nothing to the giver but are everything when they're given. There's me, mad as hell with Billy, for complaining about money, making me feel terrible guilty for spending his last bob, then those two fellers lift me out of it. Just as well. Got to figure out what I'll tell Alice tonight. God, I always thought I could make up stories. No trouble at all with stuff for the wee ones or lies for the nuns but this is hard. Remembering is bad enough but filling in the rest, bits I don't know, from story books and school, is nigh impossible. The lady in Clayton library gave me such a look the other day when I asked for books on India, Africa and Malta. Reckon she thought I couldn't even read.'

I've told my girl about the Avoca, only cobbled from what I've seen or heard, and yet another library book. All that nonsense about St Kevin came from Sister Angela, a tale she'd tell every time she'd remember I came to them from Wicklow. She, God bless her, was one of the nice ones.

Even this next part will be difficult because I was alive but don't properly remember, I was too young. I'll just have to tell it like the others, almost as though the baby Maria and me are different. I could try to explain to Alice, but it won't make any difference to her.

The memories that *are* mine will be hard enough to tell when we get there.

*

The ten minutes past five steamed away from Rathdrum platform with a deafening blast of its whistle, up the line to Arklow, Wicklow and Bray and eventually in to Dublin before seven o'clock. There'd been only six get off, five regulars home for the weekend, and a commercial traveller who asked the way to his lodgings.

Edmund obliged with directions, then trundled the empty mail truck along the platform, rolled it down the ramp to cross the tracks and strained up the other side again. At the top of the second incline he'd paused for breath, just for a minute, hoping no-one could see him from the ticket-office window. He'd been feeling better for the last few weeks, having picked up when they'd moved to Rathdrum and Hannah had told him she was pregnant. Enough to make any man's health improve.

He'd been glad to get the job on the Dublin, Wicklow and Wexford Railway, even though it meant moving from home and disappointing his father. John must have known Edmund had never been happy working on the FitzTemple estate. That's why he'd left for the Army in the first place. Sure, he'd enjoyed working alongside his father, most of the time, but he felt stifled. He envied the old man's ability to forget his travels and settle down into the country life, with the biggest excitement being the changing colours of leaves in autumn, or new shoots pushing through the ground every spring. Edmund knew he'd seen less than his father in his army career, but still, he'd escaped from the townland and wasn't content to stay there for the remainder of his life after he'd returned. Working on the estate had been hard, out in all weathers, and badly paid, not to mention precarious. One mistake or a misplaced word and FitzTemple would have had him out, possibly his father too. No, it was better to leave when he'd had the chance, under his own control. He knew that with a new wife, and a baby on the way, it had been the right decision.

When Maria did enter the world she didn't do so easily. Despite all of Mrs Houlihan's experience, and the encouragements of Hannah's mother, who'd come up for the confinement, the doctor had to be called and was none too pleased with being brought out in such awful weather. Rain and hail had been lashing down, and the late snow of the previous few days had turned to slush, the ruts in the drifts overflowing with water. Dr Gillespie had stamped his feet on the mat and thrown his sodden overcoat in Edmund's direction.

'Filthy night, Mr Byrne, where's your wife?' Within seconds his question was answered by Hannah's shrieks escaped from the Byrne's bedroom. 'You stay here. I presume the ladies have everything prepared?'

Edmund told him that they had. Gillespie pulled open the door and Edmund caught a glimpse of Hannah on the bed, sweat pouring from her and fear in her eyes, mother on one side and neighbour on the other. When the scene was taken from him, he stood, shaking, one hand on the kettle, unsure if he should make tea for the doctor or boil more for the imminent birth.

It was a long night, with much pacing from Edmund and much screaming from his wife but as the first flecks of grey dawn appeared, he heard the baby cry and a few minutes later Hannah's mother called him in.

'It's a girl, a lovely baby girl. She's your eyes and your dark hair, there'd be no mistaking the father of that one.'

Hannah's face was blotched and her damp hair spread across the pillow, but Edmund thought she'd never looked so beautiful. He leaned over and kissed her forehead, then did the same to the pink child at her side.

'Maria, we'll call her Maria.' His wife whispered. Edmund squeezed her hand and nodded without reply.

Dr Gillespie washed his bloody hands in a basin, dried them, then slipped on his coat, warming by the stove. 'She had a difficult time there for a while, Mr Byrne, and will need to rest for a few days. You've someone will help look after her?'

Edmund looked towards his mother-in-law and she nodded.

The rain of the night had moved on and when the doctor stepped into the cold morning air he turned to Edmund with parting words that froze the new father deeper than the frost laying on the hedgerow.

'I thought we'd lost her you know. You'd better both think twice before you put her through that again.'

*

Hannah was sitting outside the cottage when Edmund turned into the lane. She didn't spot him so he stopped behind the barn and watched her. A bowl of vegetables sat on her knee, potatoes, carrots and swedes which she was peeling for their dinner. On the grass by her side, Maria, barely a month old, lay on a blanket, with three chickens nearby, clucking and pecking away at the ground, picking up scraps and tugging out the occasional incautious worm. Hannah put down the knife into her bowl and ran her fingers through her hair. He couldn't believe how beautiful he found her to be and hoped she'd be proud of him with the news he was bringing home.

Edmund began to whistle, his usual calling card when he walked. Hannah always said that it brightened her day when she heard his tune coming down the road. At first he said he never knew that he did it but now, sometimes, he stopped on purpose, hoping to catch his wife unawares. It wasn't that he expected to find her doing something he would be unhappy with, simply that it was fun to surprise her and to admire her from a distance.

When she heard Edmund, she stood, put the food she had been preparing onto the seat, and walked to the gate to meet him. When he stepped through she flung her arms around his neck and kissed him.

'My, what was that for?'

'I missed you today, love. We've been so lonely here without you.'

'I'll have to go to work more often then.' he said, grinning.

Hannah took her husband's hand and led him into the house. 'Sit down, I'll put on the kettle. I've something to tell you.'

'That makes two of us.'

Hannah scooped three large spoonfuls into the brown pot and lifted the bubbling kettle from the stove to make the tea. 'You first' she said.

'No, you, mine is very special and we'll need to talk about it.'

'What makes you think mine isn't special?' Hannah laughed 'It's not only you can have something important to say, you know'.

'Because you can't keep a big secret for a minute longer than is necessary. You'd have blurted it out as soon as you clapped eyes on me. So sit down and tell me what happened in your day.'

'Mammy came on the bus to see me.'

'But you said you were on your own all day.'

'She was only here an hour then had to get back.' Hannah swallowed hard 'She's expecting.'

'What? I thought your daddy couldn't move with his back.'

'She thinks it happened on one of his better days.'

The two laughed so long and hard it left Edmund wheezing and clutching his chest.

'Oh dear, dear, me, that might even be better than my news. Funnier anyway'

She was pleased that he'd taken it so well. When she'd told him she was expecting Maria she'd thought that he had been happy but hadn't been sure.

'Are you telling me the truth, Edmund Byrne? You're not just saying it because you think it's what I want to hear?'

Her husband affected a mock frown. 'Mrs Byrne, how could you say such a thing? I'm hurt.' The furrowed brow gave way to his bright smile. 'Good luck to them I say. Your mammy's no spring chicken but she's not old neither. Still got her looks. Everything's going to be perfect. You, me, Maria, a new sister for you … and a new job for me.'

Edmund told her how Station-master O'Donnell, a Donegal man, had approached him earlier in the day.

'Said he'd be sorry to see me go, but there's a

new train guard's job coming up in Dublin in the summer. There for me if I want it. Much better than being a porter and a few more shillings every week, not much, but enough to rent us a little house maybe. And it would be in the city, Hannah, not locked away out in the middle of nowhere like this. What do you think?'

For two hours they talked about it, first while she made their meal, then after they'd eaten, on their stools at the kitchen table, catching the final rays of evening sunshine on their faces. There were so many things to consider. Would they really have enough money to find somewhere nice in Dublin? What about his parents, they weren't getting any younger? And her mother, now that her daddy was almost crippled with the back, how would she manage at her age with a new baby?

Edmund's enthusiasm for the move was infectious, and though Hannah would never admit it to him, she'd do anything to make him happy. So the decision was made. They went through it one more time, snuggled together in the dark before falling asleep, but they'd already agreed. Next morning, Edmund whistled down the road to work, to tell O'Donnell he'd be accepting the offer.

Day 9

My daddy was excited about moving to the city and the new job. Mammy was more wary, I think, and even then, she didn't want to leave. Her townland, Rathdrum and Arklow were all she'd ever known and she felt content there. She'd been up to Dublin only once, the time she'd had the photo taken with Auntie Bridget, and she'd thought it noisy and unclean somehow. I've been a few times and I can see why she'd feel that way. The Lord knows what she'd think about Manchester; Dublin would be heaven by comparison.

*

Hannah soon learnt that the world isn't always as we want it to be. Her father's cousin gave them an address in Charlotte Street in Rathmines where he knew there was a room to rent. Edmund insisted it would do them "until we get sorted out" even though it wasn't the nice little house he'd promised.

On a wet day in August, in the first year of the new century, Edmund and Hannah, she carrying Maria and he carrying two suitcases stuffed with all the belongings they could take with them, boarded the Dublin train. They'd have left Rathdrum a month earlier if it hadn't been for Hannah's mother losing the baby. Not the first she'd lost but, being older now, it hit her hard. For the first two weeks she'd eat nothing and Hannah was convinced her mother would go the way of the baby. Then, day by day, she came back to the world, supported by the love of her daughter and husband.

Edmund and Hannah took an hour to walk the mile and a half south from Kingsbridge Station to their new home, needing to stop regularly to catch their breath and to ask directions. The river, Trinity College, theatres, carriages, trams and more people than Hannah could imagine, passed before her eyes like a blur. As they moved from the centre of the city, rags replaced top hats and fine dresses, and the only respite from acre upon acre of cobbles was the oasis of St. Stephen's Green, the public park guarded by iron railings and huge stone arches. On one corner, five women selling flowers screeched into the street, competing vigorously for every customer passing. On another, children as young as five, in filthy pants and dresses, begged farthings from passers-by.

Charlotte Street was wide and lined with shops of every description and trams trundled down the middle. Edmund cursed when he saw them, saying they could have ridden from the station if they'd known and been there in a quarter of the time. When they landed on the step of number sixteen, Hannah almost wept, and was grateful they hadn't arrived a single minute earlier. The house, one of three wedged between an ironmonger and a furniture-maker, had three storeys of blackened brick with square windows which looked like they'd never seen a wash since the day the house was built several lifetimes earlier. The landlord, a man in his forties dressed in woollen topcoat, pin-striped trousers and bowler hat, greeted them in the hallway, sounding like one of the officers in Edmund's old regiment.

'Mr and Mrs Byrne I presume? I'm Gerald Fabian.'

A child's voice echoed from the first floor landing and Fabian turned to shout up the stairs.

'Will you keep that boy quiet Mrs Drury or I'll have you out, by God I will.' he turned back to the Byrnes with a humourless smile 'I'm sorry about that. Sometimes one can't always get the tenants one hopes for. I'm sure you'll not be giving me such problems.'

Hannah clutched Maria closer to her chest and stroked the child's head to make sure she stayed quiet. Already she wanted to go back home.

They agreed the terms and Fabian handed Edmund the key after they'd paid two week's rent in advance. He didn't bother to go upstairs with the family, just gave them a final warning before he left that he had a full list of everything in their room and there'd be trouble if any of it went missing or was damaged. As they climbed to the top of the house a guard of honour made up of scruffy boys and girls inspected them on each landing. Only one adult appeared, a woman on the second floor who introduced herself as Margaret Murphy and welcomed them to the house, telling Hannah to just ask if she needed anything.

Once inside, Edmund dropped the cases to the floor and collapsed on the bed in the corner of the room, his chest heaving with the exertion of climbing the three flights. Hannah stood and surveyed their new home; the green painted walls, the wooden floor, the wardrobe with the door hanging off; the tin bath and the night-soil bucket, and wondered how she could tell Edmund he'd let her down.

When his wheezing slackened, Edmund raised himself on one elbow.

'It's not what we'd hoped for, is it?'

Hannah shook her head slowly and murmured 'No.'

'We'll be fine though, the three of us. I start the job tomorrow and when we've a few week's wages under our belts we'll find something better, just you see.'

Hannah lay beside her husband and rocked Maria to sleep, then placed the infant between them on the mattress. The mother listened to the sounds of the street and the lives of her neighbours on every side, closed her eyes and saw the green fields surrounding their whitewashed cottage in Rathdrum.

*

Hannah stretched her back and wondered how she would get through another day like this. Pregnant, and so weak from coughing she felt like lying down and not getting out of bed again. And skint. So short of money she daren't poke her nose out on to the Dublin streets for fear that one of the shop keepers would see her. Like that hoor Sweeney the butcher who'd caught her on Saturday. Called her all the names under the sun, right there in front of the neighbours, just because she owed him a few bob. Not as if she was the only one, half the house would be in his debt. His, and grocer O'Keefe's, and every other fool's within half a mile who'd be daft enough to let stuff out on credit. Not to mention the landlord, God save us, though Mr Fabian didn't count. Englishman with a silver-topped cane, so he was fair game. Hannah knew for a fact that Bowsie McDaid on the second floor had pulled in a big win on the horses but still asked Fabian to wait until next week because he was a bit short. Bloody idiot believed him as well. Serves him right. If he can't keep his ear to the ground he deserves what he gets.

Still, Hannah felt ashamed of how she'd come this low. Respectable parents in a nice cottage by the chapel. Even had a little garden for her dad to grow a few veg. Sure, he wasn't fit to do much else these days after the accident. Now, she and Edmund and little Maria had been living in this one room for a year, with thirty-six others in the house, every day having to carry the night soil three floors down then bring the day's coal three floors up again. Well today she wasn't fit to do it. Let the place stink for a few hours. It stank anyway with its few sticks of Fabian's furniture and bug-ridden bed, the only thing of her own being the mahogany clock on the mantle shelf that her grandmother had left her.

At least the April sun was finding its way through the single tall window and taking the chill off the room so she could manage without a fire for a while. If it got too cold she could climb under the sheets and pull little Maria in beside her. The two of them would just cuddle there and keep warm. Perhaps the tot might stop crying for a while. Not that Hannah blamed her; the poor kitten was teething and hungry.

'It's not your fault is it my lovely? Mammy knows. Daddy will be home soon with his wages then we can sneak out and buy something for you. He'll maybe have a drop left in that bottle of his we can rub on those gums eh?'

Maria ceased her snivelling, looked up at her mother and smudged the tears and snot across her burning cheek with the back of her hand. This respite was only temporary and the child started again as soon as Hannah slumped on the corner of the bed. Hannah almost burst into tears herself.

Some days she wondered if they should pack up their few sticks and head back to Arklow but Edmund's work was here in Dublin as a train guard working out of Kingsbridge Station. The hours were long and the wages were small. Perhaps if his lungs were better he'd be able to show them what a good worker he was, it wasn't his fault he'd picked up the consumption in the Queen's service. Half the men stationed in Malta got it, according to John. The railway company should be grateful to have him.

Hannah leaned forward and wiped her Maria's eyes.

'We'll go down and see Mrs Murphy shall we? She'll maybe offer us a cup of tea, even a slice of scone. A nice enough woman, don't you think? Lucky she has the son and her fella both in work, must leave them a bob or two to spare every week. Someday we'll be like that. You and …' She patted her belly. 'this new little brother of yours will be bringing home the shillings then we'll have fresh bread every day. And meat on Sundays.'

As if she understood, and was in complete agreement with this plan, Maria chuckled and her mother smiled, each content in the other's company for the moment.

*

Mrs Murphy pulled back her front door. If Hannah had been looking for it she'd have noticed the annoyance flit across the careworn eyes of her older neighbour. Instead, she saw what they both wanted her to see, the welcoming smile of a middle-aged country woman who was pleased Hannah and Maria had taken the trouble to come downstairs to fill her morning.

'Come inside, dear, the baby looks frozen. Let's get you some tea and some milk for the little one.'

The women settled down and began to talk of the things they talked about every day. The weather, the noise from the other rooms, who had died and who was newly pregnant. On their second cup Mrs Murphy broke her news. Mr Murphy and her son, Christopher, had been told their jobs on the railway would be gone come Friday.

'The two of 'em. The foreman just strode up while they were having a smoke and told 'em they were finished. No reason given. Nor no apology. Tim says it happened to quite a few of 'em the same day. Funny your Edmund didn't mention it.'

Maria, who had been pacified hearing Mrs Murphy's soft voice, and by a bowl of bread softened with warm milk, began to wail again.

'I'd better be getting her back upstairs, see if I can put her to bed for a while.'

'You look like you need a lie down yourself.'

Hannah laughed. 'That's true enough.' She enjoyed Mrs Murphy's company. Not just for the freely given sustenance, but because she was kind, good humoured, and always seemed to see the best in everyone regardless of how they might treat her. The younger woman gave her a brief hug then squeezed her hand.

'I'm sure something will turn up soon for Mr Murphy and Christopher. I'm sure it will.'

On the stairs Hannah barely caught her neighbour's whispered reply. 'It has to, Hannah. It just has to.'

*

Hannah had left the potatoes and turnips she'd been saving boiling on the stove while she popped to the only shop in the area which would still serve her providing she had the cash in her hand. Edmund was looking after Maria, or, at least, he was keeping an ear in case she woke up. His wages would stretch to a jug of buttermilk tonight and some flour so she could bake a scone or two of bread to see them through the next few days.

The baby inside her had stopped its kicking and Hannah felt good to be out in the fresh air, the first time in half a week she'd ventured beyond the front step. The three Boyle children had been sitting on the stairs, staring at her bump when she passed, the signs of hunger clearly etched in those deep, hollow, eyes. Their father, Séan Boyle, once a navvy on England's roads and railways, and well set up by all accounts, hadn't been able to land a simple labourer's job since breaking his arm and returning to Dublin. The money had soon run out. He'd mentioned to Edmund that he was thinking of taking the family back over the water but Hannah doubted he'd have much more success over there. A man with no education and only used to swinging a pick stands no chance once he's no longer even able to do it. Doubtless the family would be in the workhouse before many more months passed, along with thousands of others like them.

Hannah shivered at the thought, despite the late afternoon sunshine on her face. In that moment she threw a prayer skywards to thank the Lord that her Edmund had a job bringing in some money every week. It might not be much but it was enough to keep them out of that place.

Edmund had been quiet when he came home, not his usual smiling self, probably just more tired than usual. If they were laying men off then it stood to reason that there'd be more work for those left to do it. Perhaps he'd have perked up by the time she returned home. He was always in such good humour in the evenings, with the three of them in front of the open fire, even though his cough would often be worse than hers.

*

'You're not yourself, Edmund, what's wrong?'

A shake of the head.

He'd still not said a word, just stared out of the grimy window into the street below. When

Hannah had returned from the shop, Maria was still on the bed where her mother had left her. Normally, by this time, there'd be some kind of game going on, with Edmund hiding behind a towel and popping his head out to make the child squeal with delight. Or he'd creep up on her and raise her at arm's length, tickling her until the giggles made her breathless.

They'd eaten their Friday fish in silence, Edmund moving the food around on his plate and picking at it without a sign of pleasure. He'd not even told Hannah how well she'd cooked it, a mealtime ritual regardless of how meagre the fare might be, words he gifted to her to say he was sorry he couldn't provide a better larder for them.

When they'd finished eating, Hannah had heated water on the stove to fill the small tin tub for Maria's weekly bath, then dropped the girl in when she was satisfied it was cool enough. Even Edmund in his sour mood hadn't been able to help a smile as his daughter had splashed and shrieked each time her mother doused the child's head with soapy water. Hannah had taken her chance to try to finally get a word out of Edmund.

'You must talk to me, Edmund. Is it something I've done? Tell me. Please.'

He covered his mouth and screwed his eyes shut before drawing a deep breath.

'The job's gone.'

'What?'

'On Tuesday I was let go. Me and another ten. Told to finish off the week and collect our last wages tonight.'

'But you're such a good worker, why would they do such a thing?'

'The new foreman's brother-in-law needed a job and he got mine. The Murphys downstairs, their jobs gone to his cousins, just moved up to Dublin from Tipp. You know how it goes.'

Despite herself, anger and panic made Hannah's words cold. 'And you couldn't share this with me all week? When did you think I'd find out?'

'I was hoping something would turn up or the foreman would change his mind. I didn't know what to do or how to tell you.' He turned away to peer sightlessly at the street below.

Hannah lifted Maria from the bath, wiped her with the towel, then slipped her nightclothes on before putting her in the bed. The mantle clock struck seven when she lifted her chair to place it behind Edmund's.

'Let's not argue. It's not your fault.' Hannah put her chin on his shoulder and wrapped her arms round his chest. He waited for the merest moment then covered her wrist with his palm.

Later, in bed, the only light in the room was the dying glow of the fire. Between them lay Maria, gently snoring and hugging the warm bump that was soon to be her baby brother or sister. They'd lain there for an hour, husband and wife holding hands, not knowing the words to use. Hannah shifted to ease the throbbing in her back.

'When the baby comes, I can take in washing, that'll help.'

'I'll find something, don't you worry your pretty head about it.'

'No, but I mean … if you don't. Or if you stay home I might find a little job in a shop or in a hotel.'

'And how do you think that would make me look? A man, looking after babies while his wife goes out to work.'

The injustice he'd been feeling for days bubbled just below the surface but Hannah wasn't going to let him get away with it.

'You'll look like what you are. A man without a job, same as so many others, and with mouths to feed at home and rent to pay. The difference would be that you wouldn't have been so stupid or proud as to let your loved ones fall prey to the workhouse. When we married, you promised to look after me, always, and I know you will. But now it might be my turn for a short while. You go search for work, it's only right, but if it doesn't come then we'll do what we have to do to survive. You, me, Maria …' She moved his hand to feel the heartbeat inside her 'and this little one.'

*

James Aloysius Byrne made his entry into the family much more easily than his elder sister had. True, he was three weeks early and his mother needed to be regularly attended by the doctor on account of the consumption that had now come upon her, but the birth itself was straightforward. He was a quiet child, spiritual from the start Hannah said, and he had the look of her father, with bright blue eyes and a cast of red in his thin hair.

Maria was fascinated by the new addition and spent hours on end playing with him on the rug by the bed, where her mother lay with increasing frequency. Hannah was watching the two of them and smiled, hoping it would always be this way, and the feeling gave her strength to fight the pain in her rasping lungs.

Edmund was out searching for work again, now the carter on Harcourt Street had let him go, saying he needed someone younger, stronger and cheaper. There'd been other scraps of work but hardly enough survive, and the rent was behind by three weeks, with the landlord, Fabian, being more and more insistent they catch up. He might dress like a gentleman but they'd heard he had some very ungentlemanly friends to help him when tenants didn't pay on time. There'd been nothing for a few days so now they had no coal and the cupboard was almost bare.

Hannah raised herself up when she heard the whistling on the stairs, and was over by the sink by the time she heard Edmund's turning of the door handle. He breezed in and scooped Maria shrieking above his head, tickling her until she was helpless.

'How're my three favourite people today?'

His wife took Maria from him, laid her back down on the rug, and threw her arms around his neck.

'You're in a good mood.'

'And why shouldn't I be when I've you to come home to?'

'Did you find work?'

'After a fashion.'

Hannah pushed him away gently and looked up into his laughing eyes.

'How do you mean "after a fashion"? Don't tell me, that carter wants you back on less money?'

'No, and if he did I'd tell him where to put his job. I'll not work for nothing.'

'So what's happened?

Edmund's grin disappeared but he took Hannah's hand and pulled her to sit beside down beside him on the bed.

'I got into a bit of trouble today but it worked out better than it might.'

She tilted her head. 'Trouble?'

'Well, as I said, it worked out fine.'

'Tell me.'

'I was up on the sidings, looking for any bits of wood or coal that might have fallen from the trucks. I'd seen fellers there doing it when I was on the trains. Anyway, out from behind one of the engines steps a policeman.'

Hannah threw her hand over her mouth. Edmund took it away, laying it on her lap.

'I told you, don't worry, it's fine. I knew McCloskey from Rathdrum, he'd called in on the station-master now and again. Said he wouldn't arrest me. This time. Said he could see I was on hard times. Asked if I'd think about moving to Liverpool for a job. His brother-in-law has a good job at the docks and says there's always work going there. So if I want to go he'll put in the word. What do you think?'

Another jump into the unknown but they couldn't stay here and starve or, worse, end up in the workhouse. Liverpool? England? Maybe a new start. Where would they live? Hannah's parents might be able to lend them the money for the boat, and perhaps a few bob to get settled. They'd send it back as soon as they could, of course. It wouldn't be quick though, she'd have to write to them in London. They'd moved there soon after the baby died, hoping her father might find some lighter work he could manage with his bad back. Hannah suspected they'd also gone to take her mother's mind off her loss.

'Let's sleep on it and see how we feel in the morning.'

But they didn't sleep much. Edmund was less sure than Hannah and every time she'd drift off, he'd raise another problem for them to think about and she'd need to put his mind at rest. So it went on until nearly four in the morning when the baby woke and needed to be fed. When she climbed back in to bed, Edmund was snoring so loudly there was nothing to be done but wait for the morning light to appear, and plan the letter to her mother.

A week later they were boarding the ferry for Liverpool, just as they'd arrived in Dublin. This time with two children, two suitcases, and hopes for a better future. They'd very little else, except for the guilt of leaving in the night without paying the rent, plus a few shillings Hannah had extracted from the pawnbroker for her grandmother's mantle clock. In Edmund's pocket, safe against his chest, he carried a letter of introduction to Constable McCloskey's brother-in-law, their ticket to a new life across the sea.

Day 10

The new century started with such hope for the family; leaving for a new country, a new job for Edmund, and two children. If only it would last.

The day had been calm and warm as the Byrnes stood by the ship's rail, watching Dublin move away in the morning sun, the Wicklow mountains grey-blue away to the south-west once they'd cleared Howth Head. For a while, Hannah thought she could see Arklow in the distance but decided it must be Bray or Greystones, though she still felt sad for the home she'd left more than a year earlier.

Once the novelty of the view and the sea journey had worn off, they settled themselves on the deck, the children between them, and watched the other passengers. Most of those sitting or lying were sweating beneath heavy woollen dresses and shawls, or overcoats and cloth caps, dressed for heavier weather and to save the weight in their crammed cases. Better dressed gents and ladies promenaded until they were out of sight of land, and the smell of their lower class fellows drove them back indoors to the first class lounge. Young, single men stood in groups, chatting and eyeing the passers-by and occasionally one would peel away to chance his arm with a lone woman he'd spied. So it went on for hours on end, all trying to grab a few winks of sleep and the well-to-do returning outside only when England appeared on the horizon.

I can see our arrival in Liverpool clear as day in my head. I was only a tot, but so much noise, so many people, would be enough to stick with anyone. Course I didn't know what was going on, no idea about why we were moving, why would I? Children have it so easy.

Now, Hannah fixed her eyes firmly on Edmund's back as they were jostled down the gangway in a sea of humanity pouring from the boat on to the docks. Nearly everyone the same as them. Poor, desperate for work, scanning the crowd for anyone meeting them, or trying to find friends and family they'd travelled with. Half the passengers, at least, seemed to be children, their laughter or crying shrill above the hubbub of the hundreds of fearful and expectant conversations of their parents.

Behind them, to the left, two businessmen in bowler hats tried to push through until a bull-strong farm labourer blocked their progress, telling them in his Limerick accent to stay where they were and "to mind the ladies".

Edmund bellowed above the racket.

'Stay close to me, Hannah, hang on to the children, we'll soon be away from here.' An instruction Hannah had no intention of disobeying. Maria clung to her hand, wide-eyed, and baby Jimmy nestled asleep, as usual, against his mother's shoulder.

The melee thinned when they hit the dockside, some of them staying with those who'd come to greet them, exchanging hugs, kisses and tears before starting their journeys homeward, others, more familiar with the area, scurrying to catch a train or tram ahead of the crowd.

The whole area was alive with people, horses and handcarts moving in every direction, and the sky was a spider's web of rigging against a smoke-streaked blue sky for as far as the eye could see along the piers. Market stall holders shouted offerings of their wares to the new arrivals; coarse bread, fruit, eggs, butter and all manner of clothing. Hannah grabbed a seat on a box at the side of one cart selling vegetables, trying to regain her land-legs.

The greengrocer smiled across at Hannah and gave a small apple to Maria, polishing it on his apron before handing it over when the mother nodded her approval. A man in a shabby jacket and cap approached Edmund.

'You lookin' for work, Paddy?'

'Not today. I think I've something arranged.' He patted his coat pocket. 'Just need to find somewhere to stay then track down this here man.'

'Well, plenty of work on the docks if you want it, by the hour or the half day, whichever suits ya.' Come back and see me if ya don't get sorted out.'

He moved off towards another man who

looked lost. Edmund grinned at Hannah.

'See, I knew I'd get a job here. Even if McCloskey's letter doesn't do the trick it looks like we'll be fine. Come on, let's look for lodgings.'

*

The streets around the docks were dark by the time they found someone who'd take them in. They'd walked past house after house with signs in the window declaring "No vacancies" or "No Irish". Some had both. Several without the notices refused when they saw the small children or heard that Edmund hadn't actually got a job yet. As they walked away from a grubby red-brick with an immaculate donkey-stoned step, a young woman lifted the sash window on the first floor and called down.

'Mrs Costigan in King Street, two roads down, number twelve, she's some rooms to rent. Nice lady. From Wexford. Clean and won't fiddle you like some of these characters. Tell her I sent you - Dolly Feehan.'

They grabbed the bags and children, almost dragging them the last few dozen yards, and Mrs Costigan greeted them like long lost friends when she answered the door to Edmund's weary knock. 'Come in come in, dears, leave your bags in the hall, I'll put on the kettle'.

Hannah almost wept for the woman's kindness. They'd been all day on the ferry, three hours before this waiting at the port in the dark, having sneaked from Charlotte Street at dead of night. Then an hour and a half knocking on doors before Dolly Feehan pointed them in the right direction. The children had become cranky, she and Edmund were tired, and they all needed a good feed.

The landlady, who was small, round and wearing a wrap-around floral pinafore, gave them a hot drink then showed them to a fine, bright room, insisting when she left that they eat with her that evening "so I can catch up on news". She returned a few minutes later with soup and bread for Maria and some warm milk for Jimmy, reminding the couple to come down at seven o'clock.

The meal was the best Hannah and Edmund had eaten in ages, boiled mutton with barley, potatoes and cabbage followed by apple tart and even a pale ale for Edmund.

'It was left over from when himself was alive and I'm sure he'd not begrudge you having it. Kevin was a lovely man, generous to a fault he was.' Mrs Costigan smiled at her memory 'Twenty years together we was when God took him.'

Hannah asked how he died.

'Accident it was. Didn't he work in the shunting yard and fall from the footplate. Icy day it was and he slipped. Should never have been working in them conditions but sure what could he do? No work, no pay, that's what he said ' the widow wiped an eye on her pinafore and sniffed. 'Now, no need for any of that is there? What's done is done. More tart Mr Byrne?, Go on and tell me all that's happening over the water. '

Hannah gave their hostess news about events in Dublin, with Edmund throwing in the odd funny story. In Bootle, the landlady was surrounded by an ever-changing mix of Irish immigrants, so would never be short of news from home, but she absorbed every morsel that night as if she'd not spoken to another soul for years. Hannah sensed she'd only asked out of human kindness, or to ease her loneliness.

*

Edmund and Maria stayed under Mrs Costigan's roof for the first three nights while Edmund found his contact and began his new job. He'd been expecting to be portering again but Ted McCloskey said any friend of his brother-in-law was a friend of his and had to be well looked after. There was a job going as a guard, checking the wagons were secure and keeping an eye out for thieving. It would need a bit of training but Ted thought Edmund could manage it and it would be a good step up. Half pay for the first week, then he'd be ready. Edmund didn't think twice, and Hannah flung her arms round his neck, smothering him with kisses, when he told her.

On the fourth day, the landlady took Hannah

to a house two doors down the street, brought her inside and led her down the hall to a green door towards the back. She handed Hannah a key.

'Here, dear, take this. Step inside and see if you like it.'

The room was large and light streamed through the window on the back wall. Hannah ran her fingers through the thin covering of dust on the table and was apprehensive.

'There's no bed, Mrs C, would we need to buy one? Only, we've no money to spare, not until Edmund gets himself settled.'

'Shush now, you just go through that door there and have a look.'

Hannah became still and almost stopped breathing when she pushed into a second room. On top of newly painted floorboards, a grey rug separated two beds, one double and a small single, and in the corner stood a wicker cot. She turned back to face the other woman.

'We couldn't possibly afford this Mrs C. It's beautiful.'

'It's only a matter of time before that husband of yours finds his feet, then you'll be fine. The room's only lying empty so you can have it the same price as the one you're in for now. You can pay me a bit more later if it all works out.'

Hannah knew she was lying. There were Irish families arriving every day from Dublin, lots of them looking for work and for somewhere to stay. The landlady could let the rooms several times a day if she wanted to.

'Why are you being so kind to us, Mrs C?'

Mrs Costigan gestured for Hannah to sit beside her at the table. She scraped at some newly-discovered, invisible, dirt on her fingernails for a moment before folding her hands on her lap and drawing a deep breath.

'When Kevin and me arrived over here we were the same as you and Edmund. Not two pennies in the world to rub together and the dog's abuse at every door we knocked. Many's the night in those first weeks we slept anywhere we could, even park benches, and I swore that if we ever got ourselves set up I'd do the decent thing. He finally got himself a bit of a job, then another at weekends and we started to save a few coppers. Within a year or two we'd enough put by to think about buying the house down the street and renting out some rooms. With Kevin working and me running the house we did all right together. Three years before he was killed we bought this place. Said it would be a nest egg for when we got older.' Now the tears began to flow, great heaving sobs which only calmed when Hannah took both her hands in hers. 'Didn't know he'd be taken that soon and I do miss him. So, I run the two houses and do what I can when I see someone needs a little help.'

Mrs Costigan stood and brushed the front of her apron.

'Will you take the rooms then, Hannah, will you?'

*

Hannah strived every day to make their new home as comfortable as she could, and never tired of telling Mrs Costigan how grateful they were for the rooms she'd let them have. Edmund settled in to his job and there was overtime whenever he wanted some, bringing in welcome extra money for treats and to pay their landlady what the rooms were worth. The children grew and on Sundays, when Edmund wasn't working, he'd lie in another hour or two, then the family would take a walk to King's Gardens or to look in the shop windows on Stanley Road. In the summer, when the weather was fine, they'd hop on to a bus to Crosby, and walk along the beach, then let Maria and Jimmy play in the sand to their hearts' content.

For a year and a half they were as happy as they'd ever been, but sometimes Hannah found herself lonely with the long hours Edmund worked, and, though she loved the children, they could be a drain some days. Then the row started easily enough, as these things often do. An unsuspecting person walks into a room and finds a storm brewing at its centre.

Hannah had been sitting in the dark for an

hour, two hours before that looking out of the window. Waiting for Edmund to come home. He finished at seven, easily back to King Street by half past at the latest. He'd sometimes call into the Oak for a pint, but never this late.

At first it had only been on a Friday night, once on his birthday, but in the last few weeks it had become more often. Not every night, he couldn't afford that, but two, maybe three nights, and getting later all the time. He'd never be drunk when he got back, just merry, in a better mood than when he sat by the fire with her on the other evenings.

Didn't he know she would like to escape once in a while as well? To be free of the endless dragging down of being stuck in the house with two crying children all day. Only twice in the last six months had he taken Hannah out without the children, once on the ferry to New Brighton, where they'd spent the afternoon in the sunshine lying on the beach and walking along the promenade. She'd wanted to go into the pleasure grounds and up the new tower but Edmund said they hadn't the money to spare. The only other time they'd been out together was two weeks earlier, when he had come home from work after calling in to the pub, declaring they were going to the music hall. Mrs Costigan had agreed to sit with the little ones, happy to be with them for an hour or so, and they'd jumped on the tram into the city. When they'd arrived at the Park Palace he seemed to be looking for someone, until he spied Dolly Feehan and her latest young man and dragged Hannah over to join them. They had a good time, with Edmund in the best of humour, telling jokes and stories from work, making them laugh so much they hardly needed the comedians and performing dogs on stage, though Eric, Dolly's companion, didn't smile much. Hannah thought Dolly was good company and could see how she'd get on well behind the bar where she worked most evenings. Afterwards, though, Edmund had wanted to go for a drink but Hannah insisted they went home to relieve Mrs Costigan and the night ended on a sour note. He hadn't said anything but his mood was darker and he hardly spoke to Hannah until he left for work next morning.

At half past ten she heard his key in the lock, scratching to find the hole then a harsh click as it turned. There was shuffling while he removed his coat and hat and hung them on the hook behind the door. When he turned he jumped at the site of Hannah's silhouette against the window.

'Christ, you scared the life out of me. What you doing sitting here in the dark' his words were slurred 'and why did you lock me out? I thought maybe you'd gone to bed.'

'Perhaps I should have. You'd hardly have

noticed would you?'

'What's that supposed to mean?'

'You know what it means. Out till all hours of the night, God knows where.'

'I've been for a pint, that's all. Ted McClosky's birthday and a few of us joined him to celebrate.' Edmund nodded his head and pursed his bottom lip 'nothing wrong with that is there? A man can have a drink now and again, can't he?'

'Until this time?'

'Well, Ted and the lads were there for a good while, then I got chatting to Dolly, she -'

'What?'

Edmund sobered quickly, sensing the attack about to come.

'You were with Dolly Feehan?'

'She works behind the bar in the Oak. I thought you knew that.'

Hannah did know, Dolly had told them the night they'd all met at the Park Palace, but she hadn't made the connection.

'That explains it then.'

'Explains what?'

'You. Out at the pub every other night. Later than a man should be with a wife and two babies at home.'

'Aye, there you have it. Taking a pint and a chat is more fun than sitting here night after night.'

'So you decided you'd start seeing that woman?

I knew something wasn't right when we just happened to bump into them. That Eric could tell something was going on as well.'

'Now wait a minute, wait one minute, I am not "seeing that woman" as you put it. She's behind the bar that's all. Granted she's a damn sight prettier than that Mayo lump, Declan, who was there before her, and she likes a laugh, but that's as far as it goes.'

'Hah. And you expect me to believe that?'

Edmund turned as if to storm out of the house but, instead, he sighed heavily and went down on one knee in front of his wife. His voice softened.

'Listen, you're the only woman for me. Always have been and always will be.'

'That's the drink talking.'

'No, no, it isn't. Honestly.'

Edmund told her of the photograph he'd carried with him in Malta, how he had hoped to see her when he came home, and was overjoyed when they met again. He said how he was sorry he'd not been able to give her the life he thought she deserved but through everything he'd never wanted anyone else. He reached up and wrapped a stray curl around his finger.

'Look at you. You're beautiful. How could any man want for more? Please don't think I prefer Dolly Feehan over you. Nothing is happening with her.'

He clasped his hands in front and burst into a line from a song they'd heard in a romantic duet at the music hall "When first I saw the love-light in your eyes, I knew the world held nought but joy for me ..."

A smile lifted the ends of Hannah's lips.

'I'll even change pubs if that will make you happy.'

'I'd prefer it if you weren't going to the pub at all. Come home to me once in a while. I need you.'

'And I need you' he laughed 'but I do need a pint now and again.'

So that was it. They kissed and made up. In fact I think they probably did more than kissed. That night would have been just about nine months before baby Emer came and everything changed.

PART TWO

Day 11

We're now at my life where I remember things, just bits and pieces, from when I was two or three years old, more like pictures than anything, not much before then. Some of it must be from what my mammy or daddy told me. Actually, I think there must be a lot of that.

Memory's funny isn't it? We think we saw or heard something in all its detail but really we've made a lot of it up to turn it into a good story, or we're just remembering it second-hand. A tale heard on our mother's knee. I've seen you children do it, stuff you never witnessed, or were too young to have taken in, and then telling it like you were there and taking part.

This is how my next stories will be, I expect. I'd not stand up in court and swear they are all true, only as I remember the events or how they were told to me. You'll need to make up your own mind which is which.

*

Some of the spark went out of Daddy for a while after the night Mammy told him off. I don't know if there was more to him and that Dolly Feehan than he was saying, or if it was missing the freedom of going out on his own, but after the row he'd spend his nights in front of the fire, dozing or gazing through the window. Sometimes his cough was very bad. If the evening was warm enough he might carry a kitchen chair outside and sit in the sunny yard dangling Jimmy on his lap.

He worked long hours and I'd never see him on weekday mornings and, unless he was ill, he'd be out of the house early, but I think he liked his job. He and Ted McClosky had hit it off from the minute they met and McClosky had taken Daddy under his wing. The older man worked in the signal box on the sidings and was a cousin of the boss who gave out the jobs, so McClosky had lots of friends. He'd bring one or two round to King Street some nights and I'd hear them all talking and laughing on the other side of the bedroom door. One of them might throw out a song, then they'd clap and shout until Mammy gave one, though, truth to tell, she'd not a very good voice. Daddy would seem to be in a brighter mood on these nights and after they'd all gone he and Mammy would whisper and giggle in their big bed long into the early hours.

One day, Mammy lay Jimmy in his cot and asked me to sit beside her on the armchair. She put her arm around my shoulders and pulled me close.

'Mammy has something to tell you darling. You're going to have another little brother or sister soon. That'll be nice won't it? '

I don't know if she expected some kind of reply from me but she got very little. I'd have only been three or four years of age and not much idea what she was telling me. I suppose I understood the idea of a new baby, we had Jimmy after all, but I'd no thought about what this birth might mean for the family.

*

Mammy lies sweating on the bed, Mrs Costigan and a woman in a pink striped frock with a white apron are on either side, one holding her hand, the other mopping her head. I don't remember which was which. They're both telling her to relax, to take deep breaths, but all Mammy does is scream. Then there is blood. A lot of blood and it goes quiet. The two women look at each other and shake their heads.

The next thing it seems, though there must have been days in between, I'm in our room, the curtains are drawn, and I'm surrounded by grown-ups in black. Daddy has me on his knee telling me we'll be all right but I can see by the damp tracks on his cheeks that it isn't. I am asking for Mammy and can't understand why she's asleep in a wooden box in the corner. He tells me to shush.

There's a line of people walking past Mammy, all moving their lips and crossing themselves. After they pass her they come across to Daddy and me, saying 'Sorry for your trouble' then looking away. Mrs Costigan and Dolly Feehan are handing round cups of tea and slices of apple pie. I think it must be a party but no one is laughing.

*

Eighteen months gone and another move. This time back across the sea and me able to remember it all. I was six years old by this time.

Daddy had tried so hard to manage after Mammy went, but Mrs Costigan was taken into hospital and couldn't look after Jimmy and me anymore. He knew he must pack in the job and head for home where he might get some help.

When he told me we were leaving, I cried and cried and asked him why we couldn't get another Mammy. He cried himself and said it wasn't as easy as that. I didn't see why not, after all, that Dolly had being around lots of times and I could see Daddy liked her. Why couldn't he just marry her?

It was pouring down the day we left. Jimmy was in the pram with a suitcase balanced on the back. He kept complaining he was old enough to walk but Daddy told him to be quiet and it was easier this way. Daddy carried the other case and I held Dolly's hand. She walked with us all the way to the boat. At one point we stopped and Daddy pointed to a train shunting through one of the yards.

'See there, Maria, that's where I used to go to work. Up and down on that big old engine every day.'

I don't know why he told me then, I'd been with him lots of times, and Mammy would take us down sometimes to watch him when she wanted a walk. Perhaps he forgot, or maybe he just wanted to remind himself what he was leaving.

There were so many boats in the docks, and so many people trying to get on to ours. There were horses everywhere, big smelly beasts hauling carts loaded high in the air, and prettier ones pulling carriages. Dolly gave us all a hug before we went up the ramp, with a good long one for Daddy and I thought she had tears running down her cheeks when she'd finished.

All the seats on the deck were taken, so we walked round and round. I asked Daddy why we couldn't go inside in the warm and he said we couldn't afford it, our tickets only let us travel on the deck. When we'd passed the same place three times Daddy was coughing badly and we were about to huddle down on the floor when two men, who looked much younger than Daddy, called him over.

'Here mister, take these seats, you look done in, and you can't have the little ones down there in the damp.'

So the three of us sat on a bench wedged in beside a very old lady with a long black coat and a grey shawl. She had a ginger cat in a wicker basket which hid in the corner every time the sheep-dog with the people next to her barked. On our other side was a family like ours, except they had a Mammy with them. Their little boy stared at me for a good long time until his mammy pushed him over to say hello. He told me his name was Mick, he was six and a half, and he usually wore glasses but his sister had grabbed them off his nose and they'd broken. I didn't really like the look of him, he screwed up his eyes and picked his nose but there was no-one else to talk to so we played catch-ball until the sea got too rough. Then I sat by Daddy, taking turns in pushing Jimmy's pram back and forward hoping he'd drop off to sleep, though he didn't for ages, then it stopped raining and the sun came out. It was warm in the sunshine and I could see the steam rising from the deck floating round the passenger's ankles. Daddy lifted me on to his shoulder so I could see over the side of the boat. It was beautiful. The water sparkled all the way into the distance where it joined the land at the foot of the mountains. Daddy pointed to them.

'That's where we're going, Maria, back to where you were born.' He bit his lip. 'We'll all be fine back there, I'll find someone to look after you and your brother and I'll find a good job. We'll get a little house with a garden, you'll like that won't you?'

I wasn't sure if I'd like it or not, I didn't remember the place much from before. All I had in my head was a picture of fields all around and thought how different it was to the city, lots and lots of green and hardly any people. In Dublin and

Liverpool we'd been surrounded by neighbours, sometimes even in the same house. Out in the countryside there was hardly anyone. Still, Daddy seemed to be looking forward to it.

Jimmy woke up again so we asked the lady with the cat if she'd watch our cases while we went for a walk around the deck. She didn't look very happy but did agree when Daddy smiled at her. There was a big procession "taking the air" as Daddy called it, all bunching up when anyone stopped to take in the view. By now we were getting closer to the land, though it took hours from when we'd first seen the hills, then, gradually, it turned from blue-grey to green, and we could see buildings away in the distance. The closer we got to the landing stage, the more the passengers jammed against the front rails, shielding their eyes from the sun and squinting for a sight of friends or relatives on the dock. A crowd started to gather around the barrier where we had to get off so Daddy took us back to collect our bags from the old lady. She told him off for being away for so long so he had to say he was sorry but I could see he wasn't really sorry because he was grinning behind his serious face.

Soon afterwards there were men running and throwing ropes on to the dock and other men taking them to tie the boat to metal posts. Then the ramp was in place and everybody pushed forward with lots of shouting and waving. I was frightened but Daddy said to hold on to his trouser leg really hard and not let go until we were safely on the dock.

*

Two and half hours later we were climbing down from the bus in Avoca. We were the only ones getting off there and I looked around as it rumbled on its way. Not a soul in the street except for a man leaning against the closed door of O'Brien's bar on the other side. He waved to my dad to come over.

'Edmund Byrne, isn't it? From Ballyduff?'

Daddy looked at him then shook his head. 'I'm sorry, I can't get you, I've been away a while. Remind me.'

'Terence, Terence Doyle, I worked on the estate with your da'. You'd have seen me in the stables.'

'I have you now. So what are you doing up this part of the country?'

'Ah, you know, Edmund, you have to take the work where you can, don't you.'

Doyle used alcohol to cope with a life where he felt he'd been dealt all the bad cards. The chip on his shoulder, and the way he chose to deal with it, never failed to get him in trouble and put him back where he stood today. My granddad had given him more than one chance on the estate but Doyle's drinking and bad temper made sure he didn't last long. He was always short of money.

'Sorry for your da', Edmund. A good man.' The bolt on the bar door clattered and Doyle stuck out a hand. 'You wouldn't have the price of a jar?'

Daddy shrugged. 'Not a chance I'm afraid. Been off work myself and I've got to look after these two.'

The door now swung open and the man stepped inside without a backward glance so Daddy sat me and Jimmy on the step and followed Doyle in with the biggest case. A few minutes later he came out without it.

'Paddy O'Brien there says he'll hold on to the bag 'til I can pick it up. We've enough in the other one to see us for a day or two.'

Then we walked. Alongside the river, the same one as comes out to the sea by Arklow, up the hill past the grey chapel where Granny and Grandad were married, and out into the countryside. On my little legs it felt like miles and miles but years later I discovered it would take hardly any time to reach our destination from the town. Distances are different in the country and the city anyway. You'd walk the same length every day to school or the shops and think nothing of it, but out there, with nothing but trees and the odd farm, the road seems to go on forever.

After a while we came to a cottage set back from the lane and Daddy stopped at the end of a rutted track as if he was thinking. Jimmy started to cry and this seemed to make up his mind because he grabbed my hand and marched towards the house.

A woman a bit younger than Daddy opened the half-door to his knock and other than the long hair and glasses she looked just like him. She peered at his face, then mine, then at the baby in the carriage, and back to him.

'Edmund!' She hugged him and buried her head in his chest. 'Oh, Edmund, it's so good to see you. I have missed you.' She let go of Daddy and crouched down in front of me. 'My goodness, Maria, how you've grown.'

Daddy pushed me forward but I stepped back again.

'Maria, this is your Auntie Bridget. Say hello.'

*

My Auntie Bridget Byrne lacked Mammy's good looks and failed to see men in any kind of romantic light. They were fine for carrying out the heavier jobs around the place and bringing in a regular wage, but she didn't appear to feel the need for flowers, soft words or being kept warm in bed. In the way that often happens with young people, the plain, though not unattractive, Bridget and my mother, the lovely Hannah Quinn, became the greatest of friends. What Bridget lost in looks she more than made up for in loyalty to Mammy and a wicked sense of humour.

I think my aunt knew Jimmy was too young to understand we'd lost Mammy and I wasn't. He would have missed her, of course, but didn't grasp she wouldn't be coming back. As a result I was given special attention. Every morning Auntie Bridget would take my hand and we'd walk the garden hedges looking for eggs the hens had laid away from the coop. She'd let me carry the basket and ask me to take it into the kitchen.

'Careful now, don't be dropping any' she'd said for the first few times until I repeated it back to her, wagging my finger at her the same way that she'd done, then she laughed and we played that game every day afterwards. Some days we'd gather the tools from the byre and I'd help with the weeding. Auntie Bridget would show me which plants I could pull and which ones I shouldn't, always telling me the names of these 'those are cabbages, Maria, and these are carrots, see how the tops are different.' Sometimes I could tell the difference but mostly I couldn't and she'd grab me at the last minute before I hoked out her peas or beans. Then, if she was in a really good mood I'd be lifted under the arms and swung round and round until we both fell, dizzy and giggling to the ground, with her scolding me that I'd have us all starved.

*

My grandfather and grandmother had lived in a lovely home, down a lane on a great lord's estate outside Arklow. Daddy and Mammy took me back there a few times before we moved to England. The roof was slate, not thatch like the usual country houses then, the walls were good quality stone and they had a neat vegetable patch at the side. Auntie Bridget and Uncle Mick would be there and we'd all have tea before they'd go off for a walk, leaving me with grandad. Grandad had a bad leg but he'd hoist me up onto the good one and tell me stories about his time travelling the world as a soldier, about how he'd met grandma, and how he was injured and had to go back to Wicklow. Sometimes he'd lift me high on to his shoulders and from up there I'd look down on the blue veins criss-crossing his near-bald head and he'd laugh when I twirled the grey tufts above his ears around my middle finger.

On his sideboard he'd a photograph of Daddy in uniform, in a wooden frame Grandad said he'd made himself. Daddy looked ever so smart, with a wide belt round his tunic and a cane under his arm. He'd left the army by the time I was born but I could tell Grandad was very proud of him. "Soldiers for generations" he'd say "your daddy, me, my daddy, and even his daddy I think. Back a hundred years and more."

If the other grown-ups were away a long time, Grandad would lift a big fork from a hook on the wall, and toast bread in front of the fire. When it was done, he'd spread butter all over and we'd sit close, munching like there was no tomorrow. That toast was the best thing I ever tasted.

I don't know if the stories he told me were true, but I loved to hear them time after time, in his deep, soft, voice. He died when I was only four or five, and I'd not seen him for a while before that, so I've no memory of his face, only the top of his head and that voice wrapped around me like a blanket.

Day 12

I spent an hour on my own this afternoon thinking of more stories for Alice. Wasting time when I could lose Billy before long and should be thinking about his health. He drinks too much and he smokes too much, even though the doctors told him he should stop after the heart attack. I think he only does it because he's scared. When they called him up again, in 1939, he told me he didn't want to go. He'd seen enough killing in the First War and in Ireland to last a lifetime.

They sent him home ill, not fit to be shot at any more and I was so glad to see him, but he's different. He's mostly bad-tempered and has a look in his eyes like he doesn't know where he is half the time. Even though they've changed his job and he doesn't need to start work so early, he still takes to his bed every afternoon. Mind, I enjoy the time on my own when he does. Rose usually takes a nap then as well, so I can sit in the kitchen, or on the step if it's warm, with my own thoughts.

*

We stayed with Auntie Bridget for two months and the sun shone all the time. At first she didn't appear too happy with the idea, her cottage was small and with three more of us there was barely room to move. She must also have been worried about the extra mouths to feed from her few chickens and vegetable garden but she seemed glad to have

Daddy back so we made do for a week or two.

Luckily, Daddy soon had work when neighbours heard he was back in the area, so there was money coming in and he could give some to his sister so we weren't such a burden. I don't think he liked the jobs as much as he'd enjoyed riding the train, even though being in the fresh air stopped him coughing so much. In the evenings he'd kiss me and Jimmy goodnight, then head down the road 'to see a man about a dog'. Billy used to say the same thing when he was going to the pub so I think that must have been what my dad was up to as well. Some nights I'd hear the latch lift very late and he'd have a headache next morning, saying he was staying in bed, until Auntie Bridget chased him out of it. Then one day I heard the two of them outside the front door.

'Sure, Bridget, you know it will be for the best. I'll have steady wages coming in and a job that suits me. You know this farming lark isn't for me. '

'But what about the little ones? Another move so soon, it can't be good for them '

'Will you hush woman. I'll be the judge of what's best for my own children. '

I didn't hear any more because Jimmy started wailing and I had to go and sooth him until he settled. By the time I'd rocked him to sleep Daddy was sitting on his chair staring at the fire and Auntie Bridget was attacking the cabbage bed with a hoe.

Two days later Daddy was throwing our stuff on the back of Tommy Lynch's cart and lifting the us up beside him at the front. His friend asked if we were ready, then shook the reins to get us on our way.

How many times did I have to go through that in my life? Just settling down then having to up sticks and move on. The longest place I stayed was with the Sisters and that was hardly what I'd call a home. Bitches. Even with Billy there was nowhere steady for years.

It took us about two hours to plod down to Arklow and it started drizzling on the way so we were soaked before we got halfway there. Daddy tried to cheer me up by clip-clopping in time with the horse and it was fun for a while but the water dripping from my hair down on to my neck soon made me miserable and he stopped. We came to a stop on the main street of the town outside a big building with a window full of spades, hammers and dozens of other pieces of hardware I couldn't name. A skinny man in a long brown coat, badly buttoned waistcoat and flat cap dashed from the shop and shook Daddy's hand. It was his brother, my Uncle Mick.

'Come in, come in, Edmund, let me take one of those bags.'

He slipped a few coins to Tommy Lynch for his

trouble and took us inside, where he introduced us to his boss, Mr Jenkins. He wore the same kind of coat as my uncle but was much fatter.

'This is Edmund, my older brother, sir. He can start straight away, even this afternoon if you want him to' he looked at Daddy, who nodded to confirm 'and you can see the children are only small so there's plenty of space in the room upstairs for the three of them.'

The boss took Daddy to one side and asked him a few questions then shook his hand and smiled at Uncle Mick.

'He seems a good man, Mick, so he can have the job. There's no need to begin until tomorrow so take him up and settle him in. You can take a tea-break now and explain what he'll be doing.'

Before we climbed the stairs, Daddy started coughing, and had to put Jimmy and the case down. Mr Jenkins raised an eyebrow at my uncle.

'He'll be fine sir, just caught something in his throat. Now you come on Edmund and we'll have a chat.'

*

Daddy wasn't working behind the counter like Uncle Mick, instead, he unloaded deliveries into the stores and helped customers carry their orders out to their carts and carriages. Every morning before they opened he'd swish the broom around the red-tiled floor of the shop, sometimes chasing

me with it for a bit of fun. He'd polish the counters
and wash the window of the front door, all in time
for Mr Jenkins to open at nine o'clock. Then Uncle
Mick's wife, Margaret, would call to collect Jimmy
and me to go to her house for the day.

She had four children of her own, all older than
me, two of them already working as delivery boys
in the town. The others were kind to us and played
when they had nothing better to do, though Auntie
Margaret kept them busy helping her most of the
time. In a shed at behind their cottage she had a
table with a loom on top. She'd bend over it for
hours on end, her hands skipping backwards and
forwards, weaving cloth for a man who'd pick it up
once a week. The children, Molly and Grace, would
hand her the brightly coloured wool when she
called out for it and stack the finished bolts in
baskets ready to be taken away. At the end of each
length, we'd all be asked to help check for snags,
though we'd rarely find any. If we did, then Auntie
Margaret would curse and set to repairing the fault
unless the damage was too bad, in which case it
would be thrown in to a box in the corner to sell
more cheaply or for her own use. All of the
children had skirts or jackets made from the
discarded material and one day, when Jimmy and I
arrived she handed us a cap each, with flaps to keep
our ears warm. I wore mine for days, inside and
out, because I thought it looked so pretty, until

Daddy said I should take it off and save it for special occasions.

We'd walk every evening back to the shop with my aunt and Daddy would be waiting, usually sitting on the bottom step, smoking and peeling the spuds for tea. I'd hear him whistling before I saw him and it would always cheer me up no matter the weather.

These were good days, some of the best we had. There was food on the table and Daddy seemed happy most of the time. I'm sure he missed Mammy but he put on some weight, the colour came back to his cheeks and his breathing improved a lot.

On Sundays he'd sleep later if Auntie Margaret didn't come round to drag him out to Mass, then in the afternoon we'd go for a walk, sometimes out to Ballyduff where he'd been born, or along the river to watch the boats going out to sea.

One Monday evening after we'd been in Arklow about six months we arrived home and he wasn't there but Uncle Mick was. He whispered a few words to my aunt and she lifted Jimmy to follow him upstairs, telling me to hurry on behind them.

I could hear Daddy coughing before we got to the top. He was in bed, pale and sweating, and could hardly lift his head. My uncle turned to Auntie Margaret.

'He's been like this all afternoon. I went out to

the yard at about eleven o'clock and he was slumped on a sack of sawdust, gasping for breath, said he'd felt it coming on for days. Next thing, he begins that damn cough, then passes out. I helped him up here but not before old Jenkins had seen him. He warned me that Edmund mustn't be bad for too long else he'd have to get rid of him.'

'So what can we do?'

'Not much. Keep him comfortable and make sure the children are fed, I suppose, then hope he picks up. You bring some soup down and I'll sleep here for a night or two to keep an eye on him.'

All through the first night Daddy coughed and coughed, and I could see the blood on his handkerchief when he wiped his mouth. On the next he was breathing better but still too weak to get out of bed and then in the morning Uncle Mick brought him a message from the boss.

'I'm sorry, Edmund, Jenkins says you'll have to go. He'll let you keep the room for a few days until you're strong enough to leave but then he'll need it for the new man. I pleaded with him but he said if I wasn't happy I could go as well and you know I daren't, there's not so many jobs around for a man to pick and choose.'

'Where will we go?'

'I don't know, Edmund, I can't have you here, there just isn't room. Can you not go back to Bridget?'

My father shook his head. 'She's no space either. But don't worry about us. We'll be fine once I'm up and about. I'll find something else here in the town. '

"Fine" he'd said. We weren't though. Another thing that's different about Ireland is that it's like a small village. Everyone knows your business and it doesn't take long for word to get round if you're unreliable. Daddy recovered enough to look for work but no one was willing to take him on for anything permanent and with just the odd day here and there he'd no money for rent so we slept where we could. A friend's floor one night, a shop doorway the next. The few bob Daddy was able to pull in stretched to buying bread or spuds every couple of days then we'd have to manage on handouts or anything we could steal from fields and gardens. We'd no way to cook food in any case and Daddy got thin again. We all did. If we were lucky we'd find a dry byre that didn't stink too much of the cows and might be able to stay there for a while until the farmer chased us out. We were in one of these when Daddy took another turn for the worse.

He was lying on a pile of straw and asked me to sit down beside him, then gave me a small scrap of paper with a few words scrawled on it.

'This is where your Aunt Bridget lives. You remember it there?' I nodded. 'Well if anything happens to me you show it to someone and ask them to take you and little Jimmy to her. Do you understand?'

I said I did, but I didn't really. What could happen to him? I knew he was ill and I knew Mammy had gone away with the same cough but I didn't connect the two. Not at the time.

*

One Saturday night I was woken by rain crashing on the roof and lightning sent me scuttling across our bed of byre straw to Daddy. I didn't hear his breathing until the thunder died but then, straight away, I knew something was wrong. His chest was heaving, his breaths were coming so fast and when I touched his face it was cold and damp. I couldn't wake him no matter how much I pulled and pulled his arm nor how much I shouted him.

I grabbed Jimmy's hand and dragged him outside then down the track to the house near the road. We were soaked and covered in mud before we got there and Jimmy was crying all the way. I banged on the back door with my fist and got no answer. It was pitch black but I spotted a stone beside the step in one of the storm flashes. I scooped it up and bashed the door loud enough to waken the dead. A window above our heads opened and an oil lamp was swung outside. A woman's voice.

'Who's there? What's all that noise?

'Help us lady. It's my Daddy.'

Day 13

The night I told you about last time was one of the scariest I ever knew, Alice, as far as I could see, my daddy was dying. All I could think of on the road in to town was what would become of Jimmy and me.

Arklow fever hospital was a wooden building behind the doctor's house on the edge of town and someone told me later it was designed to be burned if a serious outbreak occurred. Mr Horkan, the man whose byre we'd been sleeping in, was a cousin of one the nurses and he brought us there on the back of his cart, where he'd lain Daddy on some old feed sacks with Jimmy and me beside him. Mrs Horkan wrapped her husband's old mackintosh round us to keep out the rain but the worst of the storm had blown through and the stars were twinkling where the clouds had broken. There were still flashes of lightning from time to time, away in the distance, and the thunder wasn't anywhere near as fierce by the time we stopped at the gates.

Mr Horkan rapped on the door for the doctor, telling him he'd a sick man with him though wasn't prepared to go in to the hospital himself for fear of catching something. The doctor went back inside and a few minutes later two men arrived with a stretcher.

No-one seemed to bother about us so we stood by the gates when Mr Horkan left, trying to keep warm. By the time it was light we were shaking so much with the hunger and the cold that a passing nurse took us through to the kitchen and gave us tea and bits of stale crust. She said she'd try to find out about Daddy and left us by the fire for a few minutes.

As he thawed and his belly filled Jimmy stopped snivelling and even managed a grin. I looked at him and wondered what people would think of the two of us. Both unwashed, in clothes that had seen better days, and, without a doubt, smelly. Underneath it all, Jimmy had the brightest eyes and an innocent way about him. He'd a habit, which Daddy had tried to get him to stop, of pulling on his ear whenever he was nervous or happy, and was tugging away while he sat warming himself.

When the nurse came back, she said Daddy would be in the hospital for a few days and we must go home. She said she was just finishing her shift and asked where we lived so she could walk with us. I lied and said we were staying with my daddy's sister who'd just moved down from Dublin. The three of us walked in silence along the river until we crossed the bridge. I pointed down the quay.

'It's down there. We'll be fine now. Thanks.'

I grabbed Jimmy and we ran, turning once to wave goodbye, then dashed in to the first side street. Round the corner I dragged my brother hard against a wall and counted to ten. Then counted again before popping my head round to make sure the nurse had moved on.

We went first to Uncle Mick's shop, hoping he'd take care of us, but it was Sunday and the doors were locked, and though I'd walked it many times I didn't know the way to his house.

A nicely dressed woman on her way to church asked me if we were all right and I showed her the paper that Daddy had made me keep in my dress pocket.

'Do you know where this is, lady? We need to get there.'

She explained which road we needed to take out of the town and said we must knock at houses along the way to make sure we were still heading in the right direction. One of the ladies where we called was very nice and gave us something to eat, though others chased us from the doorstep with nothing. It took us all day, then Jimmy could walk no more. We slept under the trees by the river that first night, huddled together and shivering.

Sometimes Billy says I'm a hard woman. He wouldn't be so surprised if he knew everything I've been through.

By the middle of the second morning we arrived at the house of a neighbour of Auntie Bridget, who looked the two scruffy urchins up and down then took us by the hand and led us past the last couple of fields. My aunt was a picture of embarrassment when we arrived and I think she only took us in just keep face with the neighbour. She scrubbed us and fed us, washed our clothes and made us sit wrapped in towels then asked what had happened to her brother. When I told her, Auntie Bridget stayed quiet for a good while before turning to me.

'You can't stay Maria. I've not the cash to keep two children, even though I love you both. I'll scrounge some decent clothes from a neighbour and you can stay for three nights but then you must go back to wait for your daddy.'

When I look back, I think how cruel it might seem but they were different times. My aunt was so hard up she could barely provide for herself, let alone put food in two more mouths, however small. Perhaps she was hoping Uncle Mick would to take us in if he knew Daddy was ill.

So that's how it was. Jimmy and I stayed until the Thursday morning after breakfast when Tommy Lynch turned up to transport us back to Arklow. Our aunt gave us a bag of scone bread, jam and butter, pressed a few pennies into my hand, kissed and hugged us both, then went inside and closed the door without seeing us set off.

Mr Lynch dropped us at the hospital gates, where I rang the bell and a nurse answered. She checked and told me Daddy would need to stay in a while longer, perhaps a month or more so we went to look for Uncle Mick at the shop again.

'Gone. Left last week. Upped sticks and took the family to America.' Mr Jenkins clearly wasn't pleased. 'I always had him down as a reliable sort of a man and then he does this. Said he thought he'd be able to better himself over there.'

The shopkeeper was able to give me directions to my uncle's house so I took Jimmy's hand and walked out, turned left along the road and towards the river. As we got closer I recognised the area and soon found the house. It was locked but it didn't take much to smash a window at the back and climb inside then I stood on a chair to pull back the top bolt on the door to let Jimmy in. Our uncle and aunt must only have been able to take a few things with them because the house was more or less the same as last time we'd been. We wandered from room to room, poking in cupboards, where they'd even left some dried foods, and testing out the furniture and beds. It felt so strange to be there on our own, though we giggled and giggled at the idea we might have somewhere decent to stay for a while. After we tired of our exploring I went outside to gather sticks to light a fire and soon we were warming our toes, Jimmy asleep in one armchair and me in the other.

*

It's a mystery to me how we were never discovered.

We made no secret that we were living in the house, lighting the fire every night when we returned home and playing games in the field when we had the strength. Perhaps the neighbours knew we were there and knew who we were so left us to it, not willing to take us in and not wanting to see us sleeping on the streets.

We slept in the big bed, under two old coats left behind until, one day, on our way back from town, I spied some blankets drying on the line outside a big house. I hushed Jimmy and nipped across the yard, pulled two down, then ran as fast as I could to dive out of sight. They were still damp but they dried quickly enough and we slept in luxury after that.

Three months we were there and they were almost the happiest days of my life. We had no money and we had no-one but it was one big adventure. Imagine it. Two children with their own house, free to do what they want and to go where they want. To go to bed when they like and to get up when they like, with no grown-ups ordering them about. For the first few weeks we'd go to the fever hospital to ask about Daddy but the story was always the same. He was very ill and needed to be looked after. The nurses could never say when he'd be coming out and they wouldn't let us see him, said children weren't allowed. So after a while we stopped going.

We'd spend our days begging for pennies, or for scraps from the shops, running for our lives if a policeman appeared in the street. Sometimes we'd wander down to the quay and I'd help unload the fish. I hardly ever got paid for it, though they would give me a mackerel which was damaged so couldn't be sent to the market. Three or four of the shopkeepers were very kind and might throw in a lump of cheese or some eggs and stale bread as long as we didn't pester them too often. I made a point of buying from them when we'd copped some money on the street. Mr O'Leary, the greengrocer, was especially nice and would always let me have a bag of vegetables once a week. He'd tell me how to cook them, or how to make a good soup, and then, once I got the hang of it, we'd eat well for a few days.

On a Wednesday in June, Jimmy and me were sitting on the corner of an alleyway off the main street, stopping passers-by and asking them if they'd a ha'penny to spare. Jimmy was really good at it and could put on a face so sad it would melt the hardest heart. Men were always easier to cadge from than the women, especially if they'd a drink taken, and I'd be good at spotting the likeliest then send Jimmy off to waylay them. On this morning he was in a sour mood and didn't want to ask anyone, so I was telling him he'd get no dinner if he didn't. As a result, neither of us had bothered to keep a look-out and the next thing was that two shiny black size tens appeared, worn by the tallest uniformed bobby I'd ever seen. I made a run for it down the alley but he grabbed Jimmy then made after me. There was nowhere for me to go because it was a dead end and he soon had me cornered. Jimmy was screeching and wriggling and the policeman almost dropped him once before he raised his voice.

'You just stop that, young man.' The windows almost rattled with it. 'And you, young lady, get over here.'

It seemed pointless trying to get away. The feller was so big it would be hard to get past him and anyway, I couldn't leave my brother, even if it was his fault we'd been caught. I told Jimmy to be quiet, that it would be all right, and this brought a huge smile to the policeman's face.

'You look after him, do you? Bit of a scrapper isn't he. What's your name?'

'Maria Ann Byrne. I'm eight I think, and this is Jimmy, my brother.'

'And where would your mammy and daddy be?'

'I've no mammy, she died and Daddy's in the hospital, he's very sick and can't come out.'

'Well, you listen to me Miss Maria Ann Byrne, I've been watching out for you pair for a week or two since one of the shopkeepers told me you were around all the time bothering her customers. We can't have that now, can we? So, I'm going to take you to St Mary's where the nuns will look after you until I'm told what to do with you. Do you understand?'

I bowed my head. 'Yes, constable.'

Then we each held the policeman's hand whilst he walked us down a path which led us to hell.

*

Our spell in St Mary's was the first time Jimmy and I had been separated since he was born. I tried to hang on to his arm, kicking and spitting, but it was no use. One nun just slapped me hard and he was pulled away by another. I didn't know where they went, and I was taken to a room at the back of the building. There were clean sheets on the bed and the air smelled sickly-sweet, something I later came to recognise as carbolic, used for scrubbing away the head-lice.

A nun calling herself Sister Consolata showed me a sink, the soap, a tin bath and a bucket to fill it with.

'Now I'm going to leave you here and you get yourself washed, hair and all mind.' She pointed to a grey woollen smock dress and knickers on a chair. 'Put those on when you're finished and brush your hair a hundred times. If I come back and it's not done properly, or if there's a speck of dirt anywhere, then I'll do it for you myself and you won't like that. Am I clear?'

I knew better than to argue. 'Yes Sister.'

The water was freezing but I shivered myself in to it and by the time I climbed out I was enjoying being clean for a change. I remembered Mammy sitting me on her knee and singing one of her little nursery rhymes "This is the way we brush our hair, brush our hair , brush our hair ...' and for the first time since my father went into hospital I sat on the side of the bed and wept, great gulping sobs that I thought might never stop.

I knew if Sister Consolata came back and found me like this I'd be in bad trouble, so I pulled myself together and started the brushing. I hadn't a clue how to count to a hundred and just carried on until every single snag had gone and my hair felt shiny. Then I just sat there, looking around and wondering how long I'd have to wait before they'd bring Jimmy and we'd get something to eat. The walls of the room were painted white and on one wall hung a wooden cross with a very sad looking Jesus. On the windowsill stood a simple statue of Our Lady, dressed in blue and white and wearing a beautiful smile. Mammy had taken me to Mass every Sunday and I'd always stared at a similar, much bigger one high on the altar behind the priest. My mother would squeeze my hand and smile when she saw me looking up. I could feel myself about to burst in to tears again when the door handle rattled and the nun returned. She told me to stand, checked behind my ears and ran her fingers through my long dark hair.

'Very good, Maria. Now doesn't that feel a whole lot better?' She sounded much less stern than when she'd left and even smiled. 'I'll take you down to the kitchen shortly for your tea.'

'Will Jimmy be there?'

She shook her head. 'No he won't. He'll be staying with Mr O'Neill, the caretaker, while he's here and eating with him. You'll see him again in a day or two.'

The meal was the best I'd eaten in a long time and even though it was only leftovers from the nun's table there was a small chop, potatoes mashed with butter and some cabbage. Afterwards I was taken back upstairs by a younger nun who told me say my prayers then climb in to bed. She put out the lamp and closed the door behind her, leaving me beneath the covers thinking that, apart from being away from Jimmy, I could get used to the luxury of this life.

In less than a week I was in a different place, standing next to my brother at the back of a line of other children who were being ushered out in ones and twos to stand in front of three men at a high table.

*

Viscount Ralph Francis FitzTemple, heir to the 6th

Earl of Rathnew, was waiting and shifted uneasily in his seat. He felt like he was always waiting for something. Sometimes it was simply for dinner, or for his wife to stop talking, or, like today, for the next tale of depravity, neighbourly spitefulness or just plain badness to come before the Petty Sessions. More generally he was waiting for his father to die, or even for him to just pass on his lands and inheritance so that Ralph could go travelling. The twentieth case of the morning was just as disconcerting as the preceding ten, all of whom he'd committed to the Industrial Schools, but now it was approaching his lunchtime and talk of children starving in the streets was having an unsettling effect.

His fellow magistrates stole glances at each other, perhaps sharing similar thoughts.

'What's the case against this one?' asked FitzTemple.

'Maria Ann Byrne, my lord.' Read the court clerk. 'Found begging and destitute with her younger brother on the streets of Arklow town last Wednesday. She's eight years old, their mother is dead and their father is in the fever hospital, expected to remain there for some time.'

'And what's become of the brother?'

'Up next my lord, up next.'

At this point a second magistrate, James Murray, interjected. 'Where have they both been since last Wednesday?'

Viscount FitzTemple glared at his colleague for prolonging the proceedings, and the clerk, Isaac Foley, scanned his papers to find a quick answer.

'They were lodged with the sisters at St Mary's, sir.'

Murray ignored the discomfort of the bench chairman and pressed on. 'Is there anyone here to speak for the child?'

'A Miss Bridget Byrne, sir. The lady over there.' He pointed to my aunt seated on a stool near the back. 'She's the maiden aunt of the two of them.'

The errant magistrate addressed her. 'Please stand, Miss Byrne. Now why can't the children stay with you?'

'They did, for a while, sir, but I couldn't keep them. I've no money for myself let alone to raise two young ones that aren't even my own. They're good children, sir, but they'd be much better off in that school where you've been sending the others, at least they'd be fed and clothed. More than I could be sure of doing for them.'

The third magistrate, Timothy White, a doctor in the town, consulted his watch and interjected. 'I think we've probably heard enough. I suggest we send the girl up to that place in Dublin. What's it called Mr Foley?'

'St Gregory's, sir.'

'That's it, St Gregory's. We'll send her there

and she'll learn how to cook, sew and keep house. And the sisters will give her a good religious education to keep her on the straight and narrow. What do you say, gentlemen?'

His fellows nodded and the viscount passed sentence that Maria Ann Byrne, aged eight years, of no fixed abode, should be committed to an Industrial School until her sixteenth birthday. With the minimum of further discussion, her brother was given the same sentence. It carried a recommendation he remain in a local institution for as long as practical, so his father could visit him if he became well, and felt so inclined.

With this 'bad business' out of the way the three gentlemen adjourned the court and retired to the King's Hotel for a lunch of soup, mutton pie and apple tart, all washed down with the best claret on offer. They were in total agreement that they were deserving of this, given their tribulations of the morning, and the afternoon still to come. Viscount FitzTemple remained blissfully unaware he'd just sentenced the grandchildren of a man who'd saved his father's life, a man without whom he would never have existed.

Day 14

God, I was so tired last time. My own fault, losing the bloody bus fare. At least it was only for the second bus home, but was far enough to walk at that time of night, then having Billy ranting and raving when I got in. Not too pleased he'd missed the pub, even less pleased when I told him I thought that's why he was mad, not because he was worried. Didn't like that at all.

Can't think why it did me in so much. Not as if it's the first time I've tramped the streets for hours, good weather and bad. Part of life when I was younger. Wouldn't have met him otherwise.

*

To this day I can't understand why they sent me to Dublin, away from any chance of my father or my aunt visiting me. Perhaps there was nowhere closer. They called it an orphanage but it wasn't. It was a gaol for a hundred children with the cruellest warders in the world. Warders who claimed to serve the will of God.

I was transported from the court by the police, without a chance for a proper goodbye to Jimmy, and there were two other girls, Bernie Doyle and Kathleen Breslin, travelling with me. They were in front of me waiting for the magistrates and I'd heard their cases but I didn't know them, even though they were both from Arklow. I liked Bernie straight away. She was about my age, blond and smiling, despite there not being much to smile about. Bernie's father had died when she was five and the parish priest had condemned her mother because she was seeing another man. One day a policeman and someone she called the Cruelty Man had cycled up to the house when her mother's friend was still there. The Cruelty Man was a kind of social worker and he took Bernie away to the court. Her mother must have been so ashamed or shocked because she never spoke up for her daughter nor tried to get her back.

The other girl, Kathleen, was a year or two older than us and didn't speak the whole way to Dublin, not even when we stopped for the night in Newcastle. She'd pull a face or throw something at us if we even dared to look at her. Her knees and hands were red-raw, as if she'd been crawling about on damp ground, and I wanted to ask her about them but was too scared.

We arrived at St Gregory's early on a warm autumn evening and, when we entered the grounds, the dozens of girls working in the vegetable plots stopped what they were doing and crowded round the vehicle. A young nun ran over to them and told them to get move away but a few ignored her, following behind us, until an older woman came out and shouted.

'You girls, back to work or no supper.'

They didn't wait to be spoken to by her again

and returned to their jobs. I learned very soon afterwards that this was not someone to be disobeyed.

St Gregory's was the biggest building I'd ever seen in Ireland. It was grey stone, two floors high and had two dozen windows on the front, with ten down the side. At least twice the size of the hospital where I'd left Daddy. We were taken to the back door and into a cold room where the older nun we'd seen outside looked over the papers from the court, spoke to the policeman and signed to say we'd been delivered.

'I'm Sister Francis-Ellen and you, Bernadette Doyle, Maria Byrne and Kathleen Breslin, will be in our care until your sixteenth birthday. If you are well-behaved and attentive, you'll become good Catholic girls and able to live a decent life when you leave us. If you're not well-behaved, you'll wish you'd never been born. Do I make myself clear?'

'Yes, Sister.' Repeated three times.

'Good.' She handed us each a mohair sort of dress. It didn't look new, and a pair of knickers, likewise. 'So take these into that room,' pointing to a door across the corridor 'get yourselves undressed and Sister Ursula will help you take a bath.'

Poor Bernie screamed every time Sister Ursula poured the freezing water over her hair, getting a slap from the nun whenever she did. I imagined my new-found friend had never taken cold baths at home, nor been treated so badly in her whole life, and she was in floods of tears as she dried herself and I'd taken her place in the tub. I was determined not to show the same weakness so gritted my teeth and squeezed my eyes shut to keep out the caustic soap. I'd bathed plenty of times in cold water and even though I preferred it warm it was no major hardship. The dress, on the other hand, was different, and for all the years I was forced to wear one I never got used to the itchiness of that cloth.

The Breslin girl was up next. When she undressed, it was obvious she was a stranger to water of any kind, warm or cold, and I guessed she'd been living on the streets for a while. The nun smacked Kathleen only once when she ducked her head away from the jug, the second time, the girl grabbed the hand and sunk her teeth in to it. The nun's hand was raised again but then slowly lowered.

'So we're a dog are we, Kathleen? Well we'll see about that. There are sisters here who are not keen on little girls pretending to be animals. No, not keen at all. I think you'll be spending a night or two on your own.'

When we were finished and Kathleen taken to wherever she was to be punished, we were told it was too late for anything to eat and we'd have to wait until breakfast.

I was starving, having had nothing since mid-morning, but there was no option but to last through the night. Sister Ursula took us up some back stairs, stone stairs they were, and the walls were painted grey, I don't know why I remember this. The dormitory was painted the same colour, with an enormous crucifix above the door, and the space had a strange smell. Later I recognised it as a pungent mix of young bodies, beeswax, disinfectant and candles. There were a hundred beds in four rows, a girl standing by each one, identically dressed in grey nightclothes, and they ran from about six years old to fifteen or sixteen. Bernie was pointed to a bed near the far end and I was given one about half way down with another empty one next to it.

Sister Ursula walked to the middle of the dormitory and clapped her hands twice. 'Listen here. These new girls are Maria Byrne and Bernadette Doyle, both from the lovely County Wicklow, sent to us so they can learn how to behave properly and to love Our Lady.' She turned to one of the older girls. 'You, Helen Cullan, you've ten minutes to tell these two what they must, and mustn't do, then all off to bed. I'll be back soon to check on you all and woe betide any girl not on her way to sleep by then.'

With this she marched out, leaving our guide to give us the list.

'Up at half past six, washed, dressed, bed made and down in the dining room by seven o'clock. God help you if you wet the bed. That's the thing they hate the most. It will be a beating and no breakfast at least, worse if you do it more than once. Always address them as Sister this or Sister that, never miss out their name, ask if you don't know but don't ask twice.'

And so she went on, rule after rule for ten minutes. My head was spinning, and I knew I'd never remember it all. Bernie sobbed the whole time until Helen put an arm around her shoulder.

'Husht, don't be crying like that, you'll manage just fine. Most of the sisters are nice, and kind, you just have to watch out for the ones who aren't. You'll soon pick up who to be careful of. I've been here since I was ten and it took me a few weeks but after that I got on grand. Not to say I won't be happy to leave when my time's up in five months and eighteen days.' She peered through the window to the clock tower across the yard, then took a step away. 'You'd better get your nightdress on, then on your knees and say your prayers. Be sharp. That cow Sister Ursula will be back in a minute.'

Of all the nights I spent in that place, I think the first one was the worst. Somehow, on the streets and in my uncle's cottage, even waiting to go in front of the magistrates, I'd imagined my father would get well and come to look after us.

Now, he was still in hospital, and Jimmy had been sent to a place miles away, and I was surrounded by strangers, and it seemed I'd be there for years. I undressed, climbed under the coarse brown blanket and waited with my eyes closed until the sister had finished her inspection. Then, I turned on my back and stared at the ceiling, listening to my neighbours snoring or crying in the darkness.

*

Two days later we came back before tea and Kathleen Breslin was sitting on the bed next to mine. The rawness had gone from her knees but now she had welts on each leg and her hair had been cut short, jagged, like with poor scissors or a blunt knife. Her eyes, bloodshot from crying, had lost the fierceness she'd shown on the journey from Arklow.

'Are you all right?'

Her glance was a mix of defiance and terror, though she still didn't speak. Most of the other girls were ignoring her, you learnt to mind your own business pretty soon in that place, only one or two were watching. She'd scared me on the police cart but now she was frightened and it looked like we might be together for a good few years to come. So I took the few steps between our beds and sat down beside her. Next thing, Helen was on her other side and before long the battered Kathleen was surrounded by half a dozen of the older girls, forming a cocoon whilst the tears ran down her face. They'd all been there for one reason or another. The tears didn't last long because Sister Francis-Ellen came in and everyone scampered back to stand by their bed, staring straight ahead and arms by their sides. The nun stood just inside the doorway and addressed the room.

'I can see you've met our latest addition. Kathleen Breslin is her name and she needed some extra tuition before she was ready to join you. Isn't that right, Kathleen?'

The girl nodded. 'Yes, Sister Francis-Ellen.'

'She's been away from the good Lord for a long time but we'll bring her back again one way or another. Now, I want you all down in the gardens straight away. There's a trader coming for cabbages in twenty minutes and they'll need cutting ready for loading when he arrives. Straight line, in twos, follow me.'

Kathleen fell in beside me, halfway down the line and as our part of the snake passed through the door she dug me hard in the ribs with her elbow.

'Don't think that show in there makes us friends, Byrne. I don't like you.'

I'd spent too much time looking after myself, Daddy and Jimmy to be pushed around. I was about to give her some of her own medicine when a girl behind me called Teresa grabbed my fist.

'Don't' she whispered, pointing down the stairs

'Sister will hear and we'll all get into trouble. Settle it later when none of them are around.'

I glared at Breslin but did as Teresa asked, knowing I'd get my chance sometime.

*

Pulling cabbages was a job we did twice a week from May to October. The couple of acres of grounds were planted with vegetables which I think were supposed to be used to feed us but most of them were sold or ended up on the dinner table of the nuns. What we were fed was terrible unless there was an inspection happening, then we'd get a proper meal so the inspectors would believe we were well treated. For breakfast it would be bread, a bit of lard and cocoa, and in the middle of the day there'd be stale bread baked in pig's blood, then, about five o'clock, porridge and tea in a tin mug . That's what we lived off, nothing but scraps and rubbish, hungry all the time.

That hunger stays with me, Alice. Even though Billy doesn't earn much, I can't rest easy if I don't have more in the larder than we need, just in case. So as I know it's there.

Some of the things Auntie Bridget taught me must have stuck because the nuns soon recognised I knew about the different crops and could tell a dock from a cabbage. There were quite a few of us, but many more who hadn't a clue, so we were spread amongst the others and told to keep them in order. A lot of the time I enjoyed the work except when the rain was pouring and we were left out there, dripping wet. It would take us hours to dry when we were called in for Mass. One such day I was sent with Kathleen Breslin to fetch a barrow load of horse manure from behind the stables. She'd continued to pinch and punch me whenever she could, always when one of the nuns was in earshot and I couldn't retaliate, so I'd need to put her in her place sometime. The ground around the dung heap was swimming in mud, leaving us slipping and sliding as we tried to shovel the muck into our barrow, and it took no effort at all for me to give her a push. Before she knew what was happening she was lying in filth and I was standing over her, my pitchfork pointed at her chest.

'You'd best stop messing with me, Breslin, I've had enough. Touch me once more and you'll be sorry.' I prodded her with the fork 'If you don't want this stuck through you you'll leave me alone.'

I was shaking, not sure what I'd do if she fought back, when I heard Sister Ursula shouting our names. I looked away for a second and Breslin grabbed my ankle, tripping me into the mess beside her and we started to kick and fight, two farmyard cats covered in mud, and worse. Then the nun was standing in the yard, calling for us to stop, unable, or unwilling, to get any closer. We did stop, looked at each other, then burst out laughing. Later we were made to wash our dresses then sloshed down with buckets of freezing water, standing naked outside the back door, before two of the Sisters took us inside and treated us to the belt. The leather stung so much against my wet skin that I screamed out. When they switched to Kathleen I could see from the look on their faces that they were enjoying it and all the time Sister Francis-Ellen sat in the corner reading her missal.

After this, Kathleen and I were best of friends and looked out for each other. It was Kathleen, Bernie and me against the world, though Bernie never got into the same scrapes as we did, she was such a gentle soul.

Kathleen Breslin had been born in a room above a pub in a small town in north County Wexford, where the owner let her mother live in exchange for occasional favours. Bella Breslin didn't know if the landlord was Kathleen's father, there were so many men made their way up the stairs day and night, and it was one of these she followed to Arklow when the daughter was two years old. They'd lived in a shabby cottage for nearly three years until he'd gone out on a boat drunk, fell overboard and drowned. Bella survived another eighteen months after him, just long enough to teach Kathleen how to live on the streets, begging and stealing from shops. Fortunately, the girl had been spared from learning Bella's trade, she was still too young to be earning pennies flat on her back. At best her mother had ignored Kathleen, just seeing her as a burden, at worst she'd been beaten by the mother's man, whenever he'd a drink taken and a foul temper to go alongside. These experiences helped her adapt well to the school, where love was in short supply. Even though she'd had no education before arriving at St Gregory's she was bright and good at her lessons so at least she was spared the random violence of the classroom which the dimmer ones endured. One thing she couldn't manage was discipline. She joked that she was going to ask Sister Ursula to move her bed in to the punishment room permanently, it had become so much like home.

*

Although there were three or four cruel nuns, most of them were as you'd expect, caring and appearing to have our best interests at heart. They maintained their distance from us, and they were all more holy than we might like, but they did try to give us an education of sorts. As well as the Sisters we had what they called lay teachers, ones who just came in to work every day, and they were the best. Sister Francis-Ellen was like the head mistress, she wasn't the top one though. That would be the Reverend Mother, who lived in the convent next to the school and we only saw at Easter and Christmas. Then there were the novices, mainly young women who were given the skivvying jobs that were just above what we might be made to do. They'd work in the kitchen, or supervise us outside if it was raining, or clean the Sister's rooms where we weren't allowed.

One of these younger nuns, Sister Assumpta she was called, worked in the kitchen preparing the Sisters' food. She would pop out her head if we were passing and share out a few crusts smothered with butter, she must have known we were starving most of the time. After a while she stopped and I didn't see her again. Whether she'd been found out or moved on I don't know, but we did miss the extra rations.

There was also a teacher, Mrs McGovern, Scottish I think, and she was always kind. Taught us sewing and I was hopeless, still am, but she never got angry, explained how we'd made a mistake and let us try again. One time I was embroidering a flower on a pillow case, the nuns sold these if they were any good, and I found I'd sewn the material to my dress. Most of the other teachers would have pulled me out and humiliated me in front of the class but Mrs McGovern just sat down beside me, snipped away the threads and asked me to start again. I could see she was smiling, trying not to giggle, all the way through, though she covered it well. All the girls liked her.

There was only one man about the place, Mr

Sullivan. He did a lot of the heavier jobs and looked after the two horses. He always wore a brown suit with a flat cap and I thought he was ancient, although he was probably only as old as Billy is now. Mr Sullivan lived in a small house behind the stables, separated from the school by a high wall. None of the girls liked him much and steered well away from the man if they could.

When I was about twelve a new teacher replaced Mrs McGovern and she was quite stuck up, with a posh Dublin voice. She seemed to think it was our job to earn money for the church and I got into an argument with her soon after she started. My needlework was always rubbish, no matter how hard Mrs McGovern had tried I could never quite grasp it, never quite make it tidy enough to be sold. The new teacher, Miss Kevens, called me to the front of the class, holding up my latest effort.

'And what do you call this Maria Byrne? Look at the state of it.'

'What's the matter with it, Miss?'

'It's just plain careless. Every stitch is a different length. Even they should be. Even, not like this.'

I turned to my classmates. 'Well it looks fine to me, Miss.'

Most of them giggled. Only the two Cavanagh sisters, who were sneaks, frowned and tut-tutted, but they both had it in their heads they'd be teachers themselves one day so it was hardly surprising they'd take her side.

'You're a bold girl, Maria Byrne. Very bold. You'd better watch your step.'

I knew I shouldn't say another word but I couldn't help myself.

'I've been told you only get cross with poor work because you can't give it to the nuns to sell. Is that right Miss?

This time there were fewer giggles and several gasps. A number of the girls had their hands over their mouths and the Cavanaghs looked like they might pass out.

Thwack.

I heard the slap on the side of the head before I felt it. Then it went dark.

When I opened my eyes, the circle of faces looking down made me think I'd ascended into heaven, until I recognised Bernie and Miss Kevens. My hair was damp on one side with something stickier than water, and it was throbbing. The teacher's blow had sent me flying, bashing my head on the corner of the desk, though if I'd expected sympathy at this point I'd have been mistaken. Miss Kevens pulled me up by the ear and marched me down to Sister Francis-Ellen's room, where I got the strap across the hands for my "argumentative nature". It wasn't the first time, nor would it be the last, though I think by that time even Sister Francis-Ellen was despairing that they'd make me fall in to line.

Day 15

'That bus was awful tonight. Mrs Crawshaw from number eight kept me chatting at the gate. Wanted to know all about how you were getting on. All the neighbours have been lovely, sending their prayers and good wishes every time they see me. So I missed the one into town and had to get the next, which only took me to Ardwick Green, where the Apollo was letting out and everyone was queueing for the buses. There were no seats left when I climbed on.'

The tea trolley clatters past, the woman who'd been so kind to Maria the previous week smiles as she pushes it past the end of the bed. 'Any change?' she mouthes. Maria shakes her head and the woman moves on.

'I was talking to your dad when I got back last night. Not talking, arguing really. He asked what I did when I'm with you, says I shouldn't be here so much. Said the others need me as well, especially Tommy and Rose. I told him they've got me all day, every day, while he's out at work or in bed, and I want to be with you in the evenings. It's not as though it's going to last forever.

'When I explained I tell you stories about my life, right back from my granddad's time, he said I shouldn't. "Picking at old sores" he called it. Of course he might be right, and I know he's only worried about me - and you - but he doesn't understand. If I don't start picking those old scabs off sometime they're going to weigh me down for ever. And who else do I tell?'

A nurse lifts Alice's notes from the bed-end and moves round to take her temperature. She does this without speaking to Maria, checks her watch, then writes on the notes before moving on to the next patient. Maria chuckles.

'That's one happy in her work, don't you think?' She runs her fingers across her daughter's brow, as if they might be more accurate than the thermometer, then touches her own cheek for comparison. 'Anyway, we talked about it until he got fed up and went to his bed. Your dad can go on about it as much as he likes but I'll keep on coming and keep telling you the story until it's finished.'

*

When I was thirteen years old, Sister Ursula called me in from the gardens just before lunchtime. She took me in to a room where a clean dress was lying on a chair with a pair of decent shoes on the floor beside it.

'Get into these Byrne, you have a visitor.'

She made sure I was washed, back of the neck and behind the ears included, then, for her amusement, dragged every tangle out of my hair with a large tortoiseshell comb. When she'd decided I was presentable she led me through the school to the front hall, then in to a beautiful wood-panelled room off to the side, completely at odds with the grey and cream walls of the areas we inhabited.

My father raised himself from the chair at the head of a dining table laid with crockery and cutlery for two people. He was thinner than I remembered, his cheeks sunken in a grey face. There were no hugs when Sister Ursula left the room, just silence until she'd returned with a teapot and a platter of sandwiches and then left us alone again. He must have been as hungry as me because he dived in, eating sandwich after sandwich directly from the dish, without bothering to transfer them to his plate. When I lifted three, putting two into my apron pocket for later, he gave me a look as if I'd done him a great wrong.

After a few minutes of this he paused between mouthfuls.

'So how are they treating you, Maria?'

'Not so bad, Daddy.'

'That's good then. They don't beat you?'

'Not so much now I'm older.'

'Good, ... good.'

'Have you come to take me home, Daddy?'

He shook his head and threw out a bitter, throaty laugh.

'Home? Even if I had a home to take you to I don't think they'd let me.' He reached into his jacket pocket and pulled out a tiny parcel of tissue paper. 'Here, I brought you this.'

He watched me remove a dainty white handkerchief embroidered in one corner with a small flower, a rose it was meant to be, pink petals and two thin green leaves beneath. The sort of handkerchief that could be bought for pennies on any market. I held it to my cheek and said it was lovely. I meant it. No-one had given me a gift so precious since arriving at St Gregory's four years earlier. In fact, no-one had given me anything like it, ever. I'll perhaps bring it with me next time. Let you touch a piece of my life.

'I'm glad you think it's nice' he said 'I went to see your brother last year and I never thought to take anything with me. It was only afterwards I realised I should have done. Now they've told me he's moved from Arklow to Limerick somewhere and I can't see how I'll get all the way over there to see him again, I could just scrape together enough for the bus up here.'

As lunch filled his belly and the tea slid down he told me he'd been in hospital over and over since I'd last seen him. Getting out after a few weeks then staying with Auntie Bridget when she'd let him or sleeping on the street when she wouldn't, until his illness returned and he'd find himself in the care of the doctors again. He'd not the lungs to do the heavy farm labouring anymore, and casual lighter work was hard to come by, so he'd rarely enough money to keep body and soul together. In truth, I expect he was pleased to return to the workhouse hospital, where at least he'd be fed something every day, regardless of how meagre it might be.

While we were talking I was thinking that it must be a dream. A table filled with food, soft seats, china plates instead of the tin dishes I was used to. A room that was actually warm. Then the dream ended. Sister Ursula came back, saying it was time for him to leave. He didn't argue, he was as used to obeying nuns as I was, and just picked up his cap, slipped on his tattered overcoat and kissed me on the forehead before saying goodbye.

He never came again and a year later I was taken aside after Mass by Father Donovan and told that he'd died. It was a strange sensation. A man who had looked after me and my brother as best he could until he'd become too poorly, but who'd been out of my life since I was eight years old. I didn't need him, though I missed him and cried all night when I heard the news.

*

We heard in August 1914 that Britain had declared war against Germany, but life in St Gregory's went on much the same. In the September, only months before I left, they gave me a prize job. Most of the work to keep the school going was carried out by the girls. Everyone helped in the gardens, but the rest depended on how old and how bright you were, and if you were in the good books. The younger or more stupid children cleaned the rooms and polished the floors, then later would help in the kitchen or toil away in the laundry. The nuns' clothes went a few streets away to the Magdalene but everything of ours was sent to the cellar where the work was horrible. If you were in there you emerged every day with arms raw to the elbows from the water and the rough soap. Floor polishing was not a lot better, it was terrible hard on the knees and the wax stained our hands but at least it was dry. When you reached fourteen or fifteen you might be put on looking after the babies and I always loved doing that. Just as well, it was good practice for how many came later.

I never knew where the nuns got them but there were always half a dozen children in the nursery to be cared for. The rumours said they were from the women in the Magdalene and they were waiting to be sent off to America, to rich couples who couldn't have children of their own. I asked one of the nuns and she told me they were poor little orphans whose parents had died. Although I enjoyed working in the nursery we had to take turns with the night-time feeds and were still expected to do our lessons the next day. I always terrified me I'd nod off in class then get into trouble, meaning I'd be put to working in the cellar instead.

Daddy's death had knocked the stuffing out of me for a while, seemed to calm me down somehow, and I'd not been getting into any kind of trouble. So, I was surprised when my name was called out in class, along with another girl, and told to go to Sister Ursula's room.

I didn't know Eithne Esmonde very well, she'd recently arrived from Galway, and so we walked along the corridors in silence. I knocked on the Sister's door and stepped away in case she came out raging. Instead, she simply called us inside.

'Now girls, I've a job for you to do to see how you get on. You'll be leaving us before too long and you need to learn to shop properly so when you're in service you'll be of some use to your mistress.' She lifted a list from her desk. 'I know that Eithne has done this with her mother, before the poor woman died, so she'll be in charge. You, Maria, look after the money and make sure there's none of it goes missing. Else you'll be in trouble. Understand?'

'Yes, Sister Ursula.'

We were given directions and strict instructions for when we were to be back, then let out into the wide world on our own. The first time for me in seven years.

It was a ten minute walk to the shops on Macklin Road, if we'd not taken our time to look in every yard, garden and window along the way. A tram squealed to a halt at the corner of Mendip Lane and I imagined how wonderful it would be to be able to jump on board and never see the school again. If Eithne hadn't been with me I think I'd have chanced it, but she'd have been in real trouble for letting me go. That's probably why they sent two of us at a time.

All of the things we'd been told to buy were for the nuns themselves; wool for Sister Agatha, envelopes for Sister Dorothy and a cough bottle for Sister Helena. Everything for the school and the convent was grown or made by us, or was delivered by tradesmen.

We'd bought everything from the list and were ambling back down the street, stopping and pointing at anything catching our eye in the shop windows. The food shops were the ones where we paid most attention. Mounds of apples, slabs of cheese and butter, and, best of all, lamb, pork and beef hanging from hooks in the butcher's. We were drooling at the chops when a boy in a white coat leant in and lifted the tray. He looked from me to Eithne then back again, and winked a toothy smile, splitting his face, a picture I remembered from somewhere. Eithne clamped her hand over her mouth and giggled.

'What a bold boy,' she squealed 'come on Maria, let's go.' Her jaw dropped even further when she saw me smiling back. 'Maria Byrne will you stop that!'

I have to say I knew no better, there were only girls in the school, other than old Sullivan and the priests, and I'd been no more than a child the last time I was outside unsupervised. I've no idea to this day what attracts men to women at first, apart from the obvious. At that time I'd have my hair cut short, easier to keep clean, and was slim but not skinny, with the figure just beginning to develop. My mammy had been very pretty and daddy had the plainness of his sister, so I'd grown up falling between the two, and maybe the boy liked what he'd seen. He took the tray away to a room behind the counter, turned and smiled at me again. Even though I made Eithne wait a few minutes he didn't come back.

I hardly slept for the next week. The boy's grin kept coming back to me and I couldn't get him out of my head. The next time we went out, Eithne tried to steer us home a different way so we wouldn't pass the butcher's, but I insisted, telling her to go off on her own if she wanted. Needless to say she didn't, though I'd have preferred it if she had.

When we came near, the boy appeared outside and began filling the basket of a large, black bicycle propped against the wall. He looked round as we approached and smiled that smile again.

'Good day ladies, are you well?'

My school companion turned her head away in an attempt to ignore him. I smiled back and said we were fine.

'I've seen you before,' he said 'at the orphanage. You were working in the garden one day when we came with the delivery.'

I blushed and muttered that I hadn't seen him.

'I'm not surprised. You were hoking away at the weeds and giving orders to all the younger girls, like a sergeant-major. Do you want to come with me on my round?'

Eithne tugged at my sleeve. 'Come on, Maria, we have to go.'

'Maria? Is that your name then? Mine's Danny. Danny Walsh.'

Another tug and I glared at her. 'Give me a minute will you? Just one minute. In private. Go and look in the bookshop window, you can still see me from there.'

Scowling, she crossed the street and left us alone. I told Danny I couldn't go with him because Eithne and me would get a telling off if we were back late. He asked if I'd be back again and I said I didn't know, it would depend on what the sisters decided.

'Do they never let you out with that place?'

'No.'

'Is it a prison then?'

'Sort of. But full of children.'

'So I won't see you again?'

I peered across to be sure Eithne was still out of earshot. 'I might be able to get out. I've thought about it a lot. Almost did it one night when Sister Ursula was being even worse than usual. But where would I go?'

'I finish here at about half past six every day. I'd be up your road in a quarter of an hour. Could you get out for seven o'clock? Friday?'

Tea was at five, Mass at six. I'd need to be there for those else I'd be missed. Bed was at nine o'clock and I'd have to be back by then. I knew there was a gate to Park Road from Sullivan's garden and, if I was careful, I could get in there over the wall by the stables, then make my escape to meet Danny on the corner. I told him it would be easier a little bit later when we'd be sure it was dark and Mr Sullivan would have settled down for the night.

Danny looked over my shoulder, keeping his eye on Eithne, and touched my hand. 'Quarter past seven it is then, by the big tree on the corner of Park Road.'

With cheeks burning I turned and skipped across the street to the girl I now viewed as my guard. She asked me what we'd been talking about and I told her to mind her own business, then she tried pinching me to make me talk but she was no match and I gave as good as I got. I didn't think

Eithne would snitch to the nuns, though it wouldn't have paid to take chances, and I warned her not to try it. She knew me well enough to take notice.

Two whole days to get through before Friday, thinking and thinking. If it was now I'd be wondering what to wear, how I should do my hair and which brooch or necklace would bring out the colour of my eyes. Then, I had nothing, only the clothes I stood up in. Instead, all I could wonder was why he'd picked me, what would I do if he tried to kiss me, and how many children we'd have when we got married? Silliness, the thoughts of a foolish girl with no knowledge of boys and the real world. I learnt about them soon enough though. Men and what they want.

I so much wanted to share what was happening but was scared I'd be laughed at or found out. If Kathleen had still been there I'd have told her, I could tell Kathleen anything, but she'd left the previous year and was living up in the city, so I'd heard. I'd cried for days when she left and hoped for a while she'd come to visit me. She never did and I can't say I blame her. I knew once I was out of that place I wouldn't want to go back. Ever.

After Mass on Wednesday night I sat on my bed braiding spare strands of wool, then hid the finished multi-coloured band in my dress pocket. When Friday came it dragged and dragged. More than once my teachers shouted at me to pay attention to my lessons, and at tea-time I could hardly manage a bite. Through Mass I fidgeted the whole time until Father Donovan put his eye on me and I knew I'd be pulled in for a telling off if I didn't stop. Afterwards I joined the other older girls who were allowed to walk the grounds before bed. A short while later I slipped away, telling them I'd a headache and was going to the dormitory. As soon as they were round the corner I sneaked round to the back near the kitchen. The rose bed was already growing dark in the shadows and I snapped two blooms from their stems, carefully putting them in my pocket with the headband. The stone wall felt rough on my back as I pressed against it, shaking like a leaf. When the chapel bell struck seven I chanced running along building and the hedge leading to the stable yard. I scrambled over the wall into Sullivan's garden, where I dropped to my knees, catching my breath before the next dash. A light in Sullivan's house showed through closed curtains, lighting my path. I stayed low when I scurried beneath his window and out to the street.

Danny was on the corner, facing in the other direction, smoking under the street lamp. In the darkness by the gate I tied the woollen band around my hair and tucked the best of the roses into it. I strode towards Danny as if I walked in freedom every day.

Day 16

On the way here I've been considering if I should tell you about that night being magical, one of the best of my life. It seems so disloyal to Billy but I've not been able to get it out of my head all day. Perhaps it was the excitement of it, I don't know, just a silly girl escaping to meet her first boyfriend.

The autumn nip hung in the air, and Danny lent me his coat when he saw me shivering as I appeared from the shadows.

'I like the rose' he'd said, and then talked about meat for ten minutes. I think he was as nervous as me, so treated me to everything he knew about butchering, which wasn't much. He worked in the shop, that's all, but he watched his boss all the time and learnt his way round the different cuts.

Danny was just a boy, and the only one I ever really loved. I owe Billy everything, even my life, and we've shuffled along as well as any man and wife I expect, though there was never the excitement of those few days I had with Danny. I might tell you later of another man, Tony. Now he was a different kettle of fish altogether.

We walked away from St Gregory's, down the side streets where we'd not be seen if any of the sisters were about, and I explained to him that it wasn't an orphanage even though both my parents were dead. I told him about Jimmy and how we'd been split, not even knowing where he was any more.

'Jesus, I'd hate that. My brothers and me fight all the time but I'd miss them terrible if they weren't here. Kevin, that's the one next to me, is joining the army and I'm going with him. He says he wants some adventure and it will be a bit of a lark this war, though our other brother, Christy, is dead set against it. He thinks we should be kicking out the British, not fighting their battles for them. Dad gets so mad when the two of them start arguing.'

'Aren't you too young to join up?'

'I'm nearly sixteen and everyone says I look older. I can't see they're going to be too fussy anyway.'

He was right, he did look more than sixteen, and I was flattered he'd even considered walking out with someone like me, a silly little girl who knew nothing of the war.

After an hour, which flew by, I told him I'd have to go and he should carry on home, that I'd be fine making my way back to St Gregory's on my own. Danny went over the directions several times until I said I'd got them, then he gave me a funny little hug, like he was scared to do a proper one, and ran off down the street.

'I'll try to get out to the shop next week' I shouted after him and he turned and waved.

'That will be great, I hope you can.' With that

he disappeared round a corner.

I was in a daze as I floated back to school and almost missed my turn in to Park Road. It was only the memory of Danny under the street lamp that reminded me where I was. Going through old Sullivan's garden was as simple as it had been on the way out, and the stables gate opened easily with the handle on his side so I was through and outside the back door of the school with him none the wiser. No light showed from any of the downstairs windows but I'd never been outside the dormitory at that time before, at least not when it was dark, and I'd no idea who might be lurking around the corridors. My heart almost stopped when I heard a creak from behind me when I tiptoed along the second landing. No-one appeared or called my name so it must have been a floorboard I'd stepped on.

The other girls were all over me when I walked through the door, wanting to know where I'd been all evening. I fobbed them off with a story about having a headache and Sister Assumpta telling me to sit in the dark with a cold cloth on my forehead until I felt better. Everyone but Eithne seemed to believe this, and she gave me a look which said she knew I was lying.

*

All week I fretted that I'd be passed over for the shopping job so I tried hard to do well in class and to avoid getting into trouble. I even put together a bouquet from what was left in the gardens and I left it in the kitchen for Sister Ursula. When she came up to dormitory that night she asked me what I was up to, she knew well enough that she wasn't my favourite, but I said they were only going to waste and someone had told me it was her birthday. She raised an eyebrow and barked that it wasn't her birthday until March, and that I was a stupid girl. The tiny grin which slipped out told me it had achieved the desired effect and my name, along with Eithne's, was called again on Wednesday morning.

This time I warned my guard to make herself scarce when we reached the butcher's. I dragged her round to buy what we wanted as quickly as possible, and then told her to take a short walk whilst I met Danny. He must have been waiting for me, because he grabbed a box when I waved him out of the shop, and came outside to his bicycle.

'They let you out then?'

'They did, but I've only ten minutes before I have to meet that girl again.'

We walked along the street, me talking twenty to the dozen and Danny wearing his toothy smile, letting on to people as we passed. He was tall and skinny, and I was taken by his hair, golden in the sun like straw it was. He walked a mile and a half every morning to work, then the same again in the evening when he finished. His father was a coalman, with his own horse and cart, helped by Danny's older brothers, who'd take over the business when the dad's back could manage it no longer, the same as he had from his dad. The mother cleaned houses for elderly residents of Sandymount who were no longer wealthy enough to keep servants but too genteel to consider lifting a broom themselves. The family were Dubliners through and through, though the grandfather came from County Leitrim, where he'd planted potatoes on the shore of Lough Melvin until they gave out two years running and he'd joined the army to survive.

We stopped on the corner outside a draper's and he leaned his bike against the window, lifting his parcel and taking it inside. He was only away a minute, but I'd already begun to panic I'd be longer than we'd agreed, and Eithne would run off to school without me.

'I have to get back now,' I said, and turned to go.

'That's fine, I'm expected in the shop myself. Come on.'

Three doors from his last delivery a black shape loomed out of a doorway and almost collided with Danny's front wheel.

'Careful young man ... Maria Byrne, is that you?'

It was Sister Ursula and my first instinct was to run, but she grabbed me before I could. Danny pushed the bike between us, the basket almost forcing us apart. I knew there be no point, she would only wait for me at the school, so I shouted for him to stop.

Sister Ursula tightened her grip and pulled me down the street by the hair, leaving Danny shouting.

'You'll soon be out of that place, Maria, come to me when you can.'

Every single time I think about that day I wish I'd let him free me, then grabbed his hand and ran with him for the hills.

*

The day after Sister Ursula hauled me from the shops, Father Donovan pointed me out at Mass.

'That girl, there, Maria Byrne, stand up' he boomed. Every head in the chapel turned in my direction. 'Come on, get up, let all the girls see you.'

I did as I was told.

'Now, Miss Byrne, tell us, do you know right from wrong?'

I mumbled that I did.

'Speak up, girl. Do you know right from wrong?'

I lifted my head, drew breath and fixed him with my eyes.

'Yes, Father, I know right from wrong.'

'Did you hear that Sisters?' Dropping his voice, he surveyed his audience. 'How about you girls, did you hear her?'

A murmur hovered on the air for a moment.

'So tell me, Miss Byrne, if you do,' the priest now bellowing again 'why have you been so wicked? Explain to all these girls, to the good Sisters,' he intertwined his fingers, glancing upward before glaring back at me, 'and to God, how it could be that you were caught in the middle of the town with a boy.'

Despite every girl in St Gregory's knowing what I'd done there was still a gasp. I knew there was no point pretending to be sorry.

'We're friends, Father. I did nothing wrong.'

Father Donovan turned an even deeper shade of purple. Sister Ursula strode from her place on the front pews, pushed her way past the others on mine, and grabbed me by the hair.

'You wicked, wicked girl' she hissed 'The good Lord will need to be at his most merciful to forgive you. We'll see if you did nothing wrong.'

With this she kicked my feet away and dragged me howling from the chapel.

I was two weeks confined to the punishment room and they didn't let me out of the grounds again, not until the end. I wasn't even allowed to work in the gardens most days and when I was, they made sure I had the worst of the jobs. All of the time they kept me indoors gave me the freedom to think about how I might escape, how I'd run out of the gates and find Danny, how we'd go away together. I imagined myself as a butcher's wife, because surely he'd become a butcher, with his own shop and lots of customers. We'd have children, and I'd serve in the shop when I could. And look after our little garden.

But it didn't happen. How could it? The nuns watched me constantly and set girls the task of being my guard-dogs when they couldn't do it. It would never be just one girl, because the sisters knew I might force her to look the other way, so every night, just before the lights were put out, three girls would be told it was their turn to make sure I was still there in the morning. This carried on for months until, I suppose, they decided I'd got the message that I wasn't going to get away and, besides, my time in the school was almost up so they wouldn't mind if I disappeared. One less problem and one less mouth to feed.

On the morning of my sixteenth birthday I was sent to Sister Francis-Ellen's office and instructed to stand outside. From the hall window I could see a shiny black car with a lady and two children on the back seat, a boy and a girl. The woman looked up and smiled when she spotted me. I could hear a man's voice through the office door, and though it was muffled I heard my name mentioned more than once. After ten minutes Sister Francis-Ellen called me made me stand by her desk facing a red-haired man. He wore a grey gabardine overcoat and a nervous expression.

'This is Mister Callaghan, Maria. You're going to work for him. You'll look after house and help Mrs Callaghan with the children when she needs it.'

This wasn't a request or invitation, it was simply her decision being communicated to me, but I was desperate to get out of the place and didn't object. Half an hour later I'd my things packed and said few my goodbyes.

The back seat of the car smelled of leather and polish, and I squashed tight against the door when we pulled away. The last time I'd been in any sort of vehicle was when I was taken to St Gregory's and I don't remember being as scared then as much as I was with the Callaghans. She'd said hello and smiled again when I climbed in beside her. The children were introduced as Patrick and Catherine, and they seemed to be very polite. It wasn't the couple or their children which frightened me, it was the newness of it all, being free from that place and driving in a motor car with complete strangers.

Soon I caught glimpses of water and, out on the horizon, a ship gushing smoke into the clear morning sky. I imagined it to be the same ferry I'd travelled on from England. In half an hour we stopped outside a large, bow-fronted, terraced house with a view of the sea and I followed the family inside. Mrs Callaghan told me to wait in the hall whilst she settled the children.

The wooden staircase and high ceiling with its fancy plasterwork reminded me of the entrance lobby of St Gregory's, though nowhere near as grand, and I crossed my fingers that it wouldn't be half as bad. A newspaper lay on a table near the front door, open at an article reporting on heavy British casualties at a place called Suvla Bay. Mrs Callaghan came back before I could read more, and asked me in to follow her. We climbed a short flight of stairs, then a couple of longer ones to the top floor, where there were two doors. She pushed open the one on the left and led me in to small room with a bed, wardrobe and washstand. A window facing the sea had an old dining chair beside it.

'This will be your room, Maria,' she said, sweeping her hand around this palace 'you can have your own things, and decorate it how you want. It will be nice. You'll like it here in Contarf.'

This was frightening in its own way. I'd never slept in a room like this and the house was so grand I thought I must be dreaming.

I expect she'd never had a servant because she was far too nice on that first day. On the other hand, she was almost always good to me so perhaps that's just how she was. She talked about my duties; setting the fires every morning, cleaning the kitchen after meals and helping to get the children to sleep. I'd also be expected to clean other parts of the house when she asked, run errands, make all the beds and give her a hand in the garden sometimes. I'd have one afternoon a week to myself and eat all meals in the kitchen after the family had finished theirs in the dining room. My pay would be three shillings a week, less sixpence they'd agreed to send back to the sisters for the first four months. I was then left in my room and told to join her in the kitchen when I'd changed into the uniform she'd left on the bed. It fitted me well and I turned circles in front of the mirror, smiling at how nice it looked, not at all like the ones from St Gregory's. I stole a few minutes more on the window seat, staring at the point where the sea met the sky and wondering where my wages might take me if I saved enough.

Day 17

It turned out that nurse, Sister McKenzie, is quite nice. Thought her stuck up and cruel, throwing me out every night at end of visiting. Only doing her job I suppose. She brought tea and biscuits tonight when I'd missed the trolley-bus, which was good of her. And the way she tidies your bed shows she's kind, I suppose

She seemed happy to chat about your brothers and sisters, and I said they wanted to come to see you. I never expected her to say they could. The hospital's very strict about young ones visiting. I almost burst into tears when she suggested I bring them to the yard below the ward. Said she'd arrange for your bed to be pushed over by the veranda if she knows when they're coming. It wouldn't be a proper visit but at least they'll be able to see you from below. With luck I'll get Billy to come as well.

I'll pick up tonight where I left off. For the first time in eight years I was free of the Sisters with a room to myself and a bit of wages all my own.

*

The Callaghan children were lovely. Patrick was curly haired, affectionate and playful, his sister, Catherine, more reserved. She, at six, was the eldest by two years and carried her responsibilities as older sister heavily. The boy was most like his father, the girl, her mother, both in looks and temperament.

Catherine would follow her brother around, constantly asking if he was all right, and telling him off if he made a mess or was getting under my feet when I was working. His only relief was when she left for school in the morning, but then Mrs Callaghan would take over the watch. She told me one time that the children had been playing on the stairs a couple of years earlier and Catherine had pushed Patrick accidentally. He'd fallen down several steps, banging his head on the floor, and was knocked unconscious. He'd been ill for a week with everyone, including the doctor, thinking the child might not pull through. His mother, father and sister had wrapped him in cotton wool ever since.

Lucky they had the luxury, just two children to worry about. Heavens knows what they'd have done with ten. Here's me, three boys away in the army, babies at home, and feeling guilty about squandering ten penn'orth of extra love on you lying here. I expect if the Almighty decides he doesn't want you just yet, I might cling to you more than the others, who knows?

*

On my second day off, a Thursday it was, I'd enough saved from my wages to take a bus into the city. I'd not seen Danny since we'd been caught by Sister Ursula, months before, and my heart was racing when I stood on the street opposite his shop. Even so, I didn't go across straight away, I was hoping he'd walk out then I'd laugh to see the surprise on his face when he saw me. But he didn't come. Instead, another boy carried a basket out of the back and started to lay meat into the window.

I ran across the road and tapped to grab his attention, waving him to come to the door.

'Is Danny here?'

The boy shook his head. 'He's gone. Not here anymore.'

'Gone where?'

'To the army. In France I heard.'

His words carried on but I heard none of them until he shook my arm and asked if I was all right. I whispered that I was and walked away. I think I asked the boy to tell Danny I'd been looking for him if when came back.

*

I'd been with the Callaghans about two months when I came upon Mrs Callaghan crying at the kitchen table, clutching a letter in her fist. She stood and wiped her eyes when I walked in and I knew it wasn't my place to be asking her what was wrong, so I pretended I hadn't noticed and she left without speaking. Next morning Mr Callaghan came down to breakfast wearing an army uniform. He left a little later, hugging the children and his wife before climbing in to a car and being driven away. Mrs Callaghan watched him from the pavement, waving until he disappeared round the corner. She brought the children inside, asked me to look after them, then went to her room, where I could hear her sobbing all afternoon. She came down for dinner at around six o'clock when her brother, Mr Dominic Kelly, called round. Her eyes were red-rimmed and she looked so pale I was concerned for her.

Mr Kelly was a huge man with a black beard, a hearty laugh and, as his most noticeable feature, a green patch over his left eye. I was told by a maid from one of the neighbouring houses that he'd lost the eye fighting with police during a big strike three years before, though this could just have been her romancing. The other eye had nothing wrong with it and followed me round the room all the time I was serving and clearing up. After this he visited the house three or four times a week, though I'd rarely seen him when his brother-in-law was at home, and at first I thought what a good man he was to come round to support his sister. Then I realised he was constantly watching me, cracking jokes in my direction and throwing in the odd wink when he thought my employer wasn't looking.

He arrived one Friday morning a few weeks later, when Patrick was in school and Mrs Callaghan had taken Catherine on a trip in to the city. I told him they were out when I answered the door, although I thought I remembered Mrs Callaghan mentioning it to him when he'd called on Tuesday.

'Not a bother' he said 'I'll come inside and wait a while. She'll likely be back soon. Make some tea, Maria.'

I scurried in to the kitchen, keen to keep out of his way, but he followed me and took a seat at the table, following me with his one good eye as I boiled the kettle and lifted crockery from the cupboard. The cup rattled so much on its saucer as I carried it across the room I was sure I'd drop it. Mr Kelly said no more until I poured his tea and placed the pot on the stand, then he grabbed my wrist.

'You're a very pretty little thing aren't you girl?' I squealed that I didn't think so and tugged to get away. 'Oh yes you are. Very pretty.'

He was strong and it took him no effort at all to pull me on to his knee then wrap his arm around to stop my struggling.

'Come on now, Maria, be nice,' His sweaty hand was now stroking my cheek and I could smell the drink on him, but I couldn't wriggle free 'I only want a little cuddle.'

'Leave me alone, Mr Kelly. Please.'

But he had no intention of leaving me alone. Instead he squeezed me closer and planted a beery kiss on my lips. When I'd been with Danny I'd dreamed of him kissing me but not like this. There was no tenderness, no love, only a drunken desire for a girl half his age. He only stopped because the front door clattered and Patrick's tiny feet ran up the hall. Kelly was standing in a second, pushing me away.

'You say anything of this to my sister and I'll tell her you're making it up because I told you off. She'll believe me over you and then you'll be out on your ear. No reference, nothing.'

I didn't wait for Patrick or his mother to come in, I didn't know what I might say to her anyway, and ran through the back door into the garden, shaking as the tears ran down my face. It took a full five minutes before I calmed myself enough to go back inside, where the kitchen was now deserted and I could hear Mrs Callaghan calling me on the landing. I shouted from the bottom of the stairs, keeping watchful in case Kelly appeared again.

'I'm here, madam.' I glanced in the hall mirror to make sure I was presentable. 'I was out in the garden gathering a posy.'

She came down wearing a face like thunder.

'I'm very disappointed in you, Maria. My brother says you put him in the parlour and didn't even offer to make him a cup of tea. You also didn't clear the table after you'd finished your own. It isn't good enough and I thought you were getting on so well. If it happens again you'll have to go. Do you hear?'

I didn't answer

'I said, did you hear?'

This time I just sunk my chin to my chest and mumbled an apology. Her brother was right, she'd always believe him over me so there was no point in trying to explain. She told me to go to my room for the rest of the afternoon and think long and hard about my attitude. As I lay on my bed staring at the ceiling I did think long and hard, not on my attitude but about what I was going to do next.

*

I didn't sleep much that night and was dog-tired when I started work in the kitchen, tending the stove and laying the table for breakfast. Mrs Callaghan was very cold with me when she came down and told me more than once to pull myself together.

'This won't do you know' she said 'I thought I'd made it clear last night that you needed to buck up your ideas. It's just not like you but I'll not put up with it for long.'

'Yes, Mrs Callaghan. I'm sorry. I will do better, I promise.'

Why I lied to her I don't know, it just seemed easier than telling the truth. Maybe that's always the case. Me telling lies and stories with no reason.

After her next words I knew I was taking the right step.

'I'm going out again this afternoon. Mrs Darcy has invited the children and I round for tea at four o'clock. Mr Kelly may call again before I get back so you make sure you attend to him properly this time, do you understand?

'Yes Mrs Callaghan.' The words would hardly come out. 'Will I get the children ready for half past three?'

She said that would be good, and seemed pleased that I appeared to be returning to my usual self. I was pleased that it would give me the opportunity to do what I needed with the minimum of fuss.

When my morning jobs were finished I slipped to my room and counted coins on my bed. I'd spent years without any money of my own, and the Callaghans had provided everything I'd needed in the way of food, so I'd been able to save almost all of my wages for the four months I'd been with them. Thirty shillings. I split it in two, rolling twenty tightly in a strip of newspaper and placing it at the bottom of my bag. The rest went into a purse, then my coat pocket.

Patrick and Catherine were in their room when I went down. The girl must have sensed something wasn't quite right.

'Why have you your coat on, Maria are you coming with us?'

I put my finger to my lips and closed the door

behind me.

'No, not today. I have to go somewhere on my own. Now let's get you looking nice for Mrs Darcy.'

I washed their hands and faces, brushed their hair and made them put on their coats and outside shoes, then stood back.

'Aren't you two the smartest children. Your mummy will be very proud.'

Mrs Callaghan shouted for them from the hallway. 'Catherine, Patrick, come on now, we have to be on our way.'

I popped my head out of the bedroom. 'Just another minute, madam, they'll be right down.'

I closed the door and threw my arms around them both. 'I may not be here when you come back but don't say anything to Mummy before then will you? I have to take a little trip and I'm not sure how long it will take. You remember Maria in your prayers, won't you? Now off you go, and not a word to Mummy.'

I waited until I heard the front door close behind them, then fetched my bag, looking round my own room for one last time, making sure I didn't leave any of my few possessions behind. On the hall table, I left a short note telling them that I was sorry but that I'd had to leave unexpectedly. I didn't go into the reason, there seemed no point, and just asked them to forgive me for the lack of notice and hoped that they would provide a reference if they were asked for one.

Every day for four months I'd watched the ferries leaving and arriving at Dublin Port across the short stretch of water below my window. After the first week I began to record their times because I knew that one day I'd leave the Callaghans' home, either as my choice or, like now, by having no alternative. I'd spent years skivvying for the sisters and I wasn't about to spend the rest of my life doing it for other people. But what have I done since I married Billy? Year after year of cleaning house and looking after babies, cooking meals and washing dishes from morning 'til night. It's different though. I might not have much choice, just the same as at St Gregory's and Clontarf, but it's the path I chose. For myself. For better or worse.

The bus into the city trundled along tree-lined streets with large houses on either side, giving way to shops, terraces and small workshops as we drew closer to the centre. When we were almost there I checked the stop with the conductor, who was a nice man, and he asked where I was going. When I said I was heading for the port he asked if I was walking or if I wanted the bus. I had a few hours before the next ferry so it made sense for me to save the fare and I said I'd walk.

'Just follow these people here down to the landing stage' he said, pointing to a family near the front with a girl around my old age 'it won't take you long, not with young legs like yours.'

So when the family stood to get off I followed, along with a dozen other people, all carrying suitcases and bags. The area around the docks was as crowded as I remembered it from when I'd arrived with my father, though now there were nearly as many cars, vans and trucks as carts, making even more noise, and belching fumes everywhere. A line of soldiers marched past the queue at the ticket office, heading for a ship down the dock, beyond the ferry, and a sergeant barked orders as they went by. Every man carried a rifle, some laughed and joked, though just as many looked scared for their lives.

A rough youth on the back of a lorry shouted 'Come back lads, the fight's on this side of the water' and the sergeant swore at him, much to the amusement of the queueing travellers.

At the window of the ticket office the official looked me up and down. 'Bit young to be going on your own, aren't you?'

The girl from the bus, who'd gone through before me, called back 'She's not on her own, she's with us. Her dad sent money for her to buy her own ticket that's all. We're meeting him on the other side.'

I succeeded in keeping my jaw from dropping, paid the fare, then ran after the girl once I'd stuffed the ticket in my purse with the little left from the ten shillings I'd started with. I thanked her from helping.

'Nosy old crow,' she said 'what does it matter to him if you're running away?'

'Who said I was running away?

She tilted her head and raised both eyebrows 'and you're not?'

'Well maybe.' I laughed and told her my name.

'Pleased to meet you. I'm Betty, Betty Coleman. We're going to Coventry, down the country from Liverpool. My da's got jobs for us there in a munitions factory. He says he's not fit for the army but wants to do his bit.'

I didn't know it then, that there were many like Betty's father, many like the soldiers who'd marched past us, wanting to fight the Germans or help in some way in the war, and there were many like the man shouting at the soldiers, who thought Ireland should be free from England. Soon they might be fighting each other.

The Colemans were a happy bunch, the father, Dan, cracked silly jokes every minute and Betty's mother, Harriet, shrieked with laughter at every one. Their younger children, Micky and Jane giggled the whole time, playing tag and running so close to the edge of the dock my heart was in my mouth, though the parents didn't seem to take notice.

Dan Coleman was a native of Ballina, County

Mayo, and he'd moved to Clane, County Kildare, thirty years earlier to take up an apprenticeship as a farrier and blacksmith. He was willing and able, learnt all of the metal work and animal skills quickly, and he'd eventually taken over the smithy when his master could no longer manage it. Financially secure, he'd looked around for a wife, found the future Mrs Coleman and married her. Soon afterwards, Betty came along, then the others and all was well in his world until one day he noticed how many motor vehicles there were in the town. He could see the writing on the wall and knew his days of making a living fixing carts and shoeing horses were limited. Then the war with Germany came along and he heard of opportunities in the bomb factories where his expertise with metals would be in demand. A neighbour passed him an announcement in the Kildare Observer from the Ministry of Munitions and before he could say Jack Robinson, he and his wife Betty had been offered jobs at an ordnance works in Coventry, in the English Midlands. Dan did what his master had done and handed the smithy on to his apprentice, packed up house and tools, and headed for the ferry.

When we boarded, Mrs Coleman insisted I stayed alongside them. 'We'll look after you dear' she'd said, and the six of us trooped up the ramp. Mr Coleman's long years beating iron and shovelling coal into a furnace had a given him broad shoulders and strong arms, so he forced an easy way through the crowd to find us deck seats towards the front, well ahead of the smoking funnel. Betty sat between me and her mother, keeping an eye on Mickey and Jane dashing backwards and forwards along the ship rail. Every so often she'd leap up and grab the pair of them back if they were going too far, or annoying the other passengers.

'They're never tired those two, always on the go. Do you have any brothers or sisters, Maria?'

I told her about Jimmy, saying that I hadn't seen him for years, but was hoping to find him again someday. Betty's reply was drowned by a blast from the ferry's steam whistle as we pulled away from the dock, heading across the Irish Sea once more.

Day 18

These autumn evenings are drawing in, Alice. It will be dark by the time I get home tonight, and there was a definite chill when I waited at the bus stop. So, last time, I was leaving Ireland again, with some new friends, and on the ferry. Seems like I travelled there and back all the time, doesn't it?

The Colemans left me in Liverpool, with their cousin who had a millinery shop in Bootle. They'd said they would look after me and they did. The milliner, Maisy Dixon, took me on as an assistant, letting me stay in her spare room for a small rent that she took from my wages every week, and she taught me the trade of hat making. My sewing skills hadn't improved with age but Mrs Dixon kindly said I was better than so*me of the girls she'd had over the years, and she was a patient teacher, but I was still hopeless. I think she only tolerated my mistakes because she'd promised Mrs Coleman. After a while I was working less on the hats and more behind the counter, where I could do less damage. At least I could talk to the customers about how the hats were made and understood enough to take measurements and advise people how much work might be needed for repairs or alterations.

'You're good at this' remarked Mrs Dixon one day 'the customers like you and respect your advice. I can manage for now on my own in the workshop, business isn't as good as it was,' she grimaced. 'Except for mourning outfits. No shortage of mothers needing those these days.'

I was paid on Friday morning and my envelope was handed over with the same cheery 'don't spend it all in the same shop' every week. At half past twelve I'd turn the sign and walk two doors to the Daisy Chain cafe. Mrs Farina, who owned the place, gave a discount to anyone working in any of the shops nearby, and the food was tolerable, with a plate full enough to keep me satisfied until Saturday morning. She was a pretty redhead, probably ten years older than me and, in her broad Liverpool accent, always ready with a saucy line for the male customers. Tony, her husband, scowled every time he heard her, though she just pulled a face and made fun of him. There was nothing to her flirting, it was just her way, and I expect it was good for business. He was from Sorrento and had trained as a chef in the Hotel Santa Maria on the waterfront there, as he never tired of telling the customers. He was exotic and handsome, which meant the female customers also had something to keep bringing them back, and all of the women, from girls to grandmothers, would sip their tea doe-eyed, hanging on his every word. He had three fingers missing from his left hand and always wore a leather glove, heightening the air of mystery around him.

The cafe owner was easy to like and she gave

the impression of caring about each and every one of her customers, a skill I'm sure was crucial to the success of her business. It didn't take long for her to recognise me as a regular and start up a conversation when I was ordering.

'What'll it be today, love?'

'I'll have the fish please, Mrs Farina.'

'Just like every Friday, good Catholic girl I daresay. And call me Daisy.' She nodded in her husband's direction. 'That's my name over the window not his. You work at Mrs Dixon's don't you?'

I said I did and told her my name. After that she used it every Friday lunchtime when I went in, bringing me "the usual" without me needing to ask. If the café was quiet, she'd take a seat and ask how I was getting on in the shop, or just chat about the weather. She told me she loved my accent and that her mother was from Cork.

When I'd been with Mrs Dixon for about nine months she was waiting when I came back and told me to leave the door locked because she wanted to talk to me.

I looked around the shop to see if I'd left it untidy when I left. 'Have I done something wrong, Mrs Dixon?'

'Not at all Maria, not at all.' She cleared her throat nervously which got me even more worried. 'You've been so good in the shop these last few months. Business has picked right up but ...'

I knew right away what was coming.

'... I need someone to help in the workshop and I can't afford two assistants. I'm afraid I'll have to let you go. You can stay until I find someone though and I'll not have you out on the street.'

I was so upset I hardly slept that night, wondering what I might do. Next day I bumped into Daisy in the street and told her what had happened. She offered a possibility.

'I've a friend just got a job up in Morecambe, half an hour up the coast from here. Filling shells she is, says there's plenty of work up there. You could try that.'

Daisy gave me her friend's name and address, and within a week and a half, I travelled north to take up my new job.

*

White Lund was a massive place, the size of sixty farms at home and though I never counted the buildings I heard there were well over a hundred buildings scattered across it. Shell filling went on around the clock and every shift change there were around two thousand people pouring out of the sheds, with the same pouring in to replace them. Some laughing, some just talking, most so exhausted after a twelve hour stint that they could barely put one foot in front of the other. One of the women worked out that each day she'd trolley five tons of shells across the shed. This type of work, on top of the mile walk into the factory then back to the digs at the day's end, made sure there were not many sleepless nights around the Morecambe guest houses where most workers stayed.

Only a month after I started, the word went round that we had to make our areas spick and span because there was to be a special visitor. Rumours got up straight away. It must be the mayor, or the boss of Vickers, or the Prime Minister. At three o'clock the factory whistle blew, then we were marched outside and told to line the road. A half an hour we were standing there, shivering in an easterly wind, when several cars turned the corner and I could hear everyone cheering as the visitor passed the far end of the line. I'd only ever seen pictures of them but it was clear who it was from the whisper which rippled along the road. It was His Majesty, and Queen Mary, smiling and waving from the front vehicle.

Needless to say, I wasn't in the party that greeted them when they climbed out of the car in front of the factory. That was only for the likes of the managers, supervisors and a few of the posher girls who it was expected would know how to behave. King George wore full army uniform, complete with medal ribbons, and I wondered why, there was no chance he'd ever be on the front line. The Queen was dressed in a beautiful costume of navy blue, with a three-quarter length braided coat and fur collar, and wore a hat trimmed with pink and mauve roses. All the workers were craning necks to see and straining ears to catch a word. The visitors soon disappeared into one of the huts and we were ushered back inside, being told to get back to work as quickly as possible. I was wondering why we'd bothered to clean up, when the doors swing open and King George and his wife came in. The pair were surrounded by men in suits. One I recognised as the factory manager, the rest, I suspected, were other supervisors and civil servants, bowing and scraping like so many chicks around the mother hen. The couple promenaded along the line, asking questions of the girls along the way, he about the shells, she about their families and how they liked the work. Neither spoke to me. They were in the shed less than ten minutes then were whisked off to who knows where.

There were pictures in the papers of their visit the next day and everyone was going through them, trying to see themselves but there wasn't much chance. One of the older women on my line claimed she spotted herself, but all I saw was another small, round face appearing from under another uniform headdress. These uniforms were even uglier than the ones we wore at St Gregory's. They were a muddy brown, with baggy trousers and covered us from head to toe. The hat was shapeless, designed only to keep the filth or powder out of your hair and I never worked out if the whole outfit was to make us look unattractive, or to protect us from the mess we worked in. Those who were handling the powder wore gloves and face masks. "Canaries" we called them because the explosives caused their skin to turn yellow and everything they touched turned the same colour.

*

I shared a small room in a guest house on the seafront with a girl, Winnie, from Manchester, and very fond of the men she was, always flirting in the canteen and at the dances in the Winter Gardens. I only went there once because the blokes seemed rough and tried to get us to go out the back with them all the time. What did I know? They were only the same as all men given half a chance, young fellers out for a good time, a few drinks and a cuddle before catching a bus home.

Mrs Cope, the landlady, made it clear there were to be no shenanigans in her "respectable house".

'You're only young,' she'd say in the parlour, surrounded by faded chintz and stuffed birds 'and I feel responsible. I'd want to be able to look your mothers in the eye if ever they came calling.'

There was no Mr Cope. He'd died with a heart attack and a decent insurance policy ten years earlier, leaving his wife well set up to move to Morecambe and open her business. She provided bed and board at a reasonable price, never tired of telling us she was happy to do "her bit" for the war, and locked the door at half past nine. We had to let her know if we were likely to be later and it always felt to me like we were asking permission. If I was on an evening or night shift, Mrs Cope would give me a key, tied to a dolly-peg, to be returned on pain of death when I switched back to normal times.

On days off I'd lie in as late as I could get away with. The landlady knew we were all exhausted by the end of the week so she'd be lenient with breakfast times, as long as it didn't inconvenience her too much. If it was a Sunday I'd walk along the prom in the afternoon. Not far, just to the stone jetty, where there'd always be a crowd, or in the other direction to find a teashop where I'd have a little treat if I could afford it. Sometimes I'd meet girls from the factory and we'd go on the beach, splashing through the tide, then lying in the sun if the day was warm. We chatted about anything and everything, but mainly about work and men.

'Did you see the new feller yesterday?' one would pipe up.

'I did. Face like a pig.' Would come the reply. Laughs all round.

'Ah, he'd not be so bad.' Might come another.

'If you say so. I forgot you were brought up on

a farm. Pigs'd be quite attractive to you I expect.'

And so it would go on, sparking off each other, the whole crowd collapsing in giggles every few minutes.

The job was boring but so dangerous you'd never relax. The powders and detonators were explosive. Even the empty shells would break a leg, or worse, if they fell on you, and the machinery was so noisy it would send you deaf. I worked in a shed assembling the fifteen-pounder field gun shells and the arms would be aching from swinging a mallet after the first hour, getting worse all day long. Though the pain kept me awake some nights I was thankful I wasn't breathing in all that foul powder day after day.

It all came to an end one night in October. I was on a late shift on my supper break at about half past ten in the canteen when sirens started going off and a man ran in shouting 'Get out, get out, there's a fire.'

None of us needed telling twice. Outside, I could see a shed burning at the far end of the site with flames lapping through its windows. Everyone was surging away towards the beach when something exploded behind us and we all ran faster, lots of the women screaming. By the time we reached the sands the sky was glowing and one corner of the factory was completely alight. Every so often there'd be another flash and the air would thud into us. We were there most of the night, far too scared to try to go back in to town, and the explosions got louder and louder. At about three o'clock in the morning there was the biggest bang I've ever heard when one of the main storage sheds went up, and half the crowd were knocked to the ground with the blast.

Next day we were all paid off and sent home. They put on special trains and I don't think the factory ever opened again. The papers were saying it was a Zeppelin air raid but we all knew it was probably someone smoking in an area they shouldn't have been. I'd been outside with a group before supper and they'd happily flicked their fag-ends away when they'd finished, taking no notice where they ended up.

I went to another shell factory after that, a bit further up the coast, where the work was just as heavy. When the war ended, they went back to making bicycles and I stayed at that for a while, still lifting and loading all day long. Then the men came home and were looking for work so, before long, the women were laid off to let them in. I was one of the lucky ones who held on for a while before I was given my cards. So I was on the move again, back to Liverpool because I couldn't think of anywhere else to go, and hoping I'd pick up a job pretty soon.

Day 19

Overnight thunderstorms have given way to a muggy day threatening more rain and Billy hadn't wanted to accompany Maria to the hospital. He'd said the weather made it difficult to breathe and she didn't argue too much, even though she'd been looking forward to them making an afternoon of it. In some ways she's happy he is staying home, it means she needn't struggle with little Rose. At two, the toddler would be difficult to take on the buses and carry round town, and she'd take no benefit from seeing Alice, who's been ill for most of the youngest's short life.

Ruth and Brian, the two older children still living at home, aren't able to take time off work, so Maria scrubs Lizzie, Tommy and Ann, dresses them in their Sunday best, and marches them round the corner to the bus stop.

Tommy whines 'Can we sit on the top deck?' over and over while the four stand at the stop, despite filthy looks from the queue and Maria's pleas for him to be quiet. To avoid embarrassment she capitulates when the bus arrives and they climb the stairs, Tommy and Ann taking the front seat, Maria and Lizzie the one behind.

The boy, like all seven-year-olds, delights in every sight, grinning and pointing out each bald head, shop window and bicycle to his long-suffering sister, Ann, who, at twelve, would rather keep her nose buried in her book than take in the scenes of east Manchester.

Maria stops his antics for a moment and points down a side street to a building with a three-storey brick cube at each end and a yard between.

'That's where your dad works, the one nearest us. It's the sorting office. The one on the other side is the telephone exchange.'

The children crane their necks, even Ann, who's taken Billy's sandwiches there more than once when he's left without them in the early hours.

The middle child asks if they can get off the bus and go to see her father.

Maria snorts.

'Do you have nothing at all between your ears, Elizabeth Garner? Didn't we leave your dad at home only twenty minutes ago?'

This sets Tommy laughing at, and teasing, his sister, even after Ann tells him to be quiet and not so cruel to Lizzie. The boy continues, on and off, until the bus arrives in the city centre, leaving him open-mouthed, looking down on Piccadilly from his window, pointing out all the buses, trams, cars and people beetling across the square. His mother's been travelling this route for weeks and taken in nothing, all her thoughts with Alice. In the moment, she's sure the lad's right and the world can be a wondrous place when you're young.

There are so many on board it takes the family almost as long to file off the bus as it did to travel the last two stops. On Oldham Street, even Ann tucks the book under her arm to wander open-mouthed round Affleck and Brown's. All the children know not to pester Maria to buy them anything, though Tommy shoots a glance at her whenever something catches his eye. They've witnessed their mother and father arguing about money often enough to know there's none to spare for impulsive spending

After an hour they've all had enough and Maria gets her wish to rest on a bench in Piccadilly Gardens. They've brought a bag of stale bread and Tommy runs around, scattering the crumbs for the hordes of pigeons, whilst Ann tries to concentrate on her book. Liz, as always, sits by Maria's side and stares into the middle distance. The afternoon is hot and Maria mops her brow then turns to Ann.

'Look after these two for a minute, I need to fetch something.'

Soon she returns, carrying four small ice-cream cones topped with raspberry sauce.

'Your dad slipped me half a crown before we left and told me to treat you. Make it a proper day out, he said.' She passes the cones round. 'Tommy, you sit down and stay still for five minutes, don't be dropping it or else.'

The boy does as he's told and the four sit in

silence, savouring the drips as they run down the sides and on to their fingers. As each child finishes, Maria wipes their chin and hands with the handkerchief she's pulled from her handbag. A man's, large, starched and brought especially to keep the children presentable for their visit. When all are done she tells them to form a line in front of her for inspection.

'You'll do. As long as no-one looks too close.' She glances at the terminus clock and stands. 'Come on, we'd best be moving else we'll miss that bus.'

*

Maria leaves Ann, Tommy and Lizzie in the yard and climbs the stairs to Alice's ward where a nurse accosts her at the door.

'You must know by now Mrs Garner that visiting isn't until six o'clock.'

'But Sister McKenzie told me she'd make an exception if I was bringing the children.'

The nurse tut-tuts and tells Maria to wait in the corridor. Minutes tick past before the sister comes out.

'You might have warned me of the time, Mrs Garner, Alice isn't ready. Come through and give me a hand.'

Maria follows her inside and the two tidy Alice's bed before wrestling it through the double doors on to the veranda.

'You can have half an hour. No more.' Sister

McKenzie's parting shot is clear and Maria knows she means it. She could weep at the knowledge there's never enough time. Even with so little left.

Maria leans over and waves to the children below.

'Is she there?' Ann shouts.

'She is.'

Tommy leaps up and down, clapping. 'Can we come up Mam, can we?'

'Not today son. Maybe next time.'

His mother turns away, knowing her daughter will be laid out at home soon enough. They'll all see her then. Even Billy.

'Give me a minute and I'll get Alice so you can see her.'

Maria slides her arm behind her daughter's back, lifts her, and slides another pillow behind. She repeats the exercise until Alice is almost sitting upright, then hugs her close, tilting the girl so her face can be seen over the balcony. Maria looks over and sees tears streaming down Ann's cheeks. Tommy, bewildered, joins her. Lizzie stares upwards, unmoved.

*

Will I tell my girl the next bit? What's the harm after all this time? Poor lass probably can't hear a word in any case, state she's in. Why am I doing this, pouring my heart out to her in a hospital bed? It's not as if I've talked about any of this before, not to any of them. They don't even know I'm Irish. The older ones think I was in an orphanage because my parents died, that's what I told them. When the nuns visit I pretend I'm over the moon, it's what's expected. Perhaps that's it. I bottle it all up to protect the children, so they won't know there's so much evil in the world. Or perhaps it's myself I'm protecting, burying it all away so it doesn't hurt.

I hope she won't think badly of me for this.

*

Daisy Farina threw her arms around me as soon as I entered her café. 'Maria, how are you?' She moved me back to arms' length and checked me out. 'My God, you're looking good. So fit. What have you been up to?'

I gave her the full story over tea, salad and brown bread, which Daisy dished up. It was a quiet time, an hour after the busy lunch period, and her husband dealt with the few customers who came in while we were chatting. She laughed her head off when I told her the story of the munitions factory explosion and when I'd finished telling her about the bicycle works she rested her chin on her hand and raised an eyebrow.

'So you'll be looking for work?'

'I am. Do you know of anything?'

'Actually, you've come at a good time. That girl, Sally, the one who was here before you left, you remember her? Pretty in a skinny kind of a way. Blond.'

I nodded. She'd been friendly with all the customers, though always hanging around gossiping with Mr Farina when she wasn't busy.

'She got herself in the family way and I've had to let her go. Stupid girl. And no father to look after her and the child.'

'Would you be interested in the job?'

I thought about it for less than a second. 'Well it would be better than that old factory. At least you'd not be poisoning me or breaking my arms every day.'

Daisy laughed. 'I'd hope we wouldn't anyway. Can you start Monday?'

So I did. Big mistake.

*

Daisy's husband, Tony, or Antonio as she'd call him when telling him off, was so good looking. And so persuasive. When you're young and the handsome older man pays you attention it has the desired effect. He wasn't aggressive, just persistent. Nothing happened for the first month, then there were just the two of us in the café one day when Daisy went to the bank. There were no customers and he asked me to sit with him and take a cuppa. I refused at first, saying I'd get on with the dishes, but he insisted.

'Ah, always the busy Maria. Leave them for now, they'll still be there when we're finished.' His words rose and fell, almost like he was singing. He'd been in Liverpool a while and his English was good, but there was still the trace of his Italian accent. 'We've been on our feet all the morning. Don't you think we deserve a break?'

I poured us two cups and piled three sugars into his, the way he liked it. I suppose I should have suspected something wasn't quite right when he stood and flipped the snib on the front door.

'There, we'll not be disturbed now.'

*

The first couple of times it happened we just chatted. He'd ask me about Ireland or Morecambe, then tell me about Sorrento; the sun, the Bay of Naples and the volcano rumbling away only a handful of miles from the town. He'd talk of how he'd like to get away from Liverpool, anywhere. He hated the place and hated working in his wife's café.

'It's so dreary, Maria. Day after day making the same cheap food for the same poor people. I'm meant for something better than this.'

I'd say something encouraging, telling him he should be proud being able to cook so well, but he'd shrug it off.

'Oh, don't. Isn't that the point I'm making. Stuck here when I should be in a smart restaurant, cooking for rich people who'd appreciate me.'

Then came the line I later figured out he'd used

a dozen times before.

'But she won't let me.'

'Who?'

'Who do you think? Daisy. She doesn't understand, never has. The lady thinks it's all about making money, not the artistry. You understand though, don't you, Maria.'

The first time he said this I told him to hush and not talk that way, that Daisy loved him and he loved her, but in bed at night I'd wonder if he meant what he was saying. Then I began to watch. Although Daisy was my friend, as well as my employer, I could see that she sniped all day at Tony. He'd be taking too long with an order, the eggs were overdone, or he'd let them run out of potatoes, any little thing she might pick up. It soon began to seem to me that he was the one doing all the work while she was just bring out the food and chatting with the customers. In my silly head he looked like a slave and was the butt of all of her jokes. I suppose I was gullible and it didn't take too long for Tony to convince me to meet him in the evenings.

He had the habit of going out for a drink around seven o'clock, so said Daisy would never suspect anything was going on. In the café I tried not to blush whenever I spoke to either of them, for different reasons, and I made up stories to tell her about what I'd been doing on the nights I was out with Tony.

Mostly he and I would go to the park or round the back streets, somewhere we'd not be seen. Never the pictures or the pub. It would always be only for an hour because he'd need to go to have at least one pint so Daisy wouldn't wonder why he didn't smell of beer. The third time we'd met, I'd made a real effort, buying new lipstick and scent for the occasion. Tony stayed an arm's length away the whole time we were out, instead of linking like normal. When I asked him what was wrong he said Daisy would get a whiff of my perfume if he came any closer. Next day she looked at me oddly once or twice and I was expecting her to say something, but she didn't.

After that he was bolder, he must have taken my wearing of the scent as a signal that I was very keen on him. He'd pull me into the bushes in the park and plonk a kiss on my lips whenever he could. We then started meeting more often, sometimes two or even three nights a week, and we'd find a quiet corner where we could cuddle without fear of being seen by anyone we knew.

One lunchtime when Daisy was out at the bank again, he called me behind the counter.

'Can we meet tonight?' he whispered.

'But it's Wednesday, we never meet on Wednesday.' It was cheap night at the City Picture House so I'd go every week to laugh at the antics of

Charlie Chaplin and Harold Lloyd, or imagine myself alongside Douglas Fairbanks on one of his adventures.

'No, but tonight's different. Daisy's going out at six and won't be back until ten o'clock. We can be here by ourselves where no-one will see us.'

I'll never know why I agreed, it was obvious even to me that it wasn't a good idea. But what do they say? Love is blind, and by this time I was very much in love with my Antonio, or so I thought. Since then I've learnt differently. Love isn't about some childish crush on a man who talks nicely to you.

He'd prepared a salad and plonked two glasses of wine on the table. How could I fail to be impressed? We ate slowly and talked the whole while, him repeating over and over how pretty he thought I was and how he loved the sound of my voice. After the meal, he poured something he called grappa into small glasses and told me to drink. I thought I'd faint with the smell. Later, when I was as drunk from the flattery as the alcohol, he asked me to go to the bedroom with him, and I followed without protest.

*

A few months later the bump started to show when I slipped out of my nightdress in the mornings. I'd only been with Tony the once but I'd caught easily. So it always was. With Billy I began to think I only had to pick up his trousers to wash them and I'd fall, no sooner over having one than expecting again.

I wasn't stupid, but I was innocent. There'd been enough banter in the factory and on our weekend excursions for me to know the way of the world, though I'd never been with a man the whole time until Tony. To hide my condition from Daisy I considered binding myself like they did to the girls at St Gregory's, though it didn't seem right. I didn't want a baby but I didn't want to hurt it either. It was mine.

I was looking forward to telling Tony before he spotted it himself. He'd been cool with me after that first night and I'd told him we couldn't do it any more, that it was a sin and a betrayal of his wife. He'd begged, then he'd sworn, then he'd just shaken his head, telling me it was fine, that he understood. I was so sure he was in love with me I lay awake for nights worrying about how Daisy would take it when he told her he was leaving her for me. Pathetic really. I cornered Tony when she was out.

'How can that have happened?' he whined. 'We only did it the once.'

Beneath the fear there was anger in his voice and I knew he'd not be leaving Daisy to set up home with me. I felt my neck flush. 'Well once must have been enough.'

'How can I be sure it's mine?' I think it was the questioning grin he adopted, as much as his words, which made me react. I slapped his face and stormed to the door.

'You're not going to tell Daisy are you?' he bellowed after me as I left. He could have sacked me there and then but then he'd need to tell his wife why he'd done it, and that would have been difficult. She knew there were no problems with my work.

Of course, it didn't take long for Daisy to notice my condition. Even under my overall it became obvious in a few more weeks. One morning she called me through to the storeroom, closing the door behind us. She pointed to my swelling waist.

'I thought you were my friend.'

My shoes suddenly became very interesting.

'I am.' I mumbled. 'Why would you think I'm not?'

Daisy laughed. A harsh, mirthless sound. 'You're not the first, Maria, and don't think you'll be the last. Did you think I didn't guess something was going on between you two? You wearing cheap perfume and not being able to look me in the eye. He's a charming man is Tony and I love him dearly but he can't keep his pants buttoned up if there's a sweet, innocent girl around the place.'

'I'm sorry, Daisy. I -'

'You know he even brought me flowers the

morning after he'd been with you. And me awake half the night smelling you in our bed. I wasn't sure whether to be insulted because he thought I wouldn't know or because he thought a few flowers would buy me off.'

She folded her arms and gave me her decision.

'Anyway, you'll have to go. No-one will say I put a pregnant girl on the streets so you can stay until the baby is due. If anyone asks just say its daddy was killed in the war. Buy yourself a cheap ring and no-one will know the difference, God knows there's plenty more in the same situation.' Another of those laughs. 'You'll probably get more tips if you do that.'

Daisy turned her back and began tidying shelves. She was done with me.

At lunchtime I did as she'd suggested and went to Mr Cathcart, the pawnbroker at the corner of Smithdown Road, and bought a thin gold wedding band which some poor soul hadn't been able to redeem. I've still got it with the other bits and pieces I collected in those years. I wore it every day until I married Billy. Took it off outside the church when I knew I wouldn't need it any more.

*

Poor Billy. Such a nice, kind man he was back then. I wonder if he ever really knew what he was taking on? Another man's son, and me with so much sadness inside. I can only imagine I did something good at some time to deserve him. We've had our ups and downs, the Lord knows, who hasn't, but I'm sure little Josie and me would never have survived without him. The times we were in when we met.

Here's that sister again. She'll shoo me out in a minute and I'll not give her the satisfaction. Just remember, none of the others know any of this so keep it to yourself if they come to visit. Night, night, my darling girl, I'll see you tomorrow.

Day 20

Josie was born quietly in June 1920, on the day the newspaper reported that five men were shot in Derry. A smile played on his lips from the moment he opened his eyes, ignoring all the badness in the world.

The maternity hospital was in a wing of the Toxteth workhouse, with the same drab colours as St Gregory's, though I imagined even this was better than what the poor souls next door had to face. From the window by my bed I could see them over the wall. Scrawny men, women and children in grey uniforms, mostly so sick they sat or lay on benches around the yard. The ones who were well enough were given work to do to help pay for their keep and to teach them to avoid poverty. Every time I looked out, I shuddered to think of my father's life in such a place, knowing he'd have been one of the sick ones lying out there.

The night after Josie's birth I dreamt of Daddy down in that yard. He lay on a patch of grass as green as you've ever seen, eyes sunk in his head, staring up at me. He lifted his arms, reaching out, as if to pull me to him like when I was little. I tried to walk closer but every step I took he seemed to move further away, until the ground below him shifted and he started to sink into it. All the time, until everything but his arms disappeared, he was mouthing 'I'm sorry, Maria, I'm sorry.'

I don't know what he was being sorry for, none of it was his fault. Mammy died, he got sick, and me and Josie ended up in the homes because we were poor, not because of anything he did. Rich people get consumption as well, though I don't think so many, but they end up with good doctors in good hospitals, not in the workhouse with their children taken from them. Daddy never stood a chance, not from the moment he was shipped off to that cesspit in Malta, and Mammy never stood a chance from the moment she met him.

All things considered, Daisy had been very good to me. She'd kept me on right up until my confinement, on condition I didn't speak to Tony except when I was working. That had been no hardship. Once I knew he'd just used me I didn't want to speak to him anyway. She'd even made her husband dig into his savings to put some money towards his baby's upkeep for a few weeks. When she handed it over she'd said 'It could be a lot more you know.'

'How? You've been more than generous already.'

Daisy had stroked crumbs from the tablecloth with the back of her fingers. Then, her words came barely as a whisper.

'You could give the baby to me when it comes.'

I'd struggled to make sense of what she'd said, and then it all poured out of her.

'Tony and me can't have children of our own, we've been trying for years. I think it's probably why he chases young skirt all the time, to show he really is a man, you know. Perhaps if we were a proper family, with a baby , he'd be different. Happy again, like we were before.'

'No.' I shook my head. 'Definitely not.'

'Don't refuse so quickly, Maria. Think about it. You've no job, no money to speak of, and you'll be living on the streets before too long. What kind of life is that for the poor child? With us it will be looked after, safe in a good home and able to go to school when it's older.'

I didn't reply. I was wondering if she'd had this in mind all along, from the moment I turned up in her café again without a job. Had she encouraged Tony to go after me, hoping this affair would be his last and would give her the child she so much wanted? Daisy came at me again.

'You know it makes sense. We'll let you stay in one of our spare rooms until the baby is settled and you get yourself sorted out. You'll be able to see it is being looked after.' Finally she made a desperate offer. 'If you say "yes" we can just try it out, if you're not happy after a few weeks you can take the child back. What would you think of that?'

Then I did something I shouldn't have even considered, not for a second. I gave in. 'You'll have to promise, Daisy, on your mother's life, that I can have my baby if it isn't working out.'

Daisy moved closer and placed her hand on my bump. For the first time she was smiling.

'That's what I said and I'll not go back on a promise. Just give me the chance.'

I've always told myself I was doing the right thing, that she was right and I had no choice. I would be out of a home before too long and I wouldn't be able to work with a baby to look after. The child would have a better life with her than with me. Daisy's words had made me see my son or daughter begging on the streets just as I'd done until the nuns took me in. I couldn't bear it.

So, Josie was born and I moved in above the café, along the hall from the rooms Daisy and Tony used. She brought Josie to me whenever he needed feeding and the rest of the time he stayed with her. In the night I'd hear his crying and know there'd be a knock at my door soon afterwards.

About a month into our arrangement, I was dozing when the knock came and I assumed I just hadn't heard the baby. I rubbed the sleep from my eyes and called them to come in but instead of Daisy and Josie, it was Tony.

My first thought was for my son. 'Is something wrong? Is it Josie?'

'No, no, Maria. He's fine. Fast asleep.'

I pulled the sheet right up to my chin. 'Well what do you want then?'

He closed the door and stood there in the darkness. Even across the room, the smell of booze hit me. 'You've been avoiding me and I thought we got on so well.'

'How can you say that? You ran a mile as soon as you found I was expecting. Why would I bother with a man who did that to me? Now get out of here before Daisy wakes up. She'll kill us both if she finds you in here.'

'Aw come on Maria, things are different now. Daisy's got what she wants and all that I want is a little cuddle.'

'I'll give you ten seconds to get out then I'm going to start screaming. One, two -'

He was out in the passage before I could get any further, leaving me shaking in my bed.

I didn't sleep for the next hour, then I heard Josie wanting his next feed and Daisy came in soon afterwards. I knew what I had to do. When she left, I jumped out of bed and began to pack my things. Next morning I waited until Daisy put Josie in his pram and pushed it into the back yard, asking me to mind him while she went up the street for some eggs. She'd barely left when I dashed upstairs and grabbed my bag, dived out to the yard with Tony wondering what was going on, then legged it as fast as I could with Josie through the back entries. By the time Tony realised what was happening, he was too far behind to catch us, and I was out on

Smithdown Road heading for the docks.

I'd left a note on my bed for Daisy, telling her what had happened and that I'd done nothing to encourage him. I said it was obvious her hope to hold on to Tony by taking Josie wasn't going to come true and she should get rid of him as soon as she could. I finished by saying if she threw him out, and held on to the baby, then Josie would be no better off than with me so I might as well take him. I left her half the money she'd given me and promised to pay her back. I did, years later, sending her a few bob whenever I could. She never replied to any of my letters but then I never really expected her to.

That night I was back across the sea in Dublin, looking for work and lodgings.

*

It's not hard to imagine what happened next. The remaining money stretched to two nights in a lodging house, then we were sleeping in shop doorways or park benches. In the mornings I'd go looking for work, anything, but as soon as they caught sight of the baby there was a shaking of the head and I'd be shown the door. Later in the day, I'd prop a handwritten sign against Josie's pram. WAR WIDOW. PLEASE HELP. People were generally kind and I felt bad lying to them but what else could I do? There wasn't much cash in it, and I even took abuse from some who said my husband should have been fighting for Ireland's liberty, not serving an English king.

Once or twice, groups of British soldiers walked past and asked me about my husband, which regiment he'd been in and where he'd been killed. I'd become quite good at making stuff up while pregnant in Daisy's cafe, so I'd easily convince them and they'd throw a few coppers in the tin. The bit I collected was barely enough to buy me a few scraps of food and milk for the baby. He was growing and getting hungrier all the time, but he seemed happy, the smile still there even when we were walking the streets in the rain. I'd begged often enough as a child to know to keep an eye out for policeman and you'd get the nod from others at it if any were around. When they were, I'd scoop up the sign, tuck it under Josie's blanket, then saunter along the street like a real lady of leisure taking in an afternoon's window shopping. The trick was to keep moving, look innocent and hope you'd find another good spot as soon as they'd be gone. The regular beggars didn't like it though, someone new on their patch. Less to go round, I suppose.

On my third day a woman with black teeth and a crimson scar on her cheek threatened me. Told me to clear off, that this part of town was hers, had been for years. She smelled like she wasn't lying. I told her where to go but then she'd walk by every so often and glare at me. After I'd glared back a few times she leant over Josie's pram, pointed at him, looked back at me, then dragged her filthy nail across her throat. This scared me so much I knew we'd have to get away.

I hardly ate all week, saving as much as I could for the journey to Arklow. I tried selling the pram to make a few more coppers, knowing they'd not let me take it on the bus, though no one was interested. I left it on the street.

When the bus arrived, the conductor looked us up and down and clearly wasn't too keen on letting me on board.

'You've the fare, have you?'

'I have'

'You sure? Show me.'

I wanted to punch his face but knew I'd be left on the streets for another night or thrown in gaol, so I opened my purse and emptied the contents into my palm, jingling them under his nose.

'See. Is this good enough for you?'

He turned and pointed to the back seat. 'You sit there,' the face he pulled would have turned milk sour. 'where the smell will blow out of the door. I'll give you your ticket in a minute.'

The conductor reached up to pull the bell cord, ordering the driver to take us away. Within no time Josie and me were snoring our heads off.

*

Mass was over in St Peter's and St Mary's church. We'd sneaked inside to shelter from the rain after arriving in Arklow, and having no luck finding my aunt. The priest had returned to his sacristy and the stragglers were making their way outside. A middle aged woman with a great bunch of flowers and greenery in her arms stopped beside us. I hadn't noticed her walking in the opposite direction to the rest of the congregation, though recognised her from when I came in before the service. She smiled as she spoke.

'You all right Mrs?'

I gave her the truth.

'I've been better.'

She looked towards the altar. 'You just sit there till I put this lot down.'

Her voice was soft with an accent that reminded me of my granddad. In less than a minute she was back and sitting next to me.

'We've a christening tomorrow so I'm helping to decorate the church. It's not for this little feller is it?'

The woman took in my dishevelled clothes. 'No, I expect not. Hard times is it?'

She introduced herself as Nora Halpin and I repeated the tale of my dead husband, though I'm not sure she believed me. Not that it mattered, it suited both of us to pretend that she did.

'I'm looking for my aunt - Bridget Byrne. She

lived outside the town, in Ballyduff, then moved to Avoca when my granddad died, but I lost touch when I went away.'

'Bridget Byrne? Two brothers she has, Michael and Edmund?'

'Edmund was my daddy, he died a few years past. You know her?'

'Surely. She's Bridget Rafferty now, married a man down in The Fishery. Four young ones she has. Well, two of hers and two of his. Very happy they seem.'

I asked for directions and she said Auntie Bridget usually came in to town at this time, visiting her mother-in-law who lived off the main street.

It took us only five minutes to walk there, but then Josie and I hung around across from the doorway for a full half hour before a plain woman with two children came out. I hadn't seen her since that day in court, but I'd have known her anywhere. She was stockier and her hair was cut shorter than when she'd stood in the dock and asked the magistrates to send me and my brother away, though I could still see my father in her. She pulled up, looking me up and down, when I walked across the street.

'Bridget?' was all I could say.

'You have the better of me. Should I know you?'

'I'm Maria Ann Byrne. Your niece. Daddy, Jimmy and I stayed with you when I was small. You spoke for us in the court. Remember?'

Her face sank.

'Edmund's little girl - Maria.' She leaned back against the house wall and the words tumbled out. 'I couldn't take you in. You know that don't you? I hadn't the room. I've worried and worried about what happened to you since they took you away.'

'They sent me to an Industrial School in Dublin.'

'I know, I know. That's what that judge said. Did they treat you well?'

'Sometimes. Not often.'

I could have made it easier for her, I suppose, though didn't see why I should. Twice she'd turned us away, then refused to take us when the court asked her. I hoped she'd feel enough guilt to give me shelter this time.

One of her children tugged at her skirt, bleating to go home.

'Hush now, just another minute.' My aunt looked at Josie in my arms and shook her head. 'I still can't let you stay, Maria. I've these two and two older ones at home. Henry, my husband, he's away at the fishing half the time and he'd not be happy me bringing home two more mouths to feed. The pair of you can come with me now and stay for the one night. No more. Then you'll have to be on your way. We've precious little to spare.'

She led us through the town and soon I could see the sea. The houses were shabbier here and mud-splashed children played in puddles at the roadside. In front of one of the cottages someone had dug the ground skirting the wall, and flowers of every colour shone out. This would have to be her home.

My aunt told me to go and clean myself up while she settled the younger children, then soon had dishes on the table, waiting for the fish stew steaming over the fire. The oldest child, Peggy, heated some milk, crumbled in a lump of wheaten bread, and stirred it until cool enough to feed to Josie. Once he was fed, Auntie Bridget filled our bowls, giving me twice as much as she ladled in to her own or Peggy's.

It was only when we'd finished the meal, all of her children put to bed and the tea poured, she asked me again about my life since she'd last seen me. I told her the whole lot, the two of us close to tears at times, me hoping beyond hope she'd take pity on me and my son. I thought she would, for just a moment, but then she squared her shoulders, stood, and pointed to where we'd be sleeping.

'You can take this corner here in the kitchen. I'm sorry, there's nothing else. You can lay Josie down now if you want. Henry won't be home tonight, not while the weather's calm, so we can sit and chat until bedtime.'

So we did just that. Auntie Bridget told me how she'd met Henry Rafferty soon after his first wife died. He had two children who needed a mother so when a friend told him Bridget was living on her own he went calling.

'The arrangement suited us both.' She grinned. 'He's away a lot of the time and his house is bigger than mine.' The grin turned into a giggle. 'No, I shouldn't say such things. He's a lovely, kind man and his children are real darlings.'

She told me stories of her brother - my father - and about their parents. It was Auntie Bridget who gave me the tale of Granddad's time in Africa and of his black baby. She told that one with lots of detail and excursions so I suspected she'd told it many times to her children and dressed it up a bit more each time. I've often wondered if I got my storytelling from her, changing the facts just for effect.

We got on well, like we had when I was young helping in her garden. I asked if she still grew vegetables.

'No more. I've only the patch in front of the house. The back's full of nets and pots. Even if I cleared it the salt would kill anything I'd plant.'

She collected our empty cups and walked to the sink beside the window. Even though it was pitch black outside I knew she'd still see the mess behind the cottage. 'I do miss it though. So restful and the food from the market is never as fresh. Still, I suppose I'd not have time now with the children to look after.'

Auntie Bridget hugged me when we finished the night and there was a tear in her eye when she pulled away. Mine too.

*

Next morning I got up early and dressed Josie, praying he'd stay quiet, then threw our things in to a small bag. I filled the space left with bread and bits from my Aunt's larder and, God forgive me, took a few pennies from her purse, just enough to buy us something to eat later in the day. The truth was I'd no idea where I'd go but I didn't want to give her the satisfaction of escorting us out of her house.

I scribbled a quick note, thanking my aunt for her hospitality, and left it where she'd find it on the kitchen table. I even tidied the bed before we left.

A quarter of an hour later we were on the main street in Arklow, with over three hours to wait before the shops opened, so I sat on a pub windowsill, rocking Josie and watching the world go by. When the shutters started to open, I went from shop to shop asking for work, though the result was the same in all of them. A nod to my son, a shake of the head and an apology.

All day I searched and had no luck. I even tried

Mr Jenkins in the hardware shop. Told him my daddy had worked for him but he wasn't willing to help. Gave me a few coppers to buy something to eat, though, so decent enough about it. I didn't spend it straight away, I knew from years ago of the shops who were a soft touch, so managed to beg some bits at lunchtime, then bought bread and cheese later.

About two o'clock the rain started to pour and I could see there'd be no work for us in that town. I was dog-tired as well, having been up before dawn, so dodged in to the church I'd rested in the previous day. The place was quiet, cold, and Mrs Halpin's flowers looked wonderful all around the sides. Josie and I cuddled together on a pew and soon nodded off.

I dreamt I was back in my granddad's house, warm by the fire, and him telling me stories of his life. He leant across and shook me by the shoulder, then I woke up.

'You, wake up, what do you think you're doing in here?' I opened my eyes to find a tall, fat, priest towering over me. 'This is a church, not a doss-house. Get out, the pair of you.'

It took me a few seconds to find my wits and get on my feet, so he grabbed me by the elbow and marched me to the door.

'Off you go, young lady, and don't come around here again, else I'll have you taken to the workhouse.'

He needed to say no more. I lifted Josie and set off on the road out of Arklow.

Day 21

We're coming to the last couple of years I spent in Ireland, in the third war I lived through, and another soldier in my life. It would be nice to think we're getting to the happy ending. But let's not rush, and see where it goes.

A glimmer of something bright, hardly visible, twinkled on the road in the early evening, appearing and disappearing in the drizzle swirling like mist, but becoming clearer every minute I tramped towards it. Shining red in the dim countryside, the two tiny dots offered no light but the sight of them lifted my heart.

My load was getting heavy and it had been several hours since I'd stopped for rest, even longer since we'd eaten, and I was desperate to find shelter for me and the boy. I'd heard people call their child a 'bundle of joy'. At the time that was the last thing I thought of him. The result of one night's stupidity with a man after only one thing. Josie had, so far, brought me more trouble than joy but still I felt the attachment of any mother, the love given and returned. The need for the needy.

But always that smile on his lips. So he's been throughout his life. A smile a priest would be proud of, telling the world they can talk to him and he'll listen without judging. He's at Mass whenever he can and knows his catechism as well as anyone, though sadly I don't think he'll be going down the path of Father McSorley. That smile attracts too many of the ladies.

The shape of an army truck appeared, khaki green with a canvas cover, parked at the roadside though I could hear its engine ticking over. A red cross told me it wasn't one of the usual patrols. Alongside it I could make out the shape of a soldier, his face glowing for a moment when a match flared to light his cigarette. I shouldn't be seen approaching a Brit but what choice did I have? He might have a hot drink, or some food for the boy.

'Got one of those to spare?' I asked, gently, so as not to frighten him. You'd never know how these men would react.

'Christ, you made me jump. Who's there? Come on, let's have a look at you.'

I'd been right to be careful. The soldier didn't appear to have a gun but he might, then shot first and asked questions later. He looked to be in his early twenties, not much older than me, and scared out of his wits. My life was far from easy but at least I wasn't going about constantly in fear of being killed.

'What have you there, under the shawl?'

'It's just my baby – do you want to see?' I hoped it would draw some sympathy but I knew that girls were often used to transport guns wrapped up to look like they were carrying a child. Death disguised as innocence. I knew Ireland's men were fighting for our freedom but still, so many widows and distressed mothers along the way. 'He's not really a baby any longer, too heavy for that. But he's not big enough to trudge these lanes for miles on end.'

'OK, let's have a look then'. The young soldier's hand brushed Josie's cheek as he moved aside my shawl. 'Christ he's cold. Are you sure he's all right?'

'We've been walking for a long time and this damp gets though everything after a while.'

'Well I shouldn't be stopped here, I'd only pulled over for a quick drag. But I guess another few minutes won't do any harm – do you want to jump up inside the cab and get the two of you warmed up for a bit.' He glanced up and down the road, whether expecting another army unit or an ambush wasn't clear. Either way he'd have been in trouble.

I climbed into the truck, shivering even more as the warm air showed just how cold and damp I'd been. Josie tried to wriggle free but I held him close, wanting to get some heat into him before letting him loose.

'Poor little beggar is perished' said the soldier 'here, wrap this blanket around him. Would you like a bite of food? I've only a bit of army rations but you're welcome if you can face it'.

'You're very kind, many of your lot wouldn't have bothered, and maybe even have given me a kick for my troubles'.

'Well that's not me. I've had times myself where we've not known where the next meal was coming from. That's why I ended up in this joke of an army. At least we get fed and watered on a regular basis, even if we are shot at occasionally.'

He laughed but there was no real humour there. And why would there be? A young man, away from home, hated by everyone other than his comrades. His mother would have been worried sick.

The couple of biscuits and the apple he offered were soon gobbled, washed down with luke-warm water from his canteen.

'So what's your name soldier?' The warmth, food and his generosity gave me courage.

'William James Garner, Private, 244867 – name, rank and serial number's all I'm allowed to tell you – Billy to my friends. What's yours?'

'Maria Ann Byrne, Maria to friends and enemies alike.'

'And who's this young feller?'

'This is Josie - short for Joseph. A good bible name, husband of Our Lady. But I guess you wouldn't know that, you being a Brit and a Prod.'

'Steady on girl. There's no need to be insulting me after I've been good enough to help you. I've a good mind to put you out again and I would do as well if I didn't feel sorry for young Josie'.

'I'm sorry Billy. You said you're Billy to your friends, and I'd like it if we were friends. I didn't mean to cause you offence, you have been good to me.'

He was a nice looking lad, with a smile playing around his lips, even seconds after his eyes had flashed in anger. He was slim, with his badly fitting uniform hanging loosely from his shoulders. His dark hair was cut severely in a 'short back and sides' with more than a hint of Brylcreem adding a deep shine.

We chatted for a while and I told him I'd spent the day walking from Arklow, trying to make my way to Dublin eventually, though I might need to find work and shelter along the way.

'I'll take you as far as Wicklow.' Billy's voice was shaking. 'It's only about three miles further along the road and not much out of my way. I've to get to Dublin tonight and hope no-one notices the small diversion. I'd take you right up to the city but I daren't. We'll be safe as far as Wicklow if you keep your head down. And don't tell anyone what I've done.'

'Oh my goodness! Are you sure you can? I wouldn't want you getting into trouble. You've already taken a big risk in letting me into your truck in the first place.'

'No, let's not worry about it. Come one, we'll go straight away, that way I can catch up the time more easily. Hold on to the lad, it gets a bit bumpy in this heap.'

Billy crashed the gears and headed along the road towards the town, whistling in that tuneless way he has. I kept my eyes fixed on the dark road ahead, thinking about how kind he'd been and where I might find to sleep that night. From time to time I'd catch him in the corner of my eye, looking across at me and Josie, with a broad smile brightening his face.

*

'So how did you get into this?' For a little while neither of us had spoken, except for the occasional curse and apology from Billy as the truck hit potholes in the road.

'Into what?' Billy glanced across.

'This. Here. Now. How's a nice young fella like you find himself in uniform in a strange country standing guard over the likes of us?'

Billy shrugged.

'Tell you the truth, Maria, I don't really know. I joined up when the war started, just like all my mates, to fight the Germans. Fifteen I was, not long out of school and no job. So what else was there to do but con the recruiting sergeant that I was a year older, not that he took much conning I can tell you, and to take the king's shilling in exchange for new boots, warm clothes and being fed three meals every day.' The truck jolted as it hit yet another pothole and this time my boy woke with a whimper. Minutes later he was asleep again.

'But the war finished ages ago. Why are you over here?'

'I fought for four years in Belgium and France, shooting and getting shot at. Then when it was all over half my mates were dead and gone, injured or half mad with what they'd seen or done.' His eyes dropped for a moment 'Even my older brother bought it. Only in the army for a month and he went down at Ypres. After it was all over I went home to my Mam and Dad but couldn't settle. The old feller's ill and can't afford to keep me, so with no job on the horizon I signed up for another term.'

'So you wanted to come across to Ireland then?'

'God no! I thought I'd have a cushy time up in Catterick camp pushing paper around a desk or chasing new recruits around the parade ground. I was only home from France for two weeks and didn't have a clue what was happening over here. Next thing I know I'm on a boat to Belfast. Since then I've been all over this country, north to south, east to west, getting shot at and watching fellas being blown up in front of me. At least in the war we'd known who was on our side and who wasn't. And we generally knew which way the enemy was coming from.'

'I reckon you must hate us ... the Irish I mean. I lurched forward as he hit the brakes hard. 'Why,

why are you stopping? I didn't mean anything by it.' Billy turned and in one quick movement pushed my head below the dashboard.

'Quiet. Get down. There's a patrol up ahead.'

Despite Billy's warning I couldn't help myself and peeked up the road. Sure enough there was a dim light in the distance with several figures standing around a truck.

'What will I do? We'll both be in trouble if I'm found in here with you'

'You don't need to tell me that. Jump down quickly, out of the cab, and climb in the back. You'll find some blankets in there to hide under. And keep your boy quiet. They're not likely to search the truck with me driving but if he cries they'll find you. If they do then I'll have to say you must have jumped in when I stopped for a smoke.'

Billy moved on seconds after we climbed inside, driving slowly, which gave me time to cover me and Josie before we reached the checkpoint. I knew he couldn't afford to stop for long in case they'd think he was IRA.

We rolled to a standstill and a voice barked.

'Identify yourself soldier'

'Private Billy Garner, North Lancs Regiment, Sarge.'

'Number?'

'244867.'

'Good. And what are you doing out on the road

at this time of night Private? Why did you stop down the road there?'

'Just returning from Carnew barracks, Sarge, on my way to Dublin. Been picking up supplies - medicine, blankets, bandages, that kind of thing.

'You still didn't say why you stopped back there'

'Well, you can't be too careful, can you Sarge? I spotted a light in the road and wasn't sure if it was one of ours or one of theirs. Just took a minute to check it out, that's all. I was ready to dive off into the woods until morning if I couldn't be sure.'

Another voice, gentler than the sergeant's butted in.

'Billy? Billy Garner?'

'Tucker? Is that you?' Billy answered.

'This here's Billy Garner, Sarge. I spent the last two years of the war with him. Great bloke and no-one better to depend on. Billy, how've you been?' I heard Billy's saviour step closer to the cab, followed by the slap of flesh on flesh when they shook hands.

'It's great to see you Tucker. I thought you'd gone there in France when we were split up. Things have been decent apart from Sam. Did you hear about him?'

'I did Billy. Bad business. Your Mum must have been crushed. And you of course.'

'Well it hit us all pretty hard at the time. Dad

took it the worst. Sam was a rogue but Dad always had a soft spot for him.'

The sergeant had heard enough.

'If you two old fishwives can stop chattering for a minute I've a job to do. Get on your way Private Garner. If Tucker Jeffries says you're genuine then that will do for me. Keep your eyes peeled on the road though. As you say, you can never be too careful.'

Billy and his friend exchanged a few more words, each promising to stay in touch, before Billy let out the clutch and we headed down the road.

*

It was just getting light the next time we pulled to a halt and Billy threw back the canvas flap on the back of the truck.

'Jesus, Mary and Joseph! We're frozen in here and Josie is nearly starving. I thought you'd forgotten us altogether.'

'I daren't stop anywhere in sight of the patrol and then it hardly seemed worthwhile with only a few miles to go. Sorry if it's been a bit cold, I thought the blankets would keep you warm.'

'Well it wasn't too bad, but not as good as inside the cab. Can we get back in there now?' I jumped to the ground and carried Josie to the front.

'Fraid not, Maria. We're only about half a mile from Wicklow and it wouldn't do to be seen letting you out in the main street now would it? I reckon we'd both end up collecting a bullet.' Billy frowned and scanned the road. 'You'd best try walking it in from here - unless you can pick up another lift.'

'That's grand Billy. I ... we ... we're really grateful for what you've done. You needn't have and you could have got in a whole heap of trouble on our account.' Billy reached into his pocket, pulling out some pieces of chocolate and a few coins.

'Here, take this. It's not much but it's all I've with me. At least it might keep Josie happy for a while, and the cash will buy you both breakfast.'

'God be with you Billy Garner. You're a fine man.' I perched on my tiptoes and pecked him on the cheek. 'God be with you.'

With that I pulled Josie close in, turned on my heels and set off towards the town.

I heard the engine throb into life again and the wheels crunch on the road for half a minute before slowing alongside us. Billy called out of the window.

'And you, Maria Ann Byrne, may your God be with you too.'

*

On the way home last night, I was thinking of Auntie Bridget struggling with her little garden, and it reminded me of our first attempts. We'd found a house to rent in Hulme, the other side of Manchester city centre from where we are now.

Dirty, with bugs and mice, but the best we could afford. It had a yard and in one corner someone had dug up the concrete, leaving a patch of earth where they'd planted a few bulbs before they'd left. You were only four and the rest had gone to their new school, so we went out into the sunshine and started to tidy up. You were so like how I remembered my little brother, Jimmy, back then, the same eyes and the same hair. The way you were always tugging at your ear, he did just the same.

I said 'Now, Alice, let's see if we can't get some of these flowers to grow and some of these weeds to stop growing, and you chuckled as we began the new game of guessing which were flowers and which were weeds.

You were good at it and told me the first couple I showed you. You knew flowers were pretty and coloured, so I picked a dandelion to fool you. It didn't work though and you took great pleasure in telling me it was a weed.

Without hesitating, you whispered, 'I think it's pretty but you said we can't have those in the garden. They're dandelions - and you said they make us wee the bed.'

You knew it was a naughty thing to say and I pretended to scold but you wouldn't stop. On and on you went, 'But Mammy, it's only 'wee'. Wee, wee, wee, wee … weeeeee!' You only did when I grabbed you by the waist and tickled until you could shout no more.

One of the nicest days we ever spent.

Day 22

It's finally finished, Alice, all of it. The Yanks dropped two huge bombs, atomic bombs they've called them, and now the Japs have packed it in. The wireless is saying thousands and thousands were killed in the raids. Serve them right I suppose, but you can't help feeling sorry for all those poor souls who've died. And their families.

Josie said in his last letter there were rumours everywhere that the Americans were about to do something big to bring it all to an end. He didn't have much else to talk about only the heat and the dry dust, they don't let him tell us anything about what he's doing in case it gets out.

So that was one good piece of news, I suppose, and I was so cheered up last visit, after I remembered about us in the garden, I thought I'd tell you about a time in Ireland where my life took a turn for the better when I met an old friend. Really, I met two.

I was so, so lucky after Billy dropped me off. It seemed later that the good times started when we met that night. Josie and me finished the walk into Wicklow and were heading for the church, hoping to sneak into a corner to sleep. A woman pushing a pram walked towards, then past, me, giving me a really friendly smile. Most people don't bother when you look like a bag of rags. Two seconds later she stopped.

'Maria Byrne? It is you, isn't it?'

I turned and tried to pull her features to mind. Then I had her.

'Kathleen? Kathleen Breslin?'

She'd filled out, a lot, since she left St Gregory's, and I guessed the baby in the pram wasn't her first. Her clothes were new and well pressed, and her brown curls gone, now bleached blond in the latest cut.

Kathleen hugged me and we were both in tears until poor Josie began to be upset. He couldn't understand how happy we were. She insisted I went home with her.

'Just for the night. Get you warm then we'll eat and catch up.'

You have no pride when you've been on the streets for a while. Kathleen had been there and knew I wasn't about to refuse her offer. We'd stood by each other when we were in the home, so she also knew I'd do the same for her if the boot was on the other foot.

My friend had done well for herself, marrying a lovely man, Francis, twice her age who was already successful in business. He'd a large grocery shop, with a bakery next door, on the main street, and a fine house in the better part of town. Kathleen fed us, let me take a bath, and gave me some of her old clothes to wear, declaring they no longer fit her. Whether this was true or not I don't know, but they were still a couple of sizes too big for me. Even so, I was still grateful for them.

I slept the soundest night I had for ages and next day Kathleen was beside herself with excitement at breakfast.

'I had a word with Francis in bed last night,' she gave me a broad smile and a wink, 'and he says he can give you a job in the shop. Only for three weeks mind, he's nothing permanent. You can stay here with us. Put a few bob in your purse to get back on your feet. What do you say?'

I felt dizzy. What could I say?

'Who'll look after Josie?' was all I could manage.

'Sure, he can stay with me up here. One more's not going to make no difference. Please say you will.'

So I did. Kathleen and her husband were so kind. She seemed glad of female company and we talked and laughed every night, sharing stories with Francis of the games we'd got up to in St Gregory's. Sometimes her face would darken when she remembered the beatings and bad times, and I'd change the subject or just hold her hand till she was through it.

On Wednesday of the third week, Francis called me into the room in the shop he used for his paperwork and apologised that he couldn't keep me longer. He'd a townswoman coming back after being ill and she'd been a good worker for a long time. He told me he felt duty bound to let her pick up her job again and I understood. In a small town you have to keep in with the locals or you lose business. Francis said he'd pay me to the end of the week 'with a bit of a bonus' for helping him out when he was stuck. He handed me a letter.

'Take this to James McFadden, remember that name, at McFadden's Emporium in Dublin. He's a long-time friend of mine and owes me a favour or two so he's guaranteed to give you work. Nothing fancy mind, just same as here, in the shop, but he pays well enough and is a decent boss.'

Francis passed me another sheet of paper.

'This here's a lodging house run by another friend. The rooms are only a walk away from McFadden's. The rent's paid for the first month, give you a chance to settle.'

I protested and asked why he was doing all of this for me.

'My Kathleen is the best thing that's ever happened to me. I was on my own for a long time. Too long. She's told me all about the two of you in that damned place and it seems to me the least I can do is return the favour for getting her through it.'

Three days later I was on the bus to Dublin. Me, Josie, a new suitcase packed with nice clothes, and a good few pounds in my purse.

*

I arrived in the city on Saturday afternoon, the bus conductor much pleasanter than when I'd left because he didn't recognise the woman he'd been rude to less than a week earlier. Kathleen's cast-offs, which we'd altered to fit, plenty of baths and a decent haircut had done the trick. I looked like a good, respectable shop assistant at last and he even helped me off with my case.

All the way from Wicklow I'd worried about what I'd do with Josie. If I couldn't find someone to look after him I'd not be able to take the job, and I'd be out on my ear again as soon as the month's rent ran out.

I went straight to McFadden's where the boss read Francis' letter and, without hesitating, told me to come back Monday morning ready for work. As I turned to go, he asked me to wait for a minute.

'Can I ask you what you'll be doing with the wee one?'

There was nothing I could think to say, so I looked at the floor.

'I thought so.' He smiled. 'You're not the first and I expect you won't be the last. I've a few girls here who've lost their husband,' McFadden looked at my cheap wedding ring 'or maybe never had one in the first place. Things happen in life and we're not always in control, are we? There's a woman, Mrs Brown, an English lady, lives not far from where you're staying. Looks after children while their mammies are at work. She'll help you out if you need her. Use my name if you need to.'

He gave me her address and one of his assistants lived in the same street as my lodgings so she gave me directions. It was only twenty minutes to walk from the Emporium, but it felt like I floated all the way to my new home.

*

I took Josie to Mrs Brown's every morning at half past eight, chatted and settled him for fifteen minutes, then left in good time to be at the shop. James McFadden was as helpful as Francis had said he would be. He put me on a counter selling silks, patterns and cottons for embroidery. Even though I'd been hopeless at needlework in school, I'd taken in all my lessons and understood what I should be doing, even though I had no practical skill. In the shop, the theory was good enough and, as a result, I got on well with the customers, who were often well-heeled ladies looking for something to do with their time. Within a month the word of a good, new assistant had gone round and their friends were also coming in. Mr McFadden told me he was very pleased with my work.

I had a happy time there. Most of the girls were friendly, my ladies were nice to me, and the wages were enough to pay Mrs Brown, my rent, send something to Daisy Farina, and have enough to get us through every week. Never quite enough to put much by, but you can't have everything.

One or two of the men who worked in the warehouse of the Emporium asked me out but I always refused. For one thing I was deadly tired after being on my feet for eight or nine hours every day, for another, I was away from my little boy all that time and didn't want to be leaving him in the evenings as well. Besides, at the beginning I was still hoping I might magically bump in to Danny and, even after everything I'd been through, he'd say he'd been waiting for me to come back.

A month after I was settled in the Emporium, Mr McFadden asked a few of us if we'd come in on Sunday to help with stock-taking in exchange for a day during the week. It made no difference to me which days I worked so I agreed. On my weekday off I left Josie with Mrs Brown as usual. I couldn't really afford the extra but I couldn't take him with me. Not this first time. The bus took me out towards Irishtown then it was a quarter of an hour's walk in the rain to Sandymount. Danny's shop was still there but there was no sign of him. After a while I went inside and a young man with a moustache asked if he could help me.

'I'm looking for a friend. Danny Walsh. He used to work here.'

'Not in my time, Miss. Are you sure?'

'It was at the start of the War. He was a delivery boy.'

He shrugged and said he'd ask his boss. A couple of minutes later, the butcher came through, wiping bloody hands on his apron.

'You're a friend of Danny's?'

I nodded.

'I'm sorry Miss but he never came back.'

'Do you know where he went?'

'No, no, you don't understand. He never came back from France. Killed he was. Only there a few weeks -'

The rest of the day is a blur. I think I ran from the shop all the way to St Gregory's where I hammered on the door and screamed at the nuns. I swore at them for taking me away from him when we'd have had so little time anyway. I don't know where I went after that or how I got home, though it was dark and Mrs Brown was angry I'd left Josie for so long. I wandered around for the next week in a daze, until Mr McFadden took me to one side and told me I needed to pull my socks up. Danny and I had only seen each other a couple of times but he'd grown over the years into my special one. A silly, childish, dream.

*

Every Sunday, most of the women who worked at McFadden's and had their children with Mrs Brown would meet if the weather was fine. Usually we'd just take a walk round Merrion Square, or Stephen's Green where a band might be playing in the summer. Once we agreed to save for a month and take the tram to Phoenix Park. All of the boys and girls loved the zoo, I think all of their mothers did too. Then afterwards we pushed to the front of the crowd at the barracks gates and watched the cavalry trotting up and down the parade ground in their finest uniforms.

Most of the women either said they'd lost their husbands in the war or some, like me, didn't bother to say anything. One of them, Winifred, claimed she'd left her husband because he beat her. Another girl, who knew Winifred well, told me it wasn't true and he'd seemed a quiet sort of a man who upped and ran off with a younger woman from his office. Winifred was always trying to become friendly with me though I wasn't too keen. I'd see her smiling and chatting to someone then ten minutes later would be saying the most awful things about her to me. I didn't think I could trust her so I stayed civil but kept my distance.

The Emporium was by far the biggest department store I'd worked in, with three floors and a basement, almost the biggest I'd been in, even in Liverpool, and my area was towards the back of the ground floor. One day in April, there was a loud bang out on Great George's Street, followed by a commotion at the front of the shop. Three men wearing scarves across their faces ran down the hall, chased close behind by a squad of British soldiers, all carrying rifles but not able to take aim due to the dozens of customers panicking between them and the men they were after. I was so scared when the crowd cleared in front of my counter and three soldiers lifted their weapons until their sergeant shouted to watch out for me.

One of the soldiers stopped and looked at me before running out of the back door, still trying to hunt down the brave boys. I was sure it was the soldier I'd met on the road, Billy Garner. Two minutes later a dozen shots echoed down the lane at the back, quietening the buzz in the store. It was a strange, deathly quiet, lasting ten seconds or more, before the chatter started again even louder than it had been. Mr McFadden was soon walking the floor, making sure none of his workers were hurt, and settling the nerves of his more fragile lady customers. He called me over to assist one, Miss O'Hagan, who had dropped the items she'd bought from me earlier. She looked up, alarmed, when some of the soldiers came back inside. The first was Billy and he stood by my counter for a moment, waiting for his mates to join him. I wanted to catch his eye but was afraid I'd be seen, so just continued to re-wrap Mrs O'Hagan's purchases.

When I returned to my own position, a slip of paper was tucked into the frame round the glass top.

Meet me at eight. Outside McFee's Bar. B.G.

Day 23

Billy came home cheerful tonight. Payday, so there were fags, a bottle of beer for him, sweeties for the little ones and no complaints about the bus fare. He even kicked a ball about with little Tommy in the garden when he got home from school, I had to tell him to stop because of his heart. There are times he's like a perfect father, though a woman can never be certain of these things. Billy always said he wanted children but I could see in his eyes after the first three came along that he hadn't wanted it to be his whole life. I know he loves every single one of you, yet still I think sometimes he'd rather be free. When we got together in Dublin I was just so grateful to see him again, he'd been so kind when I was desperate.

McFee's was up towards the Liffey, a good twenty minute walk from Mrs Brown's, and I was running by the time I got to the corner. I hoped my headscarf would hide my face a bit and I knew Billy would be careful, he'd as much to lose as me, but I wanted to make sure there were no soldiers or workmates around to see us together. I needn't have worried. There were no barracks nearby and it was unlikely any of my friends would be out drinking on a week night. The street was quiet and Billy was on his own, in civilian clothes, leaning on the pub wall, smoking, as coolly as you like.

'Good evening, Mr Garner.'

He threw his cigarette end into the gutter and smiled broadly.

'Well, well, if it isn't Maria Ann Byrne. You made it then?'

'I did but I had to promise Mrs Brown .. the lady looking after Josie .. I'd be no later than half past nine to pick him up. We'll only have an hour then I'll have to go.'

We went in and found a booth away from the door. There were just four men at the bar, absorbed in heated conversation about horse racing, and they took no notice of us. Billy and me chose seats where we could keep an eye on anyone coming through the door.

With a pint and a glass of port on the table between us, I told Billy what had happened since we met, and how grateful I was for his kindness. He'd been stopped by another patrol, only two miles from where he'd dropped me and this time he didn't know anyone. They tore him off a strip for being off his route and put three soldiers with him to make sure he made it safely to his destination. If I'd still been in the back they'd have found me for sure.

He didn't talk about the explosion and chase when he'd come in to McFadden's that afternoon, though I'd heard there'd been a hand-grenade thrown in to a truck full of Black and Tans. Billy's squad had been in the one behind and shot two of the three men when they caught them in the lane.

'Recognised you straight away when I saw you behind the counter, even though you've a bit more colour in your cheeks. How's the little feller?'

'He's grand. Getting big and into everything. I can hardly leave him down for a minute without he's pulling at the tablecloth or trying to eat his toys.'

So we talked about everything and nothing, and the hour disappeared in a flash. Billy walked with me as far as Mrs Brown's street, then hopped on a bus, but not before we'd arranged to meet again the following week.

*

The second time Billy and I went out, he'd suggested we went to a different pub, this time some distance from the first. McEwan's was livelier than McFee's so I asked him why he'd chosen it.

'Because we can't get into a pattern. I know all the pubs the soldiers use, so it's easy to avoid them, but your workmates could be anywhere. I reckon the odds of bumping in to one of them are less if we go to a different place each time.'

'Does it matter?'

He looked at me like I'd just fallen from outer space.

'Matter? Of course it matters. Your friends might not know me but within ten seconds of hearing me talk they'll have me down for English and probably a soldier. Then they'll ask questions to check. Next thing the word will be around and you'll be in deep trouble.'

Billy grabbed my hand across the table.

'Listen. When we were down in Cork last year one of our lads was going out with a local girl and she was found out. A gang of IRA fellers stripped her then shaved her head during the night. When her father heard, he threw her onto the streets rather than go after the blokes who did it. You don't want that happening to you.'

What he'd said terrified me but I was too taken with him to let it show. Instead, I grinned and raised an eyebrow.

'So I should stop going out with you then?'

The look on his face was priceless.

'No, that's not what I'm saying. We need to be careful that's all.'

I've always able to get him like that. Tease him, I mean. He never knows when I'm telling the truth or making it up. One of the reasons I'm so fond of him I suppose.

*

Approaching Christmas, Mr McFadden had plenty of overtime on offer and though I wasn't keen, the hours I worked were long enough, the money would come in useful, so I put my name down. It meant Josie and me could have a present each, maybe an extra one for him. On the first payday after the holiday, when most of the overtime money was due, I queued with the rest. Winifred was waiting when I'd collected my wages. She took me by the arm and steered me out of earshot of the other girls. I could smell drink on her breath.

'Any chance of the loan of a few bob, Maria? Lenny, my old man, he went out on the binge over Christmas. Blew the rent.'

I suspected she'd been bingeing too, and pushed my pay packet into my pocket.

'Can't, Winifred. Sorry.'

'Ah come on. I know you'd a few hours extra.'

If it had been one of the other girls I probably wouldn't have thought twice but I wasn't about to give my hard-earned cash to someone who'd drunk away her own.

'I said I'm sorry, didn't I? There's my own rent to pay and Mrs Brown's putting up her prices in the new year. I only took the overtime so I'd have something to get me through the next few months.'

She moved in a flash from being pleasant. Her eyes narrowed and she hissed through clenched teeth.

'I only ask a friend a favour once, Byrne. If they refuse then they mean nothing to me and I'm not going to beg. Just remember what I said.'

Winifred turned away, scanning the pay queue for a new victim, and didn't give me another look.

*

Me and Billy carried on going out at least once a week, more when we could make it. He was good company, always making me laugh, and seemed to enjoy hearing my stories about days in the Emporium. I think he was ashamed of what the British were doing in Ireland because he never spoke of his army life. One time I asked him what he'd done in the War and he said he didn't want to talk about it. All he'd say was that he'd seen things no man should have to see and done things he should never have been asked to do.

As the months went by we drew closer and closer. Billy was fond of Josie and in the better weather the three of us would go walking, always in places where we hoped we wouldn't be seen. On Good Friday the shop was closed and the April sun shone for the first time in weeks. We met Billy early and took the train from Amiens Street out to Howth. Billy sat two seats away from us and all the time I had to stop Josie running to him.

The three of us had a wonderful day walking round the harbour and eating our sandwiches overlooking the water. Then we trekked for miles along the lanes to the station at Sutton. Billy was fit, used to marching and carrying a pack, so hoisting the boy onto his shoulders and carrying him so far was no hardship to him. By the time we arrived, even he was sweating so he treated us to an ice-cream from a man with a cart on the roadside.

We made our way to the platform and plonked down on a bench with Josie between us. Then I heard someone chatting away to our left. It was Winifred. I tried to escape but she turned and spotted me. She looked from me to Josie, then to Billy. There could be no doubt we were together, Josie was holding his hand. A smirk crossed her face.

'Why, Maria, out for the day are you? And who's this nice-looking young man?'

'J-just a friend.'

Why I didn't say he was a cousin, or my sister's husband, or anything other than that, I'll never know. Those three words, and the English accent coming from Billy's lips when he said hello to Winifred, set the course for the rest of my life right there.

*

The commotion came in the small hours. Banging first, then the door kicked in. Four faces vivid in the torchlight, all of them angry. I was halfway out of my bed but a strong arm pushed me down again. Josie began crying in the corner and another man shouted him to shut up, but he wouldn't. Not for all the time they were there.

The man who'd shouted joined the other and pinned me to the bed, locking his hand across my mouth. I was struggling. Wriggling and wriggling, expecting one of the others in the house to help but no-one came.

'Now girl. Little birdie tells us you've been with a British soldier.'

Winifred.

I gave a frantic shake of my head.

'Don't you be lying to us. We were told and then we watched. Thought you were careful didn't you, but not careful enough. Now we'll make you pretty for your boyfriend.' He turned and shouted. 'Phil, the blade.'

Ten minutes it took them. Two holding my arms and one locking my head while the fourth hacked away my hair. I stopped fighting pretty soon, there was no point against four men, and relaxed as best I could so they'd treat me no rougher.

When they'd done, the one called Phil pressed his nose against mine. I could smell the whiskey on him.

'There, girl, we're finished. Now you pack your things and get out. No-one wants the likes of you around here. Not even your little soldier boy now I'll bet.'

He slobbered a kiss and went to rip apart my nightdress, but the first one spoke.

'Don't Phil. Leave that kind of stuff to the Tans. Let's get out of here.'

There was no doubt who was in charge. Phil let the fabric drop and the four left, slamming my broken door behind them. I sat on the edge of my bed shaking until my baby's cries broke through. Josie was still wailing when I picked him up and carried him to the mirror. I joined the boy when I saw the ragged tufts poking from my pink and bloody scalp.

*

It was four days later when Billy found us, huddled in a shop doorway, only a few hundred yards from his barracks at the Phoenix Park.

When the men had left, I'd gathered up my money and the little I could carry then fled when the men left. At every door in the lodgings, on every landing, the women I thought were my friends spat at my feet when I walked past. I felt so bitter that I almost turned back to my room, tell them all to go to hell, and face it out. But I knew my life there was over. My job would be gone, the landlord would put me out anyway, and Mrs Brown, likely as not, would have nothing to do with us.

There was enough in my purse to pay some rent until I sorted out what to do, but the landlady of every boarding house I knocked at turned me away as soon as they saw what was under my scarf. It wasn't that they were bad or heartless women, just that they couldn't face the trouble I might bring to their door. That first night, after walking all day in the rain, I found a small hotel down by the canal and kept my head firmly covered until Josie and I were safely in our room. It seemed the sort of place where no questions were asked but I hadn't the money to stay for more than one night so it was back into the doorways next morning. I moved as close to the barracks as I could, thinking I'd be safer with a few soldiers on the doorstep.

Billy told me later that he'd been worried when I'd not turned up for our date and went round to my rooms next day with a couple of his army mates. First off, no-one would say anything, then one of the girls told him what happened. I don't know who it was but I think she must have seen he was a decent feller and took pity on us. His friends tried to stop him but he stormed off to search for Josie and me, looking in a lot of the places we'd been together but, of course, didn't find me. Billy knew that quite a few of the soldiers would be seeing Irish women, even those with wives at home, so he went round to as many as he could and asked them if their girlfriends would listen for any news of me. On the third day he got word that a woman who'd been punished had been going round the lodgings with a child. Then one of the soldiers told him they'd seen someone like that hanging around near the barracks. It didn't take him long to find me then.

I was so grateful to see him that I didn't care who knew and flung my arms round his neck as soon as he called my name. Even little Josie was giggling by the time Billy grabbed both our hands and led us down the street.

*

Billy came to me next day. He'd given me enough cash to stay in a hotel again, somewhere he knew would be safe, and told me he'd sort something out for longer when he could. I was waiting for him in the tea-room when he arrived. He looked concerned so I asked if there was a problem.

'I don't think so. It's just that when I got back some news was out on our leaving date.'

My heart sank. 'When will it be?'

'That's just it, they don't know. We were expecting to be pulling out soon, now that this treaty's signed, but the violence seems to be starting again between them who want a treaty and them who want full independence. It looks like we'll have to stay a while to protect the RIC lads. There's about a dozen of 'em killed in the last fortnight.'

'Does it mean you're going to have to move?'

'Not if you give me the right answer to my next question.'

I leaned back in my chair sharply when a waitress arrived to ask if we wanted to order. Billy flashed a smile and said a cup of tea would be 'champion'. The girl returned his smile. I nodded for the same.

'You made a hit there. I reckon she fancies

you.'

'Now, Maria, you know there's only one lass for me' Josie climbed on to his lap and Billy grinned as he ruffled my boy's curls, 'and one lad.'

I couldn't wait any longer. 'So what's this question you need to ask?'

Billy grimaced and stroked his chin. 'I spoke with my sergeant-major last night about what they did to you and he went up the line. The message came back that they'd let you move in to one of our spare quarters. The only trouble is we'd have to get married.'

The words could hardly force their way through my lips. 'Oh, Billy. I couldn't ask you to do that for me. It wouldn't be right.' I was shaking like a leaf.

'Not right? What wouldn't be right about it?'

'Well ... well we've never talked about it and ... and there's Josie. Why would you be willing to saddle yourself with someone like me with a young boy who's not your own?'

'Because I love you.' Words soft as duck down.

'What?'

'You must know I've been crackers about you since we met on the road. I hoped you might feel the same.'

Day 24

That's how your dad proposed and I was so grateful, but how could I tell him I wasn't sure? That I liked him a lot but didn't know if I loved him enough?

We hardly knew each other. I'd lost a man I thought was the one, and been treated badly by another. Apart from that, I had no experience to judge.

What I knew, what I've always known, is Billy was a good man and would look after me and mine. Even as he jiggled Josie on his knee, and my tiny son put his arms round the man's waist, I knew what my answer would be.

I've never regretted it, not really. Sometimes, when he comes home drunk or gets into one of his moods, I wonder. But he has always been there, right from that very first time with his truck outside Wicklow. And without him I wouldn't have my lovely girl.

*

There was no time to think, plan or worry. Billy and me had to marry next day. His commanding officer had given permission, but warned Billy they might be sent as reinforcements to the north-west where fighting had broken out. If they were, and we weren't married, there'd be no place for me in the barracks.

Billy had arranged for his best friend, Barney Connolly, and his wife Marion, to be witnesses. I wanted us to marry in a Catholic church but Billy said that wouldn't be possible, it would be safer to go to St Matthias where an army chaplain could perform the service. We weren't the only couple that day, there were three other soldiers and their wives-to-be, all, like us, getting married in a rush. The church was a dour sort of place, square, with big columns out front. The only extravagances were the stained glass windows above the altar, which blazed like sapphires when the afternoon sun shone, as Billy and I repeated our vows.

My mother and father were both dead, and I'd no relatives or friends to invite, so the whole affair was over in no time. All of the couples went back to the barracks straight afterwards and in the evening, once we'd settled in our quarters, we met in the canteen for a drink and a bit of a dance. The new wives were friendly, all Catholics and in the same boat as me, and I was glad of them being nearby in the days to come.

Billy and I didn't stay late. It had been a whirlwind of a day and I needed to get Josie off to bed. It felt so strange sharing a place with Billy. Even though we'd been going out for months we'd never spent a night together, not had more than a kiss and a cuddle in the pictures. There's no need for details on what happened on that first night but he was kind and I was exhausted, and we both fell asleep with smiles on our faces.

*

October 1922, Billy and I married and my countrymen shooting and bombing each other like they'd already forgotten the men they'd lost fighting the British. Every day there were reports of battles north, south, east and west across the country. Josie and I were safe in Phoenix Park but my new husband still had to go out on patrol most days.

The married quarters were three terraces of small cabins on the edge of the barracks, well away from the accommodation of the single men. Ours had a living room with a stove for cooking, a bedroom barely big enough for two and a tiny box-room where Josie's cot took the whole space. Most of the wives were English, with only four of us Irish, who were put together at one end, as far away from the other families as possible. Every time an Irish woman passed by an English billet she'd be called names and told to clear off out of the camp. The worst were those who'd lost someone in the three years before the Free State was established, though they'd never dare say anything when Billy was with me.

He was up every morning at six o'clock for duty, so even after I'd made his breakfast it was a long day ahead. I'd usually take a walk to the parade ground, the long way round, behind the officers' quarters to avoid any nastiness, and Josie would watch the soldiers marching. Then maybe I'd call for a cup of tea to Maggie Cunningham, a red-haired neighbour with a daughter the same age as Josie. Maggie was from Donegal, had a fierce tongue on her and took no nonsense from the English wives. She'd knocked the door with some tea, milk and a bag of sugar on our first day and we'd got on well. Two weeks after I married, Josie and me were watching the morning drill when the rain began to pour so I lifted the child and hurried home on the most direct route. Half way there, two women in raincoats and scarves came out of a cabin. They blocked my path.

'Where you going?'

'Home. Let me pass. Please.'

'Not your home though is it? British camp this. Not Irish. Not for scum like you.' She turned to her partner. 'Don't want to be British this lot. Spent the last few years shooting our lads just to tell us.'

The second woman snorted. 'That's what I heard.'

My temper was rising but I knew there'd be more trouble if I lashed out so I tried again to reason with them. 'Let me through. My little boy's getting soaked.'

'Let the little B get soaked. Bit of luck the mongrel will get pneumonia and die.'

Now I was about to lunge when I heard Maggie Cunningham's voice.

'Don't, Maria. They're not worth it.'

Maggie was by my side, arms folded and her head tilted. 'Now ladies, what's the problem?'

The women looked at each other, backed away and said there was no problem.

'Just been welcoming your friend here to the barracks.'

Maggie linked my arm. 'That's nice. I wouldn't like to think you don't want her here. Husband's as good as your man any day. Proper soldier, not some office clerk.'

The two slunk back indoors and we continued round to Maggie's. We laughed but I was shaking inside.

That night I told Billy and he wanted to go round to have it out with their men.

'No, Billy. What good will that do. They'll only get back at me another way. Can't you get me away? Over to England?'

He rubbed his forehead. 'I don't know when that will be. We heard this afternoon we're moving out next week. All of us.'

'Oh, Billy, at last, I can't believe it. I'll start packing in the morning. It will be … Billy, what's wrong?'

He was shaking his head.

'There's rumours they'll not let us take our Irish wives straight away. You might have to stay here until it's sorted out.'

'Why?'

'Because it's been said some blokes have married Irish girls for money, just so they can get to England.'

'But that's not us, Billy, is it?'

'I know it isn't but it might take a while to convince the powers that be.'

'Tell them we've been going out for ages, Billy. Tell them that... and tell them Josie's your little boy. That should do it.'

Billy looked like I'd slapped his face.

'How could I do that? How could you even ask me to do such a thing?'

I started to cry.

'I'm sorry. I don't know what I'm saying. But we've got to do something. I can't stay here without you. I can't.''

*

The rumours turned out not to be true, thank God. Five weeks afterwards we packed our things and Josie and me, along with all the other wives and children, waved off the columns of soldiers as they marched away behind the military band. As soon as they left we were ushered on to buses which joined the convoy of trucks rolling through the gates towards the port.

The journey took two hours trundling behind the soldiers, along a route lined with people waving flags and an age later we were on board, with the boat's horn wailing as we sailed away to England.

This was the last time ever I saw Ireland. The last time I ever wanted to see it.

*

Maria turns her key in the lock, pushes open the front door, and hangs her coat and scarf on the rack at the bottom of the stairs. Billy, dozing beside the wireless, shakes awake when she sits at the table. His wife's face tells him there's bad news.

'She's worse then?'

For a full minute she can't bring herself to speak. When she does, every sentence is broken by sobs.

'That Doctor Evans told me before I left that it would be tomorrow. He's a good man, took me into a private room and asked a nurse to bring me a cup of tea. Said she's not in any pain now and will just slip away.'

Maria turns away her head, squeezing her eyes shut.

"He said it would be fine for us to go in to sit with her, even outside visiting hours. Will you come, Billy?'

Her husband moves to sit beside her and takes her hand.

'I can't, love. Please don't ask me.'

'But why not? We should be with her at the end.'

'I know we should, but I'm such a coward.

You're so much stronger, always have been. I can't sit there and see my little girl die.'

Maria pushes his hand away.

'Then you're not the man I thought you were, Billy Garner. I'm going to my bed, I need to be out early. You can get yourself round to Father McSorley and tell him your daughter needs the last rites in the morning.'

She stands and drags her weary bones upstairs, undresses and climbs under the covers. Lying in the dark, Maria regrets what she said and yearns for Billy to follow, hold her in his arms, and tell her everything will be all right.

Day 25

'We're at the end of our story now, Alice. All those people and places I've told you about, all of those lives, how we got to here. How I married Billy and came with him to England, which was a hundred times better than I'd ever had it. Life wasn't easy at first, slum house after slum house, bad wages and a new baby every year or so. People can be so cruel. I'd been mistreated by my own people forever before I was married, then abused in the street by Manchester neighbours who disliked the Irish. That only got better when Billy settled in his job and they gave us the council house.'

A nurse appears, smiles, straightens the girl's pillow and pulls the bedsheets up to her patient's chin, then leaves, smiling weakly at Maria. A smile that says to make the most of her time left.

'Your dad went to see Father McSorley last night, asked him to come in to see you today. I expect he'll be in soon enough. I should go to Mass later. Do some penance. I've not been for a while and I'll have Father McSorley round telling me off. If he does I'm afraid I might give him a piece of my … Alice? … ALICE?'

Maria rushes for a nurse, then runs back with two close behind, and tries to rub some life into the cold hands of her daughter. One nurse checks the girl's pulse, grimly shakes her head at the other, and lays her hand on Maria's wrist.

'I'm sorry, Mrs Garner ...' Maria doesn't hear the rest.

Patients, those who are able, crane their necks to see what's going on. Then the whispers start, bed to bed. Fear hushes the ward when the doctor comes through, speaks to the nurses, and draws the curtain around Alice's bed.

*

A knock at the door. Maria sits alone with the kitchen curtains drawn and grips her cherished handkerchief with the flower embroidered in one corner. Ruth and Brian have pushed Rose round to the undertaker with Billy so he can make the arrangements, and the other young ones are at school. There'd seemed no point in keeping them home, even though Ann was inconsolable in the morning. Maria can hardly lift herself from the stool to answer the knocking. On the step, hat in hand, is Father McSorley.

'Good morning Father,' she steps aside, 'won't you come in.'

The priest gestures for her to go ahead and follows her to the kitchen. Maria peeks through the curtains and puts on the kettle, then notices the sink is full of the previous evening's dishes.

'You'll have to forgive the mess, Father, Billy's been here on his own and you know how he is. Typical man, begging your pardon, and wouldn't even think of asking the children to do a bit of cleaning up.'

'Don't you worry yourself there, Maria, I know it's not an easy time,' he takes her by the elbow, 'I'm so sorry for your loss.'

The room is quiet other than the splash of tea from pot to cup until she scrabbles in the cupboard, searching unproductively for a biscuit missed by young mouths. Outside, the birds sing and the dogs bark like they do every other day, neighbours hang out washing and talk across the fence, as every other morning. Somewhere there's the clack-clack-clack of a lawn being cut.

Maria wonders how this can still all go on, don't people know the world has ended?

'You've not been to Mass since we spoke, Maria, and I've been concerned, so, as I'd to visit Mrs Heron down the street, she broke her hip you know, I thought I'd call in. God knows you've had your hands full with Alice, but you're usually such a regular. I wanted to check I hadn't said something to upset you.'

'No, not at all, Father.

'I also wanted to apologise for arriving at the hospital too late yesterday. I'd a funeral on and couldn't get away until afterwards. You'd just left when I got there. I sat with her a while and said a few prayers for poor Alice's soul, and for you and Billy to have God's help to get through this time.'

'That's kind of you. I have to admit, Father,

what you said there in the church, the night I came home from the hospital, got me to thinking.'

'In what way?'

She sits and sips her tea.

'You know, Father, I can look out across my garden and see our church but sometimes it seems so very far away. That night we talked about Alice you told me it wasn't for us to question God's will, something I've always been taught to believe. I'm not sure I can believe it any longer.'

'I hear this so often when a loved one dies, Maria, especially when it's a child. It's at these times that our faith is tested to the limit, though it's also the time when we need it to be strongest. Just think, Alice has been ill for so long, isn't it merciful of Him to take her up and give her relief?'

She can tell the poor man is doing his best but that he doesn't believe what he's saying. Just words learnt at the seminary years ago.

'That's easy to say when it's not your flesh and blood, Father. Not your daughter who's dying. But if it was just about Alice I think I could understand your words, I might even agree with them, hard as it might be to let her go.'

'What is it then?'

'For months I've been visiting her, and that's given me a long time to spend with my own thoughts. Two weeks ago I was told that was all she had left and to help me cope I started to tell her stories. How I got to be sitting by that bedside. I told her of my grandfather's escape from the famine and his travels round the world. I told her of my father and mother's lives, and their early deaths, her in a strange country and him in the workhouse. And I told her about my life, every part of it, things I'd never told to anyone before.' She fixes her priest in the eye. 'Poverty, always poverty, and through all that storytelling, one question kept coming back to me.'

Father McSorley looks away. 'What's the question, Maria?'

'Why didn't God help? Just once?'

*

Children playing, kettle singing, sun streaming in through net curtained windows. Just another fine late Autumn day. Everything right in the world save for the draped clock and mirrors in Maria's home. Her hands deftly scrape skin and soil from potatoes, while she looks out of the window into her garden. Though 'garden' is an exaggeration, she knows, for with four young children and two older ones still at home, plus a man who works or sleeps all the hours that God sends there's little chance of cultivation of her tiny plot. Never will it be up to the standard of her Auntie Bridget. All she can do is try to keep the grass in some kind of order so that the kids have somewhere to play, and she has somewhere to sit when the luxury of a free moment presents itself.

With the potatoes finished and on the boil Maria goes out into the sunshine.

'Mammy?'

'Yes Tommy?' The boy, in short pants and a faded Fairisle jumper too small for his elder brother but two sizes too big for him, is her second youngest.

'Could we have a dog? Just a small one, it'd be good fun you know.'

'I don't think so love. Where would we keep a dog? There's barely enough room in the house for us all as it is. And a dog's an awful costly thing to keep.'

'But I'd love one Mammy. He could share my bed and I'd give him some of my food. He … he needn't cost us much you know.'

Maria turns away and whispers 'maybe someday soon son, but not now', knowing there is little chance. No matter how hard she tries, she's always, having to deny the children what they want. She arches her back to ease the knotted muscles and a twelve year old girl, Lizzie, pops her head outside.

'There's a man at the door, Mammy. I told him Daddy's not home but he says it's you he wants to see. He seems really nice.'

Lizzie and Tommy eye their mother with an air of suspicion, they're not sure she should be receiving men callers in the daytime.

'Me? He wants to see me? Tell him to wait just a minute Lizzie, I'll be straight through.'

Maria dashes inside, rinses her hands, primps her hair and walks through the living room to the front door. She's tempted to peek out of the bay window to get a look at the man first but realises how embarrassing this would be if he spots her.

The man is smiling in the doorway. Smiling, though Maria sees at a glance that he is nervous, something about the colour in his cheeks and the tiny tremor at the corner of his lips. He tugs the lobe of his right ear.

'Maria? Is it Maria Garner? Maria Byrne that was?'

Maria cocks her head ever so slightly, trying to decide if she knows the man. There's something about him, but she can't recall. She looks up and down the street in case any of the neighbours are outside.

'Yes, I'm Maria. Do I know you?'

He coughs, the nervousness getting to him.

'I .. I don't know how to tell you this without it being a shock. I've rehearsed and rehearsed what I was going to say but that's all now gone out of my head. I think I'll just have to blurt it out after all. I'm Jimmy. James Byrne. Your brother.'

*

Tea laid at the kitchen table, bread and butter, a

slice or two of cheap cake, hastily brought from the corner shop by Tommy. The trappings of normality in a world shaken to its foundations, twice in as many weeks. The hugs follow hard on Jimmy grabbing Maria by the arm, preventing her fainting away. As each tries to come to terms with what has just happened, tears continue to well in their eyes, words continue to choke in their throats.

'How did you find me? It's been how long?'

'A lifetime. Thirty seven years by my reckoning. Finding you wasn't easy, Maria, that's for sure. I was away at sea for a while when I got out of the grip of the Brothers. I travelled all around the world. I thought about going back to Arklow to settle but when I arrived there was nothing left for me, just bad memories. Someone sent me to Bella Rafferty, a daughter of Auntie Bridget, said she'd heard that you'd married a British soldier just before they all pulled out and moved to England with him.'

'You were in Arklow with the Christian brothers? You know I was in Dublin, at St Gregory's Industrial School? The "orphanage" they called it. Orphanage my fat foot! More like a prison. Some of the nuns were all right but lots of them were sadists. I can't tell you the beatings I had.'

'It was the same with me Maria. The first place in Arklow was the worse, when I was just a kid. They moved me down to Limerick when I reached twelve and the older boys there protected you a bit, not all the time you know, but most of the time.'

Maria shakes her head, pours more tea, for something to do with her hands rather than for sustenance, and hugs Rose close to her side. Jimmy explains how he'd taken one more trip to sea after leaving Arklow, this time ending up in Liverpool, where he'd married a local girl and settled down. He beams when he shows Maria a well-worn photo of his daughter, Therese.

'Just the one is it?'

'Aye, just the one. And you?'

'Young Rose here is the tenth. She's the youngest. Three of them are away in the army. The eldest, Josie, was on his way home. Should have been here by now. Got his boat from India, then when he arrived in Malta they diverted him to Germany. Terrible things been happening there. Concentration camps and mass graves they say. Specialist soldiers and military police need to investigate it all. As if he hasn't been through enough. The other two got leave for the funeral and went back to their camps afterwards. At least they should be safe now it's all over.

Maria rearranges the crockery and looks away. 'We lost a daughter a fortnight ago. Eighteen she was. A growth on her brain.'

Jimmy leans across the table and covers his sister's wrist. 'I'm so sorry, Maria. What can I say?'

They sit in quiet contemplation as the minutes tick by until Jimmy breaks the silence.

'Ten children? Ten?'

'And me brought up in a convent. For years I couldn't work out where they were coming from.'

For the first time they both laugh easily, sharing the silly joke. Jimmy returns to his story, explaining he'd recently met a soldier who'd been in Dublin in 1922, stationed at the Phoenix Park barracks. He hadn't known Maria or who she'd married, but he had known the names of the army outfits that had been left in the city at the end.

'From there I just wrote a few letters to the various regiments. Obviously I didn't know your husband's name then but I was pretty sure yours would come up on someone's records somewhere and, sure enough, it did. The Durham Light Infantry were kind enough to let me have William's name and last address.'

'Billy, it's Billy, not William. He'd hate you calling him William.'

'Oh, sorry, Billy it is. Anyway, from there I came over to Manchester a couple of times when I was able, found the street where you used to live and knocked on a few doors. People were very good about it and after a few tries I found someone who told me where you were living now. I can't believe that I've found you, though I always dreamed that I would.'

So they continue for two hours until Billy returns from work, when bottles are cracked open and all the stories told again.

When there's nothing left to say, Maria walks her brother round the corner, waving as his bus pulls away into the darkness. She doesn't go straight home. Instead, she takes the extra steps to her church, breathes deeply of the night air, then goes inside to pray.

Author's Note

In the 1970s I was given a photograph of a man in uniform, supposedly my great-grandfather. I found it interesting but then put it away. A decade or more later it re-emerged and I began a search for my ancestors. It took over twenty years to find what had happened to the man, a journey which took me back to 16th century Warwickshire and 19th century Ireland, to India, Malta and South Africa. It told me more of the lives of ordinary people than any history teaching in school.

When I began my writing adventure in the mid-2000s, I knew there was a story to tell but I didn't have the experience or the skill to tell it. I hope I now have.

This is a novel, fiction. Many of the situations were real, if not for my family, then certainly for others. Some of the characters are based on real people, or at least my imagining of them, but history and memory are strange places to go, and not a word of it, like Maria's stories, should be taken as true.

About the Author

Charlie Garratt lives near Ironbridge, Shropshire, in the cradle of the Industrial Revolution.

When he's not writing, he enjoys gardening, playing and listening to music, genealogy and reading.

Take a look at his website at: www.charliegarratt.com.

Follow him on Facebook at @charliegarratt.author or on Twitter at @charliegarratt3.

Sign up for his newsletter at: www.charliegarratt.com/lets-keep-in-touch.

Other Books by Charlie Garratt

A Shadowed Livery
The first book in a page-turning historical mystery series! Perfect for fans of Agatha Christie, Dorothy L Sayers, Philip Kerr and Andrew Taylor.

A Pretty Folly
Inspector Given is back on the case! The second historical crime novel in the Inspector James Given Mystery Series – a traditional British investigation set in England immediately before the Second World War.

A Patient Man
Inspector Given investigates murder at the outbreak of World War II.

Can Inspector Given lay the ghosts of his past to rest…?

Where Every Man
James Given must investigate another murder in wartime France.

Given had chosen the quiet life … until a murder case lands in his lap.

Printed in Great Britain
by Amazon

76141546R00192